THE KNITTER'S GUIDE TO BANISHING BOYFRIENDS

SWEET PEA, BOOK 2

KATHRYN MOON

THE KNITTER'S GUIDE TO BANISHING BOYFRIENDS

SWEET PEA, BOOK TWO

BY KATHRYN MOON

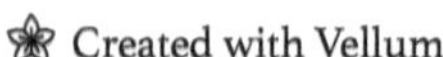 Created with Vellum

For the stitch witches who taught me their craft

CONTENTS

PREVIOUSLY, IN SWEET PEA

Shortly before Halloween in the quaint mountain town of Sweet Pea, new residents arrived. The Hell's Bells motorcycle crew was sent straight from the Bowels of Hell itself to undo the purity and charm of the little town. Their leader, King Beleth, was confident of his mission's success until he met Josie Benoit, kitchen witch and part of a local coven.

When a string of local, violent crimes pop up in Sweet Pea, Josie and her coven have their eye on the demon crew, but the rest of Sweet Pea grows suspicious of the witches.

Bell's curiosity and Josie's bravery bring them together to investigate the murders, and then natural chemistry draws them further together still. The murderer, a spiteful local angry with the town for considering selling their former family land, tries to frame Josie but ends up caught by Bell, sealing his bond with Josie and leaving them both in a slight state of confusion about where their relationship might go next.

Three months later...

1

KNIT NIGHT

Solitude. Quiet. Peace. Concentration. All the principles June Byrne valued so highly, the qualities that attracted her to the practice of knitting. The rhythm of her needles—in, wrap, out—was soothing and regular. Reliable. It occupied a part of her mind that wanted to start spinning madly when left idle.

So why, in all that was good and private and simple and clean—other concepts she was very much a fan of—had she agreed to host a knit night?

"Oh! You are *too* funny," Mrs. Montgomery crowed, the rocking chair she had installed in June's shop—*June's* shop—squeaking at a new pace with the older woman's laughter.

Yes, Mrs. Montgomery was certainly, in part, responsible for this horrible idea. She had used some kind of previously undiscovered witchcraft to pry the promise of a twice monthly—absolutely no more, not on June's life—late evening at June's sacred Knots and Knittery to host local crafters for some 'much needed socializing.'

June shuddered and flinched as the other women joined Mrs. Montgomery in their giggles and simpering.

"I never joke about medieval warfare, ladies."

More giggles, squawks, blushes. Montgomery's rocking chair—June would burn it one day—squeaking a little faster.

June tried to resist the impulse, but her eyes lifted from her project, crashing into the laughter of the demon Ashtaroth's gaze on hers.

Bastard, June thought, eyes falling back to her sweater, staring blankly at it for a moment as if she'd forgotten a basic knit in the round—a stitch she could perform in a dark theater, napping on her couch, even pick up and work a little at a stoplight.

Ashtaroth was, undoubtedly, the other influence to blame for arranging the knit nights. He hadn't missed one. And oh, he drew them in. The young women who'd left their children with their husbands for a few hours of respite, the local matrons—like Mrs. Montgomery—who only came in to wrinkle their nose and ask for acrylic, even June's stalwart customers, who stashed beautiful wool yarn like dragons and appreciated a good heritage blend with her when it came in from the farms. Oddly, the demon was one of the latter category. Even June could admit that the sweater he'd been working on since the first day she'd met him was a real thing of beauty.

In spite of the fact that he seemed hell bent on sabotaging his own project.

The giggles trailed off as footsteps thudded over to her refuge behind the desk. The group of women had invited her out to join them in their gossipy little circle the first few nights, after the coven's success on Samhain had driven up her potential popularity. June refused the offers every time. She might be expected to actually *talk* if she joined them, and that just sounded exhausting.

A shadow draped over the desk, blocking out the noise of the conversation still humming along in the circle. June dreaded these moments. They came with the soft scratch of the demon's power—like a kitten begging at a glass window—but also with relief. The force of Ashtaroth, Ash as the women all knew him, blocked out the entire rest of the world. For June, who often found the world dizzying and tiresome, he was an untrustworthy shield.

"Looks like I got myself in a bit of a pickle," he rumbled.

June blinked and set her own sweater down as Ash rested his project on the desk in front of her, a labyrinthian tangle of yarn presented on his needles.

"A pickle," June repeated, fingers digging into the lush weave of the lattice cables Ash had stitched in panels on the ribs of his sweater. A feat managed *without* a pattern. Asshole.

"Mhm."

She shouldn't have looked up. She knew better. Ash's beard was twitching, full mouth curling, eyes narrowed with laughter.

"Wendy could help you," June said, not for the first time.

Ash sank into a crouch, revealing the women behind him, letting a little of their noise filter toward them. His eyes studied her as June flinched at a sudden rush of laughter.

"You're faster."

"That's because these mistakes you make are physically impossible," June muttered, sighing and picking up the sweater at last. She couldn't let him ruin it. It was too beautiful, even if he was only goading her.

She slipped the right hand needle down, several rows below, and wove it through a few stitches, pulling Ashtaroth's mess off the left needle. *Does he know that this is my favorite part?* she wondered.

The tangle of yarn unraveled on the surface of her desk into a swirling illustration of a bird in flight, belly fat and wings stretched, even the details of feathers included. The more she tugged the strand, the faster the bird flew, shrinking into an imaginary distance. June's finger followed the trail of yarn as it slipped over the edge of the desk, wistfulness sweet in her chest. And then she remembered her audience, Ashtaroth's shockingly vibrant aquamarine eyes watching. She hunched over the needles, knitting up the bars of loose yarn until they were whole and tidy again, barely marked by the correction.

"That'll block right out," she murmured, passing the sweater back to him.

Ash grinned at her, and June reminded herself that this was a demon who wanted to destroy her home, her coven, herself. And her sister, Imogen. He was charming. He was built like a wall, which June had only recently discovered was a *thing* for her. He had impeccable taste in yarn and knitwear, which was downright *arousing*. And if he took one step against anything she loved, she would dig her nails into those pretty eyes of his and tear them out and use them to work the magic to banish him back to the depths of Hell. No matter what it cost her to do so.

"Do you know what I think?" Ash whispered.

June swallowed hard, blinking at him, half terrified of letting him continue, and then the wards of her shop tugged and June stood up from her seat with a grateful gasp as the door opened and a young woman stepped inside.

"Excuse me, I need to see if she needs any help," June said in a rush, Ash chuckling and rising from his crouch —*god, those thighs*, but June shook them out of her thoughts.

The women of knit night were already greeting the arrival, a pretty young woman with sheets of black hair and startled dark eyes, who skittered back to the door before finding June at the same moment that June's wards offered a belated little *burp* of warning.

"June Byrne," the woman—no, the *girl* breathed.

June blinked, drinking in a dozen details at once. The red rimmed eyes, the lack of coat, of purse, the hand still clasped around the handle of her shop door, ready to run, the women of knit night's curiosity. The demon standing behind June's back ripe with power like a visible pulse.

"Your special order just came in yesterday," June said, drawing up the rare but functional 'retail smile' she tended to forget to use. Wooden, yes, but it did the trick. "It's in the stock room, if you want to follow me."

The girl blinked, shoulders sagging, shooting Ash another wary glance, but she nodded. She was spelled, June realized, as she passed the younger woman and led her toward the small pantry room where she kept excess stock— or the yarn she wasn't prepared to part with yet. Protection charms draped over her shoulders that chimed happily with June's wards, but hexes too, and June wasn't sure if they were pointed outward or inward, not without digging into the girl properly.

More Imogen's speed, June thought, and she stepped aside to let the girl walk in first. She hesitated on the threshold, testing June's magic, and then sighed, the two of them closing the door on the crowd of women and the demon outside. June sealed the door with power, tracing a privacy sigil over the grain, and the girl whipped around, eyes widening.

"So we won't be overheard," June said. "Who are you?"

"You're June Byrne?"

June's lips pursed at her ignored question but nodded her head.

"You were part of Brett Lohman's coven?"

June's hand tightened around the knob of the door, his name a physical strike against her, the urge to react as if she were punched in the belly sudden and almost irresistible.

"Who are you?" June repeated, breathless this time.

"Please. I—No, you're right. My name is Amira. I've been with Brett for the past three years, and I can't—I can't—" Dark eyes filled with shining tears, Amira's head shaking, her hands fisted at her side. It took June too long to realize this wasn't reluctance or shame. It was one of the hexes, tying the girl's tongue in knots.

"Oh."

Amira gasped for air, body heaving, tears spilling over. "Please. Please, I need your help. He can't keep doing this."

Doing what? It was on the tip of June's tongue, but so were the answers. She had met Brett Lohman at her parents' funeral. Charming, handsome, gently magical—a sweet relief after the grueling practice she'd been raised in. He had comforted her, done a little centering spell after someone had tried to force her to look at what was left of her parents in their caskets. Exactly what she needed.

And then at the library, while she was anxiously studying for school—in a real high school for the first time in her life due to foster care, overwhelmed by everything she hadn't been taught—he had caught her crying. He had comforted her again. Reminded her how calming magic was, at least when it was done with him.

Over and over, June had found herself bumping into Brett, being comforted by him, retrained in magic.

Grooming. That was what they called it. She understood it now, but at the time...he'd been the one thing to hold her together, give her the strength she needed to help Imogen survive too.

Imogen.

"I can't help you." Her voice sounded calm, steady, gentle even.

Amira blanched, fawn brown skin taking on a greenish hue as June shook her head.

"He has you—"

"No, he can't touch me," June said, the words crisp in her teeth. "But it's been nine years and I..."

She had a life and a business. Imogen was...halfway right in the head most days, and there was the issue of the demons in town—little as they had accomplished since the wards were placed on Halloween. She didn't *want* to go back to that time in her life when the cracks digging their way through her, threatening her sanity, outnumbered the actual pieces she had left.

Amira's brow furrowed. "But they said—"

"They. Who's they?" June snapped, stepping forward, the younger woman rearing back.

How old are you, June wondered. Probably the same age she had been when Brett had decided it was time to move on. Was that what finally stirred Amira? Not the wrongness of a grown man cultivating a relationship with an underage girl, but being *left behind* by him after?

"There's still women in his coven," Amira whispered, starting to tremble beneath June's shadow. "Ones he's convinced would have nothing if they left. But they said that you and your sister—"

"We can't—I can take his hex off," June said, falling back a step, turning to the side to break the itchy feeling Amira's pleading gaze gave her. "But we won't...come forward. Stay away from my sister," she added for good measure, but she tried to soften the tone of her voice again.

For the first time since Amira had walked into the shop,

June caught a hint of the girl's magic. Fiery, a little wild, licking warmly around her and giving her the support to stand straighter, to nail those dark eyes to June's face until her cheeks burnt. Yes, Brett would've liked her.

"You have power. You have a coven. You could *do* something—"

"I did do something. I left," June murmured, glaring at Amira. "And I took my sister with me. I don't think about—I put that behind me. I can remove the hex for you. What you do after that is up to you. If that's what you want, you can come back on Sunday after I close," June said. "I need to get back to my customers."

Amira's eyes flashed, lips parted, and then they pressed shut again, a heavy breath exhaled through her nostrils. She nodded once. "Fine, thank you."

June's nails were biting into her own palms as they left the stockroom, one hand sliding into her pocket to tie a few knots for confusion and distraction on a bit of scrap yarn she kept handy. The knitting circle—all but Ash—puzzled over their projects with sudden concentration, only the demon still propped against June's desk watching as June escorted the other witch to the door.

Amira paused at the threshold, sharp cheek angled in June's direction, but eyes out on snowy Main Street. "He won't stop."

June opened her mouth to say something awful and shut it again. It might not have been her problem now, but there was no doubt in her mind Brett Lohman *was* a problem. The real issue was that she couldn't bring herself to care. About protecting herself and Imogen? Absolutely. About putting a stop to Brett and his coven of predators?

Why not? a voice whispered in her thoughts, pushing in her head. The snow and the lamplights and the retreating back of the young witch who hadn't waited for her answer spun in front of June, the world suddenly turning too fast.

A heavy hand landed on her shoulder as Amira's bright yellow driver side door slammed shut, and June blinked as the dizziness passed.

"What happened to her special order?" Ash asked, laughter in his voice.

His touch was warm, as strangely settling as Imogen's was sometimes, and June tore herself away. Ash's face was inches above hers, and June took one brief glance to make sure the knitters were occupied before slamming a wave of frustrated magic at the demon. He grunted, eyes widening, but it was even more infuriating that he barely swayed back from her.

"Stay the *fuck* out of my business," June hissed through her teeth.

Ash's eyebrows bounced in genuine surprise, and June marched back to the safety of her desk, fingers working in her pocket around the strand of yarn, twisting up one ward after the other. Thirty six minutes of knit night left, and pity the person who tried to get another word in her ear.

2 DESTRUCTION UNDER CONSTRUCTION

"Progress?"

Barbie passed Ash a beer over the bar top as Ash rolled his head on his neck, a sick satisfaction taken from the generous cracking sounds of his human disguise. He opened his mouth to tell Barbie about the new witch who had appeared to ruffle his little stitch witch's feathers, and then shut it again. If anyone needed to hear about the development it was Bell, and Bell was...

Ash's eyes scanned the bar, which was occupied by demons and a few of the younger locals who'd been won over by Danny Lin's bizarre fusion menu—Ash couldn't decide if chicken lo mein tacos were a blessing or a sin, but Danny said they were banned from his parent's kitchen—and came up empty on the leader of their mission. Which didn't really surprise him. Bell had been disappearing a lot lately, especially in the evenings. Ash had his suspicions, but also he didn't give a shit what the demon king was up to.

"No," Ash grunted, taking a long swig of the beer.

Barbie just nodded...or twitched, it was hard to tell.

In general, Hell's Bells MC, the elite army of Hell which

had been sent to destroy bucolic Sweet Pea, Virginia, had been striking out. They had five recruits for the MC, but January in the Virginia mountains was hardly riding time, so mostly they only saw Danny, who worked their kitchen and was deeply terrified of disappointing his traditional Chinese grandmother. Danny had brought in one of his friends too, who might've been up for a little trouble, but only on a dirtbike. There was Cornell and Thurman too, their cheerful neighbors who gave legal advice and flirted with Dante and Barbie. Of all their recruits, Becks was the only one who could really be considered 'hard' and had a record, but it was for beating up her best friend's abuser, and she took zero shit from any of them and had fucked off to South Carolina until the thaw.

Not promising at all.

"Where's Vinny?" Paimon asked, arriving at the bar, decked out fingers digging through his gray streaked beard.

Barbie shrugged, and Ash counted the waitresses. "Probably fucking Kimmy in the stock room," Ash said.

Paimon nodded at that. "He tried to force a crash at the stop sign, and it bounced back. He wiped out on an ice patch in the alley."

Vinny might've been a King of Hell and one of their team members, but not one of them bothered to hide their smirks. He was an asshole.

"Is it worth being here?" Barbie asked, wiping absolutely nothing off the counter. Far as Ash could tell, the only things Barbie enjoyed about this mission was being with his other half, Aim, and being in charge of the bar. He polished it like it was made of gold.

"You doubt?" Paimon asked, one dark eyebrow cocking as he glanced at the reticent demon over the bar.

Barbie's throat flexed, greasy blond strands hanging

forward in his face, the tattooed serpents spiralling up his neck squirming with the swallow.

"Does feel like we're in a bit of a stalemate," Ash said, sliding in for Barbie. "Can't work with our powers without them coming back at us. The ward's not shaking."

"We have skills outside our Hell gifts," Paimon said with a shrug. "But I take it those aren't working with June Byrne?"

Ash couldn't explain why the sound of his stitch witch's name was so foul on the other demon's tongue.

"I need Dante to take that binding off her," Ash muttered.

He'd tried to crack it on his own, but that shit was rock solid. Diamond hard. And inside there was something glittering, begging to be toyed with, if he could just find his way in. He caught glimpses sometimes, tantalizing little hints of what was being guarded. Even tonight, there was the little expression of joy as his yarn glyph unravelled and flew, the sudden trembling vulnerability as she'd watched the other witch leave, the sparkling anger she'd flashed at him when he tried to worm his way in. But they always faded a moment later, back below the smooth and impenetrable surface.

"We'll push him in that direction," Paimon said, eyes distant over the bar. "The town is in hibernation until spring anyway. He's not making progress with the officials."

Ash thought of Barbie's question again. Was Sweet Pea *worth* the fight? Maybe if the project had been a little easier to attack, he would've said no, but the challenge proved how serious the threat of goodness was here. And anyway, he wasn't quite ready to give up on the puzzle of June.

Vinny reappeared from the back room, swaggering with his belt still undone, followed by an entirely unrepentant Kimmy. Ash might've felt sorry for any woman who got tangled up with Vinny, but Kimmy had clawed her way into that trap when none of the other Hell's Bells demons had bit on her bait. She was nasty to Danny and the other waitresses, and anyone who could stand five minutes with Vinny probably had a shitty personality, not that Ash gave her the opportunity to let him find out firsthand.

"What are you looking at?" Vinny snarled at them, clearly puffing his chest and exaggerating his steps to give them more to stare at.

There wasn't any point in *resisting* the urge to roll his eyes, so Ash didn't, rewarded with Vinny's growl.

The door to the bar opened, bringing with it a flurry of snow and a gust of cold air, as well as another missing member of their number, Aim. The snowflakes melted in the immediate vicinity of the pyrotechnically inclined demon, who hadn't bothered with more than his typical leather jacket and torn T-shirt as protection against the mountain winters. He wore his usual brilliant, if not slightly maniacal, grin, and stepped aside to reveal familiar faces.

"This is the saddest looking scene I've witnessed all week, and I had to attend two funerals," Cornell announced, shaking off the cold as his husband, Thurman, shut the door on the night, lips twitching. Cornell's hair was short-cropped and gray, allowing snow sprinkled over his head to blend in. He reached a hand up to his fogging glasses and pulled them down, Thurman handing over a tissue.

"Business is slow," Paimon allowed.

"Business is always slow this time of year, but that doesn't mean you need to sit around looking like you're about to clip your toenails," Cornell replied brightly.

Barbie snorted and pulled out the designated bottle of wine they reserved for their neighbors and club members.

"No, save that, Barb," Thurman said and waved his hand. Ash's beard twitched with laughter at Thurman's nickname for Barbatos. He'd eventually done his research and discovered why all the humans thought Barbie's road name was so ridiculous, but he was saving the reveal to the others for a special occasion.

"We come bearing gifts!" Cornell cried, spreading his arms wide before dropping them quickly. "Well, a gift. But come on, I love having handsome men act grateful to me."

"He makes a point of it," Thurman said with a nod.

Ash grabbed his beer and rose up from his stool with Paimon at his heels, even Vinny reluctantly following their path to the windows.

"Told Aim about the upcoming repo auction, thought you boys might need something a little more road worthy in the winter than your bikes," Cornell said, opening the door.

Ash ducked out, ignoring the bite of the cold—he liked winter and he'd built his human body to bear it well. There, idling in a parking spot in front of the sidewalk, was a beast of a vehicle, with tires up to Ash's thighs. It was a horrific shade of yellow green, with blacked out windows and headlights that threatened to blind oncoming traffic, and it practically vibrated on the pavement like a dog waiting for its master's pat on the head.

"Some crazy ass up in the peaks was stocking up on military grade supplies, waiting for the end times," Cornell rattled off. "Up to his bushy eyebrows in debt on it all. This is a little overkill for our Sweet Pea roads, but I thought it looked just about your style. And you're gonna get yourselves killed if you keep riding your bikes."

They wouldn't, of course. Maybe, if they weren't paying attention, they would wipe out. But being killed in something as simple as a road accident was too mundane. Not that Cornell or Thurman would be expected to know that.

"This is..." Paimon blinked through the thick framed glasses he wore, at an equal loss of words as Ash.

This was thoughtful. Friendly. From two men they intended to do their best to manipulate and corrupt—current failure notwithstanding.

"They're verklempt," Thurman said to Cornell, smiling mildly as Cornell seemed to almost bounce in place, waiting for their reaction.

"Thank you," Ash said at last, turning to the small man and offering his massive hand.

The car was, at the very least, impressive. A monster of a machine. The gas mileage alone would be a sin.

Cornell was suitably flattered by the handshake, although he was still waiting on the others. Ash glanced at Barbie, who had always seemed a little partial to the older couple, but he found him facing in the opposite direction down the sidewalk, watching a small bundled shadow's approach.

"Do we owe you anything?" Paimon asked, very seriously.

"I paid for it," Aim informed him.

"Pft, maybe a favor," Cornell said with a dismissive wave of his hand.

Paimon's lips pursed, but he nodded his head in acknowledgement. "Very well. Thank you."

Aim moved to their new beast of a ride, jumping up into the driver's seat and dulling its roar with a turn of the keys.

"Guess you guys have a cage now," Thurman said, grinning at them.

The demons of Hell's Bells all stiffened. Paimon's head whipped in his direction. "A cage?"

Thurman blinked back at him. "Is my lingo out of date? That's what we used to call cars."

Ash chuckled and relaxed. "Oh, right. Yeah, never had a cage before. But this one looks like it'll suit."

"Can't fit all of you in it of course, but it's a start."

"What are you doing out?" Barbie snagged their attention, voice gruff as he interrogated the bundle of scarves that had almost reached them.

"Um...is...um, is Danny working?" a small voice asked, muffled through layers, large dark eyes blinking out of a gap in all the fabric.

"Mona, don't tell me you walked here," Cornell called.

Huh. Mona. "You don't look as scary as I expected from what Danny told us," Ash greeted her, opening the door as Barbie glowered down his nose at the young woman.

"I can surprise you," Mona answered. "And I figured walking would be safer than driving with my tires."

Barbie shoved his way in front of Ash, following Mona closely, Aim barely inches behind.

"Go on, I'll just wait here," Ash said, waving everyone in with another roll of his eyes.

"Such a courteous young man," Cornell said drily with a glance over his glasses that reminded Ash of Pie's looks.

Mona Lin was growing smaller as she shed her layers, piling them on an unoccupied stool by the bar, ignoring the heavy stares of the men surrounding her.

"Sister's here," Barbie rumbled through the small window that peeked into the kitchen. He returned to his station behind the bar, glare flicking up at the woman who steadfastly ignored him.

Her cheeks were bright pink, possibly with cold, but they darkened with one look at Barbie. "Soda with—Oh!" she said as he set down a fizzing glass with lemon on the rim. "Thanks."

Barbie grunted, turning away as Danny dashed out of

the kitchen, hands raised at his side as if he were being arrested.

"What are you doing here?"

"I was hungry and didn't want to cook."

"Oh. Okay."

"*Why*, Danny? What are you doing?"

"I'm cooking! It's my job, *Mona*."

"Then why are you being weird?"

"You're being weird!"

Ash crossed his arms over his chest, all the demons in the room watching the siblings curiously as the humans went about their business. Mona barely made it to Danny's chest height, and she looked about the same age as him to Ash's eyes, although he knew she was a good handful of years older from his stories. She pulled a pair of bright green glasses out of her pocket to glare at her brother through, and Ash thought she was about the least intimidating thing he'd ever seen in his life, but Danny looked guiltier by the second.

"Don't make me call Mom," Mona said, voice going dark, one eyebrow arching.

Danny gasped. "*I wasn't doing anything, I swear!*" he bellowed, face bright red.

Mona's shoulders dropped and she shrugged. "Good. What are you cooking?"

"Why?"

"Because I'm hungry, doofus, why do you think?"

"Oh. Uh. Burgers."

Mona nodded and sipped her drink before taking the slice of lemon from the edge of the glass and biting directly into it, face betraying no change of expression. "Cool. Nothing weird. Onion rings."

"Yeah," Danny said, nodding and breathing a sigh of relief. "Kay."

Families are strange, Ash decided.

Also strange was the way Barbie's gaze tracked Aim as he slid onto the booth seat next to Mona with a dangerously feral expression. The two demons were generally inseparable, although it was often difficult to understand why. But Ash had never seen *that* look exchanged between them.

"We might as well eat too. Then we can give you a ride back," Cornell said to Mona, who brightened at the offer, throwing her coat down to the floor to make room for the two men on her other side.

"This isn't working," Pie whispered to Ash under his breath, pale eyes bouncing between Aim and Barbie, Vinny, who was back in a giggling Kimmy's ear, to Mona and Cornell and Thurman chatting cheerfully at the bar.

"No," Ash agreed with a shrug and a swig of his beer.

No, their destruction of Sweet Pea's wholesome core wasn't working. But it was kind of fun anyway.

3
SLEEPOVERS

Josie squirmed, trying to wiggle her way out from under Bell's warm frame, especially his mouth on her collarbone, licking and nibbling and sucking on her skin.

"Enough. No more," she panted, swatting at his back.

It was so unfair that he never got sweaty, although it was also kind of nice. And he seemed fascinated by her sweat. Demons liked salt—it was one of the useless facts she'd discovered since the fall. When she baked Bell salted caramel brownies, she always added extra.

"I'm cuddling," Bell said, and her lashes fluttered at that warm perfect rasp, the one that had been pouring sweet filth in her ear as he fucked her limp on the couch, and then the floor, and finally her bed.

"You are fucking not, you're trying to—Mmph!"

Demons are dangerous, Josie reminded herself for what was surely the seven millionth time. Possibly just that month. *They're bad. They want to...*

Her warning thoughts dissolved as Bell purred into the kiss, rolling to the side. His arms were wrapped around her, carrying her with him to rest on his chest, but he was slowing down at last. She glanced at the clock as he let her escape for air. Shit.

"I have to get up in like three hours, Bell," she groaned, dropping her forehead down to his shoulder and taking a deep breath. She was getting used to this scent of smoke. Addicted to it even.

"I will make your sleep very restful," he said, kissing the side of her head and then rubbing one massive hand up and down over the bristles of her shaved hair. "It's growing out again."

"Hair does do that," Josie mumbled, giving in and snuggling down into his side. He'd sneak away when she was asleep. Might as well enjoy him while he was here.

"Mine doesn't," Bell mused.

Which Josie hadn't thought about before now, and it was a bit weird. Demons didn't need haircuts. She'd file that in her collection of entirely useless information that she definitely couldn't use to defeat the demons plotting against her town. One of whom was stroking her back. The one who had been in and out of her bed for months. Who'd been quizzing her about theologies and gobbling up her unsold bakery wares. The one she was getting a little—a lot, so much, painfully—confused about in her heart.

"I suppose it could," Bell continued. "What do you think? Longer? Shorter?"

Seriously, Bell? she thought, but her lips were twitching. "I like you fine as you are."

Bell stiffened beneath her, and Josie suffered a brief moment of grief. Was this the too far line in their...whatever they were doing? A little absent compliment, and her demon would finally remember they were supposed to be on opposite sides of a battlefield?

And then Josie was sitting up in a rush, Bell wrestling her over his lap, greedy hands pawing and stroking her everywhere, his mouth licking and sucking on her throat as he growled into her skin.

"Bell!"

"I changed my mind, Cupcake," Bell hissed, dragging his nose up to her ear to nibble on the lobe. "No rest for you tonight. I have too big of an appetite."

That's not all that's big, Josie thought, a hysterical giggle escaping her mouth. Bell's calloused hand reached up to cover a breast, teasing the nipple between two fingers, and Josie arched with a moan. Sleep was for the weak and Bell was—

"Oh, fuck, Bell," Josie gasped as he shifted her over his lap, drawing her down onto his cock until the strength and pound of him echoed all the way to her throat.

Bell wasn't the only one with an appetite.

Josie caught one deep breath and braced her hands on Bell's broad shoulders, finding his gaze glowing in the dark and holding it as she started to ride.

BELL, YOU REALLY FUCKIN' overdid it on the energy, Josie thought the next day as she bounced on the tip of her toes to the jazz playing in her patisserie.

She'd jumped out of bed at five that morning, after what couldn't have been more than forty minutes of sleep, to no sign of Bell in her apartment and the energy of a five-year-old on Christmas morning. Energy which was just not letting up. If Bell was going to wreck her sleep schedule, she'd prefer he did it with great sex rather than magical demon buzzes.

On the upshot, the shop was now spotless and she had already prepped as much as she could for tomorrow morning. If he didn't reappear in her apartment tonight, she might actually get some sleep. Provided this magic wore off, which she was beginning to worry it wouldn't.

Reason number 98729 why my demon should learn to text.

The other reasons had mainly to do with the number of times he'd scared the shit out of her by showing up without warning.

The bells over her shop door chimed cheerfully, a sharp wind whipping over the counters to reach Josie in the kitchen. She sighed, eyes closing and enjoyed the shiver that ran through her as the door jangled shut. Lively tendrils of magic, shy and playful, appeared from the front of the shop. Rosa Velasco, her green witch covenmate, fellow Sweet Pea business owner and best friend, had arrived.

This was another unexpected effect of Bell's little energy trick. Josie's magic had received its own boost, and it was like her spidey senses were on high alert.

"Go ahead and flip the sign for me," Josie called to her friend with a glance at the clock.

Rosa was bundled from the colorful, chunky stocking cap she wore—her singular knitting effort at June's urging—to the massive red snow boots on her feet. Dark curls were trimmed with ice, shoulders dressed with rapidly melting snow, and she was peeling herself out of her layers with a relieved sigh, only to reveal more draping fabrics.

"Fuck winter," Rosa said.

Josie's lips twitched at that, and she hummed in half-hearted agreement. Rosa, green witch by night and florist by day, was certainly not a winter girl, in spite of growing up in the area. Josie remembered sunny and rainy winters in New Orleans with her mémé, but she enjoyed the snow, and while it wasn't tourist season in Sweet Pea with the roads so dangerous this time of year, locals gave her good business over the holidays. Especially with the upcoming Valentine's Day rush.

"Here," Josie said, dipping a ladle into the small pot at her stove and pouring a generous serving of sipping chocolate into a mug for Rosa. "This should cure your winter woes. Pick out whatever you like from the case too."

"All of it," Rosa hissed, hurrying behind the counter and grabbing a dinner plate to serve herself. "So what happened to you last night?"

Of course she noticed, Josie thought, wincing. June had activated their chat group **what up, witches!** sometime during the marathon of Bell's 'appetite,' and Josie hadn't seen any of the texts calling for a coven meeting until she was getting ready this morning.

"Just crashed," Josie lied. "But all the sleep had me extra chipper today."

Rosa stood, plate piled with macarons and madeleines, cream puffs and chocolate shortbread, and arched a dubious eyebrow at her friend.

"You need something savory with that," Josie said, rushing to cover Rosa's suspicion with the distraction of quiche.

"Well, at least you suggested meeting here instead. I hate Imogen's place," Rosa said with a shudder. "It's creepy."

"It's sad," Josie corrected.

For over four years as a coven, Josie had never once seen the inside of Imogen's cabin up in the woods. Not until the demons had arrived in Sweet Pea that fall and Imogen had taught them how to summon the one named Vine to discover their purpose in town—nothing short of destroying the goodness of the town itself. The cabin was a *little* creepy, but mostly because it seemed like no one had lived there in years, as if Imogen was a ghost in her own house.

"Any guesses to what the meeting's about?" Josie asked. June's messages were curiously vague, even for her, and only said 'something's come up.' "Imbolc just passed, and it's a little early to start planning for the equinox."

"Last night was knit night, maybe she's got a demon update," Rosa suggested, mouth full of pastry and lips now lined with chocolate.

Josie's stomach turned queasily. How shitty of her would it be if she was *sleeping* with one of the demons and still not the coven member who brought information? Not that Bell stuck around for sleeping. Which she was surely not bitter about.

Josie took a sip of her own mug of chocolate, savoring the warmth and burn of the spices on her lips every bit as much as Bell's kisses.

There was one brief warning, bright as sunlight and sharp as a blade, and then the back door to the kitchen was opening, the Byrne sisters arriving. Josie's eyes widened as they entered. Damn, Bell's power was doing something weird to her.

June was glowing, the outline of a prism shining around her like taut strings of yarn pulled into a net, and inside she was the cool, placid surface Josie had come to know, to rarely witness faltering. Behind her and in direct contrast, Imogen was obscured in smoke, like a coal burning up from the core, shedding soot on the floor behind her. The Byrne sisters sometimes seemed psychically entwined, able to communicate without so much as a blink, but Josie was realizing now how wildly different they were and how...almost frightening they both were. June untouchable, and Imogen just one brush away from burning them all up.

Imogen's eyes met Josie's and the smoke drew in on itself, gathering back into the young woman, leaving an almost two-dimensional impression behind that made Josie's head hurt. And then Imogen's gaze traveled over her, brow furrowing and head tipping, and Josie realized, like an idiot, that once again Imogen was aware of Bell's mark all over her.

"Chocolate, anyone?" Josie asked, wondering if she was imagining Bell's magic starting to crash and leave her wobbly and worn out at last.

"June..." Rosa's head ducked to try and catch the other woman's gaze. "Why didn't you ever tell me about this guy?"

June was tracing a circle around the lip of her mug, eyes blinking calmly down at the crumbs of her quiche. "I left. It was over," she said with a shrug, but Josie thought she caught her wincing.

Bell's magic had definitely started to wear off, and exhaustion gave June's story a hazy, removed quality, like Josie was hearing this from a stranger. It was hard to reconcile the calm, restrained woman Josie knew with the young girl June must've been when involved with this asshole Brett.

"But you know—I mean, I told you about..." Rosa whispered, leaning across the table, frowning as June refused to look up. "You could have talked to me too."

There was a thick lump, hard as a rock in Josie's throat, as her gaze darted dizzily between her friends. She'd only ever known about June and Rosa's relationship as it pertained to the coven, but it sounded now like they shared a great deal more. Or at least, like Rosa had shared.

"I told her I would take the hexes off her so she could speak," June said softly, sitting up.

"No," Imogen replied immediately.

"What? What do you mean, no? Of course we have to help her," Rosa said, spine straightening.

"We stay out of this," Imogen said, voice whispery in her sister's ear. "We stay away from him like you said."

"Imogen, it is absolutely your and June's choice on whether or not you want to come forward about this man, but that doesn't mean we, as a coven, shouldn't help a witch who—"

"This isn't your business," Imogen growled across the table at Rosa.

Josie's head was spinning. June and Imogen had not only lost their parents as children, they'd then been preyed on by another witch. That she could wrap her head around, much as it hurt her to do so. This new thread between Rosa and June? Josie didn't know the details yet, but she could imagine. Rosa didn't really date as much as she joked about men, and Josie had wondered before if staying single was more than just about being picky or busy for her friend. Even this feral version of Imogen wasn't such a surprise, although Josie had only seen it once before when Imogen had faced off against the seven demons of Hell's Bells. But all of it combined?

"It's coven business now," Rosa snapped back at the younger woman. "And to be perfectly frank, any woman asking for help is another woman's business. You don't have to take the spells off, but *I* can."

"You don't have the power," Imogen said so simply, it took Josie a moment to realize how cruel the words were.

Rosa reared back as if struck, her cheeks flushing pink with embarrassment.

"All right, hold the fuck up," Josie mumbled, stretching both hands out to the middle of the table. June's shoulders sagged at her sudden intervention. "Let me just...put this in bullet points. June, this girl—"

"Amira."

"Amira, wants your help?"

"Yes, but—"

"No—" Imogen said to her sister again.

"Stop," Josie said, and the word was so firm, it hit her tongue like a slap, shutting Imogen up and making her glassy eyes flare with life. "June, the help you are willing to offer is undoing the magic preventing this girl from speaking out?"

"Yes."

"And you're asking if we will help you?"

"Yes," June said, nodding this time.

"Do you need all four of us?" Josie asked.

June's eyes flicked in her sister's direction, but not long enough for Imogen to snag her. "No."

"Then Rosa and I will be there. Imogen, your involvement is your choice, but you can't stop us." Imogen was glaring at her like she planned to do exactly that, and Josie continued, "I understand you wanna look out for your sister, but I think we all know June can do that for herself, and she has us for backup, yeah?"

"Fuck yeah," Rosa said firmly.

June offered her one fragile, grateful smile before the peace was broken. Josie was staring at Imogen, and the anger on the younger witch's face slipped away into something cold, one brief strike of worry hitting Josie too late.

"You really want the witch who's fucking a demon to be the one helping you, June?"

The words were cool and slippery like oil, settling in the

air between them, a long moment of confusion left behind with silence.

"What?" Rosa asked, blinking.

June let out a weary sigh, head rolling toward her sister. "Imogen, you said you weren't—"

Imogen let out a ragged bark of a laugh, still watching Josie, seeing the heat creeping up her throat and into her cheeks. "No, not me this time. It's Josie. Josie and King Beleth of Hell."

"What?" Rosa repeated, a little louder this time.

"Once is okay. I've been there. But damn, Josie, look at you. You must be—"

"Shut the fuck up, Imogen," Josie snapped at last, but her cheeks were flaming.

"*Whaaaaaaat*?" Rosa hissed out on a breath.

June was staring at Josie now, head tipping, eyes narrowing for a moment and then widening as she discovered what her sister already had.

"I am not in league with the demons," Josie bit out slowly.

Imogen arched an eyebrow. "Don't tell me you've convinced yourself that *you're* using *him*?"

No. No, she certainly wasn't under that misconception.

"Imogen, I had no idea you had enough personality to be this much of a bitch," Josie spat out, standing from her seat with a screech of rubber feet on tile. "Get out of my shop."

She didn't mean for the flash and spark of her magic, likely amplified by Bell's power sharing, but the crackle was audible in the room and it made everything so much worse. Josie released it with a weary groan, covering her face with her hands.

"Shit, you guys, it's not what it sounds like. He's not—He swore me his protection. And we don't talk about this stuff, honestly," Josie moaned from behind the shield of her palms.

"His protection?" Imogen asked, leaning forward with narrowed eyes. "Those were *his* words?"

Josie glared back at the other woman, but Imogen was right—the language mattered. "His exact words were something along the lines of no harm coming to me."

"We're talking about Mr. Bad News and you having actual sex, right?" Rosa asked.

Josie peeked out between her fingers and found her friend staring thoughtfully up at her. She wasn't a coward, so she forced herself to lower her hands and nodded.

"The closest we get to discussing anything to do with... with who he is and who I am and the whole mission bullshit is that he...he asks me to take out library books for him," Josie said, steadying her breath and squaring her shoulders. At least Imogen looked genuinely puzzled by that. "He's really curious about different theologies. He doesn't ask me shit about what we do."

"And you don't ask him," June said, frowning.

Josie's mouth opened and shut again, brow furrowing. She'd considered it but...things with Bell felt kind of cute, albeit in a sneaky way, at least until she thought about their positions in Sweet Pea. "I don't."

"Would you? If..."

"If I ever feel like it's necessary to protect, yes, I would manipulate Bell to do so," Josie said, trying to push down the icky churning feeling in her belly at the admission.

June's lips pursed for a moment before she shrugged. "I don't judge you. But I am concerned about the possible effect his power may have on your magic when it comes to undoing these hexes. You'd better...not worry about helping. At least until we can do some tests?"

"June, you're not still thinking of—" Imogen whipped her head to her sister.

"Yes, I told her I would. I can do it by myself."

"No. No, fine. We'll help her," Imogen bit out.

Josie's hands were wrapped around the back of the metal chair, the shame squatting in her mingling sourly with her simmering spite at Imogen. Maybe she shouldn't have expected the other witch to keep her secret, but Imogen's manner of spilling the beans was more like a toxic waste dump than truth for the sake of it.

Rosa's gaze bounced between Josie and the sisters before settling on June. "I can still..."

June's shoulders squared, and she shook her head. "The problem is really about us. We'll handle it. Josie, we can... figure things out next week?"

In all honesty, Josie had expected June to be the harshest with her over the demon fucking thing. The offer of an olive branch was a pleasant surprise, but the air in the room was thick with tension and Josie was more interested in shooing Imogen out before she was tempted to start fighting again.

"Sounds good," Josie said, even though it actually sounded like the beginning of the sky crashing down. Was she really going to be able to keep doing this...whatever it was with Bell, or had the bubble burst with the secret?

Imogen rose from the table, and Josie thought for a moment that cold, slippery disguise cracked, revealing a frightened girl beneath, but then her head ducked as June brushed past her, the sisters trailing quietly back through the kitchen, setting their plates down in her sink with a soft chink.

Rosa made no move to leave, and Josie sank wearily into the chair again, tracing a finger around the rim of her mug to catch stray traces of chocolate.

Rosa waited until the door shut and let out a great huff of breath. "Shit, that was ugly, babe."

"Rosa, I'm so—"

"I'm not really surprised, Josie," Rosa said, wearing a fragile smile as Josie's head jerked up. "I'm the one who told *you* the pair of you had chemistry. And you have seemed kind of...well fucked lately."

"What does well fucked seem like?" Josie squawked.

Rosa grinned and shrugged. "Well, I dunno, actually. But I imagine it looks like you. Kinda always dancing and smiling, even when you've got Mrs. Montgomery bending your ear at the counter for ten minutes. I just figured if it *did* happen, you woulda shared the news," Rosa said, eyebrows waggling. She shrugged and raised a hand. "But I get why you felt like you couldn't. He swore you his protection?"

Josie swallowed hard, remembering the night Merryweather had tried to murder her and accidentally summoned Bell to the rescue. The glow of Bell's eyes on hers, her blood on his hands, his lips still damp from her kiss. She nodded. "I mean, we're both fucking around on this whole what side of the fence we're on thing. And I...I haven't been brave enough to ask, but I think he's about as confused about it all as I am."

Rosa sighed, propping her chin up on her fist and smirking. "Josephine Benoit, converting demons with her sweet, sweet lovin' since—"

"Shut the fuck up," Josie said, a bark of laughter rushing out with a wave of relief that brought little tear pricks to her eyes. "I haven't *converted* him."

"Yet," Rosa said brightly, sobering after a moment. "And he hasn't converted you?"

"Definitely not," Josie said, chin lifting. "I spend way too

much time stressing to be thoroughly seduced. You know...
mentally," she added, waving a hand around her head.

Rosa nodded, eyes widening. "Yeah. So I think in
apology for keeping this from me, you should give me some
details. On the seducing. And the general, you know, demon
in the sheets experience."

Thank the saints and the family spirits for Rosa Velasco, Josie
thought with a giggling sigh.

"The man. Does not. Quit." Josie said, articulating every
word as Rosa's eyes brightened and their cheeks both
flushed. "So next time I don't answer the group chat—"

"Oh, you sneaky witch!" Rosa howled, clapping her
hands and laughing. "Okay, keep going. You haven't made it
up to me yet."

The next mugs of chocolate came with rum and
caramel, and Josie was thoroughly tipsy as she locked her
doors and set her wards before stumbling up to her apartment above the shop. Bell's magic was fully evaporated, and
so was the last of her own energy. She made it far enough to
toe off her shoes and unbutton her jeans before giving into
the urge to sink onto the mattress.

And as if she weren't confused enough as it was, Josie
Benoit woke alone the next morning, undressed and under
her blankets, spooned around her pillow, with a hint of
smoke on the air and the memory of being held in the night.

4

WHICH WITCH?

K ing Vine of Hell hated a great many things about the little town of Sweet Pea.

The smiles on people's faces, the snow, locals greeting him, the snow, his cohort demons, the snow.

He growled into the cold air, boots stomping down the plowed road, salt gritty under his soles. His breath fogged into the shape of flames, snow melting into the seat of his pants—he had already slipped on the icy sidewalks...twice. But being out in the ass frozen end of town was better than spending time with his cohorts around a bonfire. The demons of Hell's Bells were starting to take their human disguises a little too seriously if you asked Vinny. Which they never fucking did.

The air shimmered in front of him, a hook catching abruptly in his belly, and his low growl transformed into a full snarl.

Sweet Pea certainly had its charms, and Vinny hated every one of them, but none more than what was dragging his demonic energy away at this moment.

Fucking witches.

If they liked summoning so much, they should try being on the other end of it. His human shape split with a visceral shredding and a fiery evaporation, the hook of the call snarling into the shriveled core of his perfunctory soul and dragging him skidding through the ragged edges of space. He forced his own resistance down and popped through the other end of the summons, simmering with anger in another dark and compact room reeking of incense and beeswax and stress.

There was just one witch this time, shrouded in black and wearing a mask, holding a yew branch wreath in her hands. Vine snorted at the sight of her and grinned as she flinched at the rough sound and his hot breath, backing away from the edge of the circle she'd traced on the floor, her shoulders bumping into the wall behind her.

"Why bother hiding your face now, witch? I already know how to find you," Vine hissed.

The witch's shroud fluttered with a panicked breathing, mask turning left and right. "You don't. You don't know where we are."

Vine snarled again but paused. No, he didn't know where they fucking were, but...but it was outside the wards. He blinked at that and straightened briefly. His power was...looser, freer, despite the binding circle. Which meant whatever this witch wanted, she needed him to be able to serve, which he couldn't do in Sweet Pea. Interesting.

He shook himself, pulling the human form back together, and crossed his arms over his chest as the witch sighed and faced him again. "What do you want then?"

"I need your strength."

"Not a fucking chance," Vinny snapped, and then he spit for good measure. It didn't quite reach the edge of the circle

—it wouldn't—but it sizzled as it landed and left a satisfying pockmark on the dark cement floor.

This must be the one Dante called 'basement witch.' He thought he remembered her packing a little more oomph in her summonings.

"You are the demon king, Vine," the witch whispered.

Vinny shrugged. "I am."

"You...you are the only demon permitted to take a soul without heavenly granting."

Vinny's eyes narrowed and he let his body stretch, warping the confines of the small room. Fuck, it was practically a closet. It even still smelled like cleaning supplies.

"I am." And yet here he was, stuck inside of a chalk circle, bound by herbs and a wreath and a witch who looked about two growls away from pissing herself.

"And you hate witches."

"I sure as hell do," Vinny said, lips slanting in a poor imitation of a smile.

"I need your power to kill a witch."

Well now, that was...unexpected. Were the witches infighting? Did he care? "Which witch?" Vinny asked, because he wasn't an idiot and if the coven had enemies, maybe the demons had allies.

"It's not your place to know."

"Your enemy is my—"

"My enemy is a witch and all witches are your enemy, demon. If you refuse this work, I *will* find another, but you can have her head in your count if you do as I have ordered." Black gloved hands twisted branches in their grip, and the binding around Vinny tightened to a painful bite on his throat and tongue.

Vinny bared his teeth at the witch, but she was right— she would just call one of his brethren from Hell, or worse, someone like Bell or Dante, who would rub it directly into his face the next time he saw them. Worst case scenario, he assisted the witches and blackened their souls at the same time.

"Your soul is mine too after this, witch," Vinny warned in a soft growl.

Her breath shuddered beneath the shroud again, another tangy whiff of stress perfuming the air.

"I understand. Do you consent, King Vine of Hell, to lending your power for my working?"

Vinny thought he might like to wipe himself out of the demonic ledgers on Earth. He was getting too much traffic these days. But work was work and his crown was only lightly placed upon his head, gifted rather than gained. Serving up two witches in one day wasn't going to do his reputation any harm in the Bowels.

"I consent," he said, and the floor trembled with the weight of the bargain.

The witch sighed, and Vinny howled as she twisted the branches in her fist, warping them into a circle and then unfolding them open into two loops. Twin twists appeared on his wrists, blazing hot and carving into his flesh, a tattoo of her control.

Her chant began, the old black tongue of the Bowels, and Vinny braced himself for the gutting sensation of being drained.

THE WITCH BANISHED him after stealing her fill, and after another violent shift through space, Vinny was dropped unceremoniously into a snowdrift in Merryweather Preserve.

Fuck witches, and fuck snow. His ass had just thawed before being kicked out of whatever closet he'd been summoned to.

Vinny marched himself back to the entrance of Merryweather and down the little street of old Victorians up to Grimsby House, another of the many features of Sweet Pea that he hated. Mansard roofs and scrollwork, spindles and knobs, with a painted lady smack in the middle, gargoyle face screaming down at him. They assumed the house had been some kind of prank on Morningstar's part, a frilly classic Victorian pre-furnished with the most atrociously pink and decadent historical furniture. Vinny had banished the majority of what he'd found in his bedroom, and Hell could pay the bill when the mission was over.

The others were waiting for him by the fire, demons disguised as men, drinking beers and lounging on garden furniture in their distressed denim and leather and tattoos.

"Well?" Bell asked, dark eyebrow arching.

On second thought, Bell might've been what Vinny hated most of all in Sweet Pea. The Warlord King. The pompous dickhead was a better title for him. The figurehead of the mission, who seemed to care shit all about getting anything done and who was barely ever around to show his face.

Vinny weighed the possible pros and cons of keeping this news to himself for a moment, but there was Paimon, watching him over the rim of round glasses, bearded chin tucked close to his chest. Paimon was worth taking seriously and certainly worth not pissing off, according to the Bowels. He was as brutal with his brethren as he was with angels, the Enforcer of Hell, the shadow you didn't want darkening your doorway.

"You've been drained," Ashtaroth noted, studying Vinny with the squint of laughter at the corner of his eyes.

"A witch summoned me."

"Obviously," Bell huffed out.

"To kill another witch."

The whole group stiffened, silent, and then as if they were all one being, Vinny's six cohorts leaned forward in their various seats.

"Which witch?" Paimon asked, eyes narrowing.

"Summoned me? I don't know. Small dark room, I assumed it was the shadowy one," Vinny said, shrugging.

"Which one is getting killed?" Bell snapped.

Vinny shrugged again, and Beleth stood, snarling with teeth bared. Vinny had to hold himself still, not recall Beleth's grip on his life or how it had felt to have his weak human body choked to death and left in the cold grass for dead like the last time he pissed Bell off.

"You don't know much," Ashtaroth said with a snort.

"Not really seeing basement witch as a stone cold killer," Dante said, falling back into the wrought iron tea chair. He raised one heavy boot to rest over his knee and shot Vinny a dubious look. "You sure you got the right coven witch?"

"How many other witches you know around here?"

"The wards should prohibit—"

"We were outside the wards—"

Bell scoffed and reached a hand up to comb through black locks. "Then you know shit all. Great work, Vinny."

"I claimed two witches!"

"Man, sounds like you just got used, and you don't even know who for," Aim answered, slick grin on his face as Barbie glared at Vinny in dark silence.

"Oh yeah, name one remotely useful thing you've done in the past two months," Vinny snarled. "You know what, name one thing *any* of us have done. Who gives a shit if I helped the right or wrong witch kill off another fucking witch? It's more action for Hell than any of us have managed so far!"

"That's lazy thinking," Bell said with a roll of his eyes. Vinny's hands cracked with how hard they clenched. "It's also the reason why you're still a dog on the leash rather than the one in charge."

"Fuck—"

"Don't finish that unless you want to piss those jeans you're wearing. Ash, go scout the mountains. Take that monster truck thing. See if you can get any tastes. I'll check town."

"I said they summoned me from outside the wards," Vinny snapped, frowning.

"Sit down, Vine. It's time for details," Paimon ordered, his low and smooth voice catching Vinny by the ear like a school marm.

He scowled as Bell and Ash both headed for the driveway, sweeping past him. Ash clapped Vinny on the shoulder, laughing as Vinny snarled at him.

"Hey, like you said, at least it's action," Ash said.

Bell didn't even bother looking at him.

Fuck this mission, fuck this town, and fuck his supposed fellow soldiers. Vinny would tear Sweet Pea down one soul at a time if he had to, just to get his ass back to Hell where it belonged.

5

OVER THE EDGE

I mogen floated around the knit shop, helping herself to trying on some of June's samples, inspecting the magic embedded in the stitches. June studied her for flashes of the anger she'd displayed in Josie's bakery at the coven meeting, but in typical Imogen fashion, the mood had evaporated and left no trace behind.

"What time is it?" Imogen asked.

"Seven-fifteen," June said, without glancing at the clock.

"She's late," Imogen said, eyes flicking to her sister.

June hummed and glanced out the windows to the dark and barren Sweet Pea street. There was a storm settling in for the night, fat golden snowflakes illuminated by orange street lights, spiraling on the wind before smacking wetly to the ground. Amira was late, but not by much, especially considering the snowfall.

"Maybe she changed her mind," Imogen mused, and June's fingernail scratched absently over the wood finish of her desk at the bright tone in her sister's voice.

She'd turned off the overhead lighting after closing the shop, not that anyone had been by since the morning, and that was only one of her regulars stopping by for a little mountain chit chat over how long the storm would hold.

"Or maybe they already closed the roads."

"The news said ten," June muttered. "Gin. Why did you go after Josie like that?"

Imogen lifted a hank of Rambouillet off the shelf, drawing it to her nose for a long sniff and ignoring the question until her eyes slid to June's. "You would've rather she kept lying?"

June resisted the urge to roll her eyes at her younger sister. Did Imogen think she was stupid?

"I would've rather she told us voluntarily, but she wasn't great at hiding that something was going on," June said, thinking privately, *Not like you are.* Josie's magic had been irregular lately, but it had still been *Josie's*, seductive and playful, curious. Positive and helpful.

"We should be staying away from him, Junie," Imogen whispered, voice only as loud as the dull thud of snow on the window.

For a moment, June thought Imogen was talking about Josie's demon. But of course not.

"We are staying away from him, Gin. And we're helping another woman do the same," June said, glancing out the window again, searching for headlights on the road.

"And if he follows her here to you?" Imogen asked.

"He's always known where to find us," June said, shrugging. Brett was fascinated with their father. He'd visited the cabin. He could've tracked June down after she and Imogen left. It wasn't even a long drive. "He doesn't come because—" She swallowed the words. *Because he is afraid of us.*

He didn't have to be, not of June at least. June wasn't that kind of witch. She'd never been as good as Imogen at turning off the part of herself that worried about consequences to what their parents had taught them. Imogen had been *too good* at turning off that conscience and taught too young, as if Pearce and Celia Byrne had decided their mistake with June had been not starting her training when she was younger.

"This is good magic," June said at last, sighing.

Imogen didn't answer that, just propped herself against the shelves of yarn and stared at June through the dim light of the shop. "I'll apologize to Josie."

"Good. If she *is* at risk, it's not going to help to push her away," June said and then winced, because that was her policy with Imogen. Tolerate the drugs, the occasional slips into manipulative or corruptive magic, just to keep her hold on her sister and not drive her over into the dark temptations that chased Imogen.

"I was just playing chess," Imogen murmured. "Testing the pieces."

"We don't do that with people," June said automatically.

"I'll apologize," Imogen repeated.

Little poisonous thoughts flitted through June's head. Familiar thoughts. Was it too late for Imogen? Had the games their father made up to coach Imogen into her power shaped her beyond repair? Was Imogen only obeying June rather than understanding her?

"The vow *is* interesting," Imogen continued, rolling to face the windows, crossing her ankles and stretching the sleeves of the borrowed sweater down to cover her fingertips.

"How so?"

"He swore her *no harm*. He's a demon, so he'll probably choose a literal, physical interpretation, but he is bound to it. Not only can he not harm her, he has to protect her from the others too."

June's eyebrows raised. That sounded...like more than fucking around, as Josie had termed their sex. "She forced him into it?"

Imogen's lips quirked, head shaking, long braid slipping over her shoulder. "No. He offered it willingly. So maybe Josie *is* the key to unraveling their mission."

June bit down on the inside of her frown. Imogen was still thinking in terms of people as game pieces.

"That's next week's project. Tonight, we help Amira."

"How much longer do we wait?" Imogen asked.

It was seven-thirty now.

"I don't know. There's sandwiches in the fridge in the back."

Imogen pushed off the yarn cubbies and headed for the back, June watching her from her desk. She should have asked Josie to come anyway. If Josie's magic was corrupted, it was still nothing to Imogen's. June didn't know what it would take to rinse the stains out of Imogen. She'd simply learned to live with their mark on her sister.

"She changed her mind, June," Imogen said as June's little car pulled to a slippery stop outside of Imogen's cabin. June had stopped thinking of it as home a long time ago, and now on the rare occasions she went inside it felt more like a museum of bad memories.

"The storm might have scared her off coming," June admitted.

They had waited as long as they could. As it was, June was barely going to make it back to town before they started to close roads.

"We left him because we're strong," Imogen said, expression a little wild in the passenger seat. "Most of them go back."

June didn't feel *strong*. She felt like a bomb that never wound down, constantly poised on the last second, warning herself over and over she was a tick away from exploding.

Imogen's hand rested on June's shoulder, and with it came the return of calm, a cool cascade burning away the urgency that tried to boil over. June sighed and nodded. "I'll let you know if she gets in touch. Don't forget to reach out to Josie."

Imogen stared at her a moment longer, eyes too big and cheeks too hollow, some of the little girl June had carried around the woods like a baby doll still there in her face but most of it eaten away with time.

"Goodnight, Junie," Imogen said, leaning in and pressing a soft kiss on June's cheek before pushing open the car door and letting in a startling rush of cold air.

June waited for Imogen to close the cabin door behind her before turning the car around in the drive, rolling slowly down the road. The snow rushing ahead of her headlights reminded June of something out of an old sci-fi movie. She remembered pretending the car was a spaceship whipping past stars as her father had driven them home from a circle at the smallest hours of the night in the winter, her body tired after keeping up with the adults, blood buzzing with magic too big for her small bones.

Up ahead on the small back road that led more immediately back to town, a road closed sign glowed white and orange.

"Shit," June hissed.

She flicked her turn signal on at the last second, fishtailing and holding her breath as she turned to the main road. The detour forced her to take the longer, wider route that led around the less steep side of the mountain and outside the wards of Sweet Pea. Her tires were already skidding on the growing coat of snow on the road, and while this route was safer, it also meant she'd be driving at a crawling pace for an even longer time in the storm.

She made it around three twists, her reliable but light and slippery Toyota wiggling nervously over the ice, before another car appeared on the road behind her, headlights high and violently bright. It drove patiently and politely back from her, but it still felt like pressure on an already dangerous journey.

June cursed as her car gave another warning squirm over an icy patch before taking her foot off the gas and coasting her way into the next overlook pull off. She'd let whoever was behind her pass first. Or maybe she would give up and call the sheriff to see if one of the officers putting out the road blocks could give her a ride back.

But the heavy headlights of the car behind followed June into the overlook parking, and her hands stiffened around the wheel as it pulled to a stop, not beside her but behind her, blocking her from exiting.

Brett was her first thought. Had Imogen been right? Had he followed Amira to find her? What would it feel like to see him after all these years?

June reached down to the knitting bag on the floor at the sound of the other driver's door slamming shut, fingers catching on scrap yarn and drawing it into her fist, mind running over every warding knot she knew.

What would Brett want from her anyway, if not Imogen? Her sister had probably always been his real goal.

A hulking shadow appeared, walking out in front of the bright headlights. Massive, broad shouldered, long legged. In an hour or two, June would chastise herself for the way her body relaxed as she recognized the silhouette. The relief only lasted a heartbeat, but it shouldn't have been her first instinct. Not when—

Ashtaroth's knuckles rapped on her window, and a moment later, his smiling face appeared. He looked like a sinful version of Santa Claus, all dressed in white after only a few seconds of being out in the storm.

"You need a ride," he called through the glass.

"No, I don't." She was too quiet for him to hear through the glass, but then again, he wasn't human.

"Stitch witch," he teased, head tipping. "Your tin can isn't going to make it down the mountain. Come on."

June waited for him to open her door, which she had stupidly left unlocked, but he never touched it, just stood outside in the thick snowstorm, watching and waiting on the other side of the glass.

"Heated seats," he said, one eyebrow cocking.

June swallowed hard.

"Truce, witch. I vow to return you to your apartment, no harm done."

The resemblance of the vow from Ash to the one Bell had gifted Josie startled her in her seat. Did he know about Bell's promise? Was he mocking it now or...?

But doubting the evil intentions of a demon was a dangerous path.

"Why offer at all?" June asked through the glass.

Ash huffed, breath obscuring her view before rivulets of snow rinsed the fog off the window. "More time together to start my corruption, of course. Are you corruptible, June Byrne?"

He'd meant it as a challenge. As bait for her to rise to, refuse. But June knew that she *was* corruptible, the damage which had already been done and then carefully cut out of her. She sighed and turned the key in the ignition, the car falling still and silent as she rustled together anything that couldn't be spared until her car could be towed.

Ashtaroth stepped back as she exited the car, his broad body blocking the worst beating of the wind from striking at her.

"Yes," she answered, catching his eye, watching them widen. "But not by you."

Ash grinned at her in the dark, haloed in the glare of his headlights, and then turned on his heel and led the way to his passenger seat, opening the door for her, a wave of heat burning her cheeks as she heaved herself up into the cab. The vehicle was massive, big enough to suit the beast of the demon driving, and shockingly tidy. It smelled of harsh leather polish and lemon, so it must've been new.

She bundled her things together on her lap, taking the quiet moments alone in the hot interior to snoop, Ash stomping through the storm outside to the driver's side. Her gaze caught on him as he rounded the front, illuminated in gold and white, dressed in rugged layers and looking every bit the mountain man. The calm Imogen had left her with fractured at the sight of him, warm arousal and sharp edged panic clashing inside of her. It was acceptable to admit that the demon was attractive. It was more concerning to find herself suddenly curious about the texture of his beard or the width of his hips between hers.

June blinked and buried the thoughts as the driver's side door opened with a gust of cold wind and the soft grunt of the demon rising to the seat.

"What are you doing out here?" June asked.

He didn't buckle his seatbelt, she noted. Was that about being a macho man or invincible?

"What would you want to do if you lived in a house with

six other assholes?" Ash answered, the massive machine around them rumbling to life and backing away from her tiny Toyota. It *did* look like a tin can from this angle.

"You're counting yourself as one of the assholes," June said.

Ash laughed, and her whole body tightened at the warm, honeyed quality of the sound. "I am. But go on, answer."

Ash was a careful driver at least, but there was also something impervious about being inside of a vehicle this big, even as its momentum carried them a little faster down the curves of the mountain.

"I wouldn't live in a house with that many people," June answered easily. She didn't even live in the house with Imogen, although sometimes, she wondered if she should've put her foot down on that. "But I see your point. I don't *believe* you, but it's a good excuse."

Ash's grin flashed again out of the corner of her eyes. "Fine. I was checking your wards."

June stiffened at that, twisting to stare at him, his profile more elegant than she always expected, nose long and straight and brow smooth. And that mouth.

"Don't worry," he continued, not realizing he'd distracted her entirely without a word. "Diamond tough as ever. Can't blame a demon for trying."

Imogen checked them regularly to make sure they were holding up. She supposed it made sense that the demons would as well.

"What got you so into warding, starling?"

June's fingers dug into the canvas bag she held, eyes blinking at the endearment, a strange kind of resonance running through her.

"What are you afraid of?" Ash murmured, leaning

toward her as they met another bend in the road, the wet splash of snow under the tires whispering with his coaxing tone.

A harsh laugh escaped June's throat, and she shook her head. "Everything. Being afraid doesn't *stop* me." She bit down on the confessions that tried to rise to her tongue at that moment. She hadn't been alone with Ashtaroth since the day they met, and there was a strange kind of calm that came with his presence. She was so focused on him, it turned down the volume on all the other things that beat at her daily.

"Tell me why, then," he continued.

"What are you afraid of?" she parried.

"Nothing. Nothing worth being afraid of," he said, shrugging.

"Being afraid keeps me ready," she said, more to herself than to him, but he answered her with a thoughtful quiet.

On a ledge at the other side of the road, a deer hesitated at the precipice, body tensing as it fought its own impulse to throw itself toward the car before the car could meet it first.

"Then that makes you a very dangerous adversary," Ash said slowly, nodding once.

The road turned, and suddenly there were lights ahead. June had a physical reaction to police lights every time. She became small again, frightened, her heart in her throat and her nails biting into her palms. Ashtaroth slowed the Humvee as they neared the emergency vehicles, and June leaned forward to hit the hazard button.

"Pull over. What did you do?"

Ash laughed at her question and obeyed the order. "Promise it wasn't me. They're probably just putting up the road block."

"Not with five officers and a tow truck," June whispered, counting the blurry figures standing on the road.

"Hmm...you might be..." Ash trailed off as he pulled to a stop. "You taste that, witch?"

June ignored him, shoving herself against the massive passenger door, letting her belongings spill over the bench seat. She gripped tight to the handle, her feet trying to slip out from under her as she landed on the road. Ash was already following her, jumping down on the other side.

She did taste it. First was the whiff of burnt rubber on the road, but there was more too. Ozone and bitter charcoal at the back of her throat, up high in her nostrils, the pinching static sensation of magic in her lungs.

"June? Is that you? What are you doing out... Oh." Mark, June's old classmate and current deputy sheriff under his mother, marched away from the ledge to meet them halfway between the cars. His gaze flicked from June up to Ash, a slight frown creasing the corners of his mouth.

"I was dropping Imogen off, and I couldn't make it back through the shortcut. He picked me up at an overlook," June said quickly. "What happened?"

Ash was crossing between them, walking up to the barricade at the edge of the drop off, leaning over to stare down into the dark. His absence left room for the snow and wind to crash onto June.

"It's not looking good we think," Mark said softly. "You guys should get back into the car and get to town before the roads get any worse."

June nodded, but she only crossed her arms over her chest and waited for one of the other officers to call Mark back to the scene. She followed the wobbling black tire tracks now printed on the pavement until they vanished. Ash was still at the edge of the road, and he shifted as she moved to join him, standing between June and the wind again. His hands cupped her shoulders as June leaned over the rickety, rusted barricade. Down on the steep incline, caught between broken trees and branches, a car was steaming, cradled in the wreckage, one headlight flashing erratically. A spiderweb crack over the front windshield obscured the view of whoever was inside, but June had recognized the bright cheerful shade of yellow on the car.

Amira's car, thrown over the side of the mountain road, tore straight through the barricade. As good an excuse as any for not meeting up at the shop. *Morbid*, June chastised herself.

"No witch's magic on the road," Ash growled at her back.

"The car then," June said, nodding, oddly reassured by the warm grip on her shoulders, holding her steady as the entire mountain seemed to tip sideways as if to take her over the edge too.

"How afraid of that girl were you, starling?" Ash whispered, breath on the back of her ear.

June's fingers itched to reach up to his, steal some of that warmth he gave off so easily. "Barking up the wrong tree, beast," she answered. Maybe she had been afraid of Amira, in her usual way of wondering when a person would ask her for something. Not as afraid as Imogen had been.

"Mm. And your sister?"

June frowned and twisted to look back at him. "Imogen was with me."

Ash only nodded. "Figured as much. Come on, let's get you back in your safe little cage, starling."

Ash's hand was bigger than she expected, dwarfing and enveloping her grip. Warm, yes, and rough in a way that made him almost believable. Those should've been hands that had worked hard, not ones created to hide the monster beneath. June followed Ash like a shadow back to the Humvee, the wind and snow wrapping around him barely skimming against her.

You're holding hands, she thought, strangely detached from the realization. They were, and it was like the ground under her feet was a little more solid, the sky above steadier, the whirling storm inside of her slowing enough for her to catch a breath until he was shutting the passenger door and she was alone in the chaos again.

6

SUBTLE CURSES

June had shared her apartment with Josie briefly in the fall, after Josie had been attacked and nearly framed by their local mountain murderer. Months later, on quiet nights after closing the shop and returning to her apartment above, June missed the company. Josie was straightforward, and while she had some of Rosa's vibrant energy, she also kept it under a lid of sarcasm. Plus, she cooked food like she was breathing and didn't seem to give a second thought to feeding June when they were both done for the day.

Now, with Josie standing in front of her holding a great stack of dishes—a soup pot, a pie plate, a loaf of bread wrapped in a steaming towel, and a Tupperware of what June was hoping were leftover pastries—June was almost prompted to make an earnest confession.

I missed you.

Mostly, she had missed having someone else breathing and moving and sharing a space with her. And the food. She had *really* missed Josie's cooking.

"I made a salad," June said weakly, staring at Josie's

armload before coming to her senses and reaching out to help with the burden.

"Good. Thanks for...letting me come over," Josie said with a nod, following June into the kitchen.

"I'll be honest and say that I have questions, but I'm not... We're not..." June's tongue went stiff as she searched for the words. Josie had once referred to them as friends—not just covenmates or fellow young businesswomen in a town that didn't like change, but *friends*—and June wondered how she'd known it was the right word and found the ease to say such a thing. "Is the sex good?"

Josie's soup pot landed on her stove with a clatter, and June grimaced. Why was *that* what came out?

"Uhh..."

"Sorry. I don't know why I asked that. I just—"

"The sex is fantastic," Josie said, tipping her chin up, the first hint of the quintessential Josie Benoit glare flaring to life in her dark eyes.

How fantastic? June wondered, cheeks heating, a familiar male silhouette in her thoughts. "That wasn't my business, I'm sorry. It just came out."

Josie softened and turned away, digging through June's kitchen drawers with all the ease as if it were her own place. She pulled out a wooden spoon June didn't recall owning and came back to the oven, flicking on the burner to low and lifting the lid. Peppers and onions and garlic, tomatoes and butter and the tickle of rich seasoning flooded June's sterile space. Her stomach rumbled immediately, and Josie's hackles lowered as her smile rose.

"Wow. Gumbo?" June's shoulder brushed against Josie's as she leaned in for another deep inhale that threatened her with a sneeze in the best way. She would be feeling that heat right down to her toes. Fuck the salad.

"Jambalaya," Josie corrected with a roll of her eyes. "It's my apology recipe. I am apologizing for the way you found out about, you know, my fuckin' sex life apparently," she finished, trailing off in a mumble.

"I'm also sorry about that, but more for your sake," June said, reaching across the warm steam of the soup to pick up the still hot loaf of bread and cuddle it to her chest. "Did Imogen get in touch?"

Josie's eyes slid sideways, her lips pursing. "Your sister and I will sort this out on our own. Contrary to what you feel and what Imogen seems to take advantage of, you are not that girl's keeper."

Yes, I am. "She wants to keep us away from Lohman," June said, because making an excuse for Imogen was second nature sometimes.

"I get that," Josie said, nodding. "And I'm sorry for what he put you through. And I'm really proud of you for trying to help someone else. I know it's not as easy as it sounds."

June opened her mouth to mention Amira and the car over the mountain, but thinking of it took her back to sitting in the quiet purr of the Humvee with Ashtaroth as he drove her home in blessed silence.

"Do you trust Beleth?" She probably only got away with the subject change because the demon king was what Josie had come over to explain.

"Bowls," Josie said lightly, and June scrounged two bowls out of her dishwasher, checking to make sure they were clean before passing them to Josie. "I...I know that I shouldn't, but yes. I trust him." The confession came with a weary sigh.

"Because of the vow?"

Josie's brow furrowed and she slapped hefty portions of rice—from the Tupperware, sadly not full of pastry—into the bowls before smothering them with jambalaya. "I think I trusted Bell before the vow. No, I know I did. That was the second time he saved my life. Maybe it started before that first time too. There was just... He broke into my apartment, and even with my wards broken, even with him trying to mean mug me and scare me, he didn't set off the alarm bells. The Loa weren't mad to have him stopping by, maybe that's my excuse?"

"It must be nice to have ancestors you can trust," June said, blinking at the steaming bowl of food suddenly in her hands.

Josie hummed thoughtfully and stared over the kitchen counter, through the living room and out the window. June ladled a full spoon into her mouth, happily choking on the burning spice, shoulders dropping as it scorched through her, drawing tears up into her eyes and snot in her nose. Josie spiced the shit out of her food, and it was like it made the whole *world* brighter.

"Pace yourself. That andouille will put hair on your chest," Josie said without looking. June took another massive mouthful, even as the first bite's fire grew in intensity. "Gimme that bread. You're gonna need it."

"I'm not mad," June said, swallowing and enjoying the numb burn of her tongue. "About him, about you. I trust you."

"I worry about it constantly. Being played. Or, you know, if he has to make a choice. When he has to make a choice," Josie said.

Those are feelings, not just sex, June thought. But Josie probably already knew that and didn't need to have it pointed out. The petite witch was rummaging around busily, cutting thick slices of bread and scowling at June's spreadable margarine before begrudgingly slathering it on.

"But sometimes I get this sense that...that he's confused too. Not just about me but about the mission. About humans in general." Josie shrugged and balanced a buttered slice on each of their bowls.

June covered her thinking with chewing until her mouth was too hot to stand anymore and she gasped for air. "Ash gave me a ride home the other night."

Josie had a spoonful raised to her own lips, and it remained there as her eyes narrowed. "Shit. You think they're trying to like, seduce us all?"

"It wasn't like that," June said. But was that true? Reasonably speaking, June knew that Ash had been doing some kind of flirting on the ride. And since she grew overwhelmed and dizzy when she thought about the demon for too long, she swapped the subject with the next thing she thought of. "There was an accident on the road. I think it was Amira. And I think there was magic involved."

"His magic?" Josie asked, growing pale and settling the bowl aside.

"I don't think so," June mumbled through another bite.

Forced to share the entire night with Josie, June ordered the events in her own mind, finding both comfort and new anxiety. Imogen had been with her since the late afternoon, and she had never met Amira so she'd have no way of knowing what car to hex. Ash had been nearby at the time and he'd seen Amira's car, but June believed his curiosity in the scene was genuine.

"June, it sounds like this guy, Brad—"

"Brett," June corrected.

"—would be the person most likely to have the opportunity. And the motive."

"Or one of his coven," June said, nodding. Brett would've been able to convince one of his crowd to take action against

Amira in order to protect their head priest, if he didn't want to get his hands dirty himself.

"Shit. No wonder Imogen was so worried about this," Josie said, leaning against June's fridge.

June considered offering to let them sit in the living room, but her bowl was almost empty and she was sure she could eat another serving before Josie got around to revealing whatever was in that pie plate.

"Do we know it was magic?" Josie asked.

"I know there was magic at the scene, something corrosive. But Mark wouldn't tell me anything about how it had happened," June said. "I heard gossip in the shop today that the driver was dead."

"Mark Nolan. You spoke to him?"

"Only for a second. He was there with the rest of the department."

Josie's gaze narrowed on her again, head tipping, and June squirmed under her stare. "You could get more out of him."

"What do you mean?"

Josie snorted, head shaking. "June, that man is dizzy over you. His puppy tail starts wagging whenever he sees you—"

"His *what*?"

"He has a *crush* on you, June. He let you take evidence from a crime scene in the fall—"

"He thought it was high schoolers."

"Pretty sure he'd show you a police report if it got him a date. Although I don't recommend being *that* direct about it."

June's nose wrinkled. Mark was... Well, she'd known him forever. He was a bit like furniture—familiar, with a few memories attached, but mostly part of the scenery.

"How direct do you think would work?" June asked.

Josie's eyebrows bounced. "Wow. Seriously? Um, well it can't be the only thing you talk to him about. And a little booze never hurt to get someone to relax. You can't push." Josie's head tipped again. "June, if it was magic and it was to do with Brett...what are you going to do?"

June frowned and took a bite of wonderfully dense, chewy, flavorful bread to stall. "I don't know yet," she admitted.

She only knew there was something *wrong*. Not just the idea that Brett might've caused a young woman's death in order to keep his dirty little habits secret.

No, what concerned June was how faint her anger was, like it was buried in thick wool to muffle the sound of her own screaming. She should've been horrified. Terrified. She should've been ready to storm her way to Brett Lohman and teach him the consequences of taking advantage of witches.

Instead she was numb. Numb and curious. She would feed the latter and see what came next.

***

JOSIE WAS RIGHT, June thought with a little note of discomfort. Mark was bouncing on his heels by the door of her shop, stinking the place up with liberally applied cologne, overdressed for the simple offer of drinks, and with a dark splotchy blush rising up from his collar to his cheeks. Or maybe that was a rash from the aftershave? He had bought her flowers. Wrapped in plastic, so grocery store flowers rather than Rosa's.

"Sorry to hold you two up," June's customer, Courtney, said, eyes bouncing between them.

"It's fine," June said softly, bagging up the last of her yarn.

Mark started to speak, but it was a bit of a nervous squeak, and instead he cleared his throat and nodded.

Maybe this was a mistake. Maybe it would've been better to work a little magic on Mark's mother for the information, rather than play a man this way when he made it ever so slightly too easy. Both options were manipulative. She'd pay for it later.

Courtney left with a grin at June and a pat of her hand on Mark's shoulder. "Nice flowers. Happy Valentine's Day, you two."

Oh. Oh *no*. Was it—? June's head turned to the wall, and she blinked three times before accepting her own error. It was Valentine's Day. She'd asked Mark Nolan out on *Valentine's Day*.

One thing at a time, she told herself. First, the flowers. "Let me grab a vase for those—"

"We could swing by your apartment, if you—"

"No," June said immediately. Her apartment was sacred. But she softened the refusal. "No, I spend more time here anyway."

She didn't have a vase, but she wasn't taking Mark up to her place, so the tall plastic cup at the top of her cupboard would have to do, and she settled them onto the center table as quickly as she could.

"You look nice, as usual, of course," Mark said.

Maybe this is *the consequence for the idea*, June thought, stifling her own cringe.

"You too," June said with a tight-lipped smile. Mark looked...like Mark. Nice, normal. Maybe even a little bit handsome? *Mundane*, her thoughts hissed.

"I was thinking maybe High Top? Grab some dinner too?" Mark said as June went about settling the shop for the night.

High Top would be full of locals tonight, possibly even Mark's parents. Courtney would spread the story eventually, but at High Top they would be constantly interrupted by familiar faces. Gunney's Tavern would rule out the awkwardness of dinner but would be even worse on the crowd of singles drinking together. There might even be karaoke.

Which only left...

"What about The Inferno?" June said.

"The...Inferno."

"I like their food," June lied. She'd never tried their food and she'd heard mixed reviews, but it was the one restaurant where none of the locals seemed to want to go.

"Uh...sure. Sure," Mark said brightening. "It's owned by that odd group of new guys. The bikers."

June nodded and hummed, wincing as Mark opened the door and she was smacked with a gust of cold before bundling her coat and scarves tighter around her.

"They're an odd group," Mark repeated, glancing at her.

She was saved from having to answer by the scarf now wrapped around her face, but she nodded. They were odd. They were demons. They were only across the road, so at the least the walk was short.

She hadn't been inside The Inferno yet. Really, she'd been avoiding the demons as much as she was able. The Inferno wasn't *much* of a better choice for this date-slash-inquisition, but June was relieved to find that the only faces staring back at her were the demons and two sullen, gum-popping waitresses.

Actually, the decor wasn't half bad. She'd been expecting those old posters of scantily clad women on motorcycles, but the bar wasn't screaming biker. It was dark, which was kind of a relief. And they hadn't decorated for the holiday, which was even better. The energy was menacing but styl-ish. And the temperature was appropriately warm, she thought, unwrapping herself. The whole place was rough enough to not be considered classy but definitely trendy, and the music playing was a gritty bluesy rock at a comfort-able volume. Come tourist season, it would probably be a hit.

"Sit where you want," one of the waitresses announced, passing them with a dubious glance up and down.

June's eyes didn't take long to adjust, and she counted the demons around her. Two at the bar and one behind it, Aim, Dante, and Barbie respectively. Beleth, Ash, and the one called Pie were at a round booth at the back. The seventh demon was absent, but June remembered with star-tling clarity that he wasn't one she wanted to run into. She and her coven had summoned him for answers months ago, and he wasn't likely to be her biggest fan.

Mark tried to steer June to one of the small tables by the window, but she marched determinedly for a booth in the corner opposite Ash and the others.

"Beer?" Mark asked, stalling by the bar.

"Gin and tonic," June said to the bartender, who nodded gruffly. She escaped to the back of the bar, leaving Mark to wait for the drinks.

Ash met her at the booth. "What are you doing here, starling?"

June blinked at him, and an uneasy thought occurred to her. Had she chosen the Inferno *because* of him, rather than in spite of him?

"Drinks," June said, sliding between Ash and the booth so she could face the front door.

"In my territory?"

"You knit in mine," she tossed back, and Ash's grin flickered through his beard.

Mark was wavering at the bar, watching them, clearly deciding between dutifully waiting and coming to defend his date.

"You're milking that chump for info on the accident," Ash whispered.

June shifted uneasily in place at being found so transparent. Maybe that was part of his power rather than just knitting beautiful sweaters.

"It's just a date," June said primly.

Ash chuckled. "Starling, that guy wouldn't have the first clue on what to do with you. He's a square."

"And I'm the circle?" June asked, frowning.

Ash ducked low, his face hovering over hers, beard looking full and tempting. Soft. "You're a prism."

June blinked at that, a rare kind of delight bubbling deep under that muzzle of confusion, worry, and numbness.

"I went back to the road," Ash continued, watching her. Out of the corner of her eyes, Mark was approaching, but she couldn't tear her focus off Ash. "They had to leave part of the car behind. No hint of magic on it."

June's brow furrowed at that. If it wasn't the road, and it wasn't the car—

"Hey, uh..."

"Ash," the demon offered, standing straight and holding his hand out. Mark had to put the drinks down first, and June scooped hers up and sucked roughly on the straw, as if it might cool the warmth on her cheeks.

Mark looked like a little boy as he tried to make himself grow bigger in front of the demon.

"Just checking to make sure June got her car back all

right," Ash said, grinning at Mark, clearly aware of the posturing and that he would always end the victor.

"I dropped it off myself," Mark said, chin bucking.

He had? June hadn't paid attention.

"I'll go get you guys some appetizers," Ash said, winking at June, who immediately tried to refuse. She only needed one drink to get her answers. "On us, since it's Valentine's Day, after all."

Fuck.

"Thanks, that'd be great," Mark said, crossing his arms over his chest and waiting until Ash spun on his heel before sitting down. "They need the business," Mark said in a low tone to June.

She wasn't sure how accepting free appetizers made them the generous ones in this case, but at least Ash had offered her the opening to the topic she needed.

"Speaking of the accident, what ever happened with that?"

Mark sighed and rolled his neck on his shoulders. "I'm guessing you heard the driver didn't make it?" June nodded, and he echoed her. "Yeah, I mean, it looked like the storm was at least partly at fault, but you always have to check. The car didn't have any failure, but there is a dent on the back corner we're gonna look into in case it was a hit and run."

"Oh wow, so someone might've hit her," June repeated.

Mark hummed and sipped his drink, waving a hand in the air. "I mean maybe, the dent could've been from another time, and there was only the one set of tracks."

"So you'll track down whoever made the dent?" June asked, resisting the urge to push her will at him, spill the answers from his lips.

"Uh, I mean, if we can. Just got started on that, but I don't do a lot of the research. I leave that to the new kids." Mark grinned and shrugged sheepishly. "We've got a lead on an ex to follow at least."

June's head spun. The ex was obvious, they would track down Brett. But would it be his car that matched the dent on Amira's? And if the accident was a hit and run, why did she and Ash smell magic in the air? Was it too far a distance and he'd had to follow? Had he been in the car with her, or did he have someone in the coven now who could—

"June," Mark repeated, laughing and waving his hand in her face until she flinched and shook herself. "Sorry, it's a morbid topic, I know. How's Imogen?"

June's teeth clenched. Imogen was often a morbid topic too. Or at least an uncomfortable one.

"She's Imogen."

"I bet it's tough on her when the roads are closed and she's stuck up there on her own," Mark said.

"I think she prefers it."

His mouth parted, but he couldn't come up with anything to answer that with and ended up nodding dumbly.

June scrambled to think of another question, if only to avoid Mark's version of small talk, but he was probably right. Any other clues would come from either an autopsy report or information on the dent, and asking for a follow-up on the evidence didn't adhere to Josie's guideline of being indirect.

Before either of them could find a new safe topic, a waitress arrived with a heavily laden tray. There were appetizers, yes—some sort of egg roll that smelled like a taco—but also burgers loaded so high, there was no physical way to take a full bite, and chicken wings dressed in ranch and covered with jalapeños, bacon, black olives, and shredded cheese as if they were nachos.

"Wow, looks great!" Mark cried, passing June the enormous plate of wings and taking the burger for himself, as if they'd put an actual order in.

June searched the room for Ash and found him leaning at the end of the bar, staring at her with a wicked grin on his lips. He winked and cheers'd a bottle of beer in her direction, cursing her to an awkward—not to mention disturbingly messy—dinner date that she hadn't wanted in the first place.

7 SAINTS AND SINNERS

He waited from the corner of the back booth, eyes on the far end of the block, until a set of lights flicked off.

"You shits have this in hand. I'm going for a walk," Bell announced.

In the three plus months of...whatever game it was he was playing, Bell had learned not to look his compatriot and fellow demon king, Paimon, in the eyes as he made his excuse for the night. There were only so many times one needed to have another person stare knowingly at them, and Bell had hit the quota months ago.

He rose from the booth, unhurried. The stitch witch was still trapped at her table, now with a monstrosity of a brownie sundae that Ash had brought her and her date. Danny's noisy and demanding sister, Mona, was at the bar, barking at their chef through the kitchen window. The path to the door was clear, and Bell let out a sigh as he stepped out into the icy cold of winter in the Virginian mountains.

Leaving the Inferno, leaving Grimsby House, was a little

like taking off an article of clothing you'd grown out of—an irksome pinch released to let the blood flow freely again. He turned right out of the door, down the dark sidewalk, as if he were about to walk in subzero weather to the preserve, and then ducked into the side alley, surrounded by brick.

He eyed the drifts that had piled up against the wall, counting them carefully until he reached the fourth. Crouching, his hands dug into the snow, heating up and rushing icy water over his knuckles until he found it.

Round and squat with a thick neck, glass etched with its seal, was the top shelf bottle of rum Bell had ordered on the sly and secreted away. The label was a little sodden now, but it would hardly matter.

Bell snatched up the bottle and then shifted sideways into the second-story apartment at the same time that Josie flipped on the lights.

"Oh, for fuck's sake!" she cried, one hand flattening over her heart.

Even from across the room, Bell could hear it pound. He shouldn't find it so funny that he startled her almost every time he appeared, but...

"Perfect timing," Bell said, grinning as Josie glared daggers at him, lips pursing in that delicious pout of hers.

Instead of rising to his bait, Josie's shoulders sagged, her eyes rolling. Damn, it was never a good sign when her eyes rolled.

"I brought a present," Bell said.

"Bell, today was Hell, I dunno if I'm..." Her eyes finally caught on the bottle, head tipping. "Is that booze?"

"Facundo Rum."

"Well...I can't say no to top shelf," Josie said, blinking slowly. She did look exhausted. Beautiful, feisty, but not with her usual bounce and attack.

"Oh, no. I never said it was for *you*," Bell said, eyes widening, the bottle raising high as Josie approached him.

"Bell," Josie growled.

He missed her calling him Mr. Bad News, and he got the impression it was a sore spot for her now. Now that he was fucking her at night and pretending to be the general of a war team of demons by day.

Am I pretending? he wondered.

"It's for the loa," Bell said, dropping the bottle into Josie's hands as her eyes widened and all the irritation drained right out of her. "Do you think they'll mind sharing?"

"The loa. *My* loa?" Bell nodded, and Josie's smile was small and simple. "Thank you. And no, I think they'd appreciate the drinking company. You open this, I'll grab some glasses."

Bell took the bottle back and headed for the bedroom, glancing over his shoulder to catch a glimpse of Josie peeling out of her coat, rubbing her hands over her face, before ducking out of sight. Was he wearing out his welcome lately?

Was he getting...*self-conscious*?! That was even worse.

Bell paused outside of Josie's bathroom door, lighting the candles on the tub ledge and starting the water with a stray thought before stepping into the bedroom.

Josie's altar waited in the corner, cluttered and clean, intricate and full of love and curious trinkets. Bell had only formally met one of the loa so far, Papa Legba, and it had been a strong shift in his demonic perspective. But Josie had spoken a great deal about the Ghedes and Filomez, her patron of prosperity and business. The loa existed outside of Heaven and Hell, outside of angel and demon, of good and evil, and Bell was fascinated.

"You were open late tonight," Bell said as Josie joined

him in the room, moving to kneel in front of the altar and to lay out five shot glasses—three for the loa and two for them.

"A lot of people leave things to the last minute on Valentine's Day," Josie said with a shrug, but she glanced at him out of the corner of her eye. There was a little bit of flour or powdered sugar behind her ear, and lots of chocolate stains on her pants.

Ah, Saint Valentine's Day. Not quite what it had been after so many years, but equally irksome.

Bell cracked the seal on the bottle and poured their line of drinks, nudging one in Josie's direction. She took it and waited for him to grab another, the pair of them quiet as they cheers'd the altar first, tapped the shot glasses together, and then took their sips. Velvety and spiced, head and syrup. Bell appreciated the craftsmanship in the rum, but even more than that, he appreciated the expression of surrender on Josie's face as her eyes fell shut and her cheeks flushed.

"I started you a bath," he said.

She nodded, sipped again, and blinked her eyes open. "Are you staying?"

They usually didn't tiptoe like this, and it took Bell a moment to sort through the puzzle. Valentine's Day was a human courting celebration, and he and Josie were...straddling some kind of undetermined line. If he stayed, it would be significant to her, which meant he should leave if he was going to maintain the illusion of control. If he left...

Bell didn't want to be insignificant. Certainly not to this petite, ornery, delightful witch.

"Who else will wash all the flour off you, Cupcake?"

Josie's lips pursed and her eyes narrowed, and Bell decided that overthinking could wait for another night. Josie was tired, and he wasn't ready to make a decision other than which of the hidden treats he would raid out of Josie's cupboards.

All of them. It was a holiday.

8 A Measure of Corruption

"**A**nd how was your Valentine's date the other night, Miss June Byrne?"

June tried to fight the scowl that came on like a reflex, but judging by Rosa's cackle, she failed.

Josie, walking ahead of June into Rosa's warm and lush carriage house, turned to shoot a sympathetic grimace over her shoulder.

"He's not your speed, baby," Rosa said, softening her teasing.

No, Mark and June hadn't meshed over their awkward dinner date at the Inferno, and even he—ever optimistic and as eager to please June as a puppy—had run dry of conversation to share with her that didn't revolve around old high school teachers she'd more or less forgotten about. He hadn't even put much effort into escorting her back to her apartment when she pushed him off, simply headed back to his car. And it wasn't *his* eyes who watched her trek across the street and to the quiet alley that would lead her home. She'd seen Ashtaroth standing at that window, still smirking, every bit as focused on her as he had been while she'd tried anxiously to dissect the strange and messy meal he'd sent her. Asshole.

"I'm not really broken up about it," June mumbled, wrestling herself out of her coat, aware of Imogen's watchful stare on her back.

The roads had been declared safe enough for travel up to the cabin again, just in time for the coven to take a closer look at Josie's magic. June would've sworn Josie was untainted by any demonic influence, but it didn't hurt to do the actual research.

Rosa's home was close and full to the brim with *life* and color, wild blooms stretching up to the light of lamps, the air thick with the scent of damp dirt and sharp growth, June's fingers brushing over a flat, fat leaf as she hung her things on a hand-painted coat rack decorated in swirls and blossoms and sunny patterns. It was chaotic and almost *loud* in the cozy carriage house, but welcoming too.

Josie draped her own coat over a chair without a glance, slapping her bag down and passing a vast tray of pastries into Rosa's greedy, grabbing hands. She stretched and took in a deep breath, eyes falling shut and face lifting up to one of the lamps as if it were the sun and she was another one of Rosa's plants. She was at home here, June realized. Comfortable and familiar with her friend's space. Was that just Josie's way?

"Date?" Imogen asked, hovering behind June.

"It wasn't. I'll talk about it later." Although, in truth, June was reluctant to bring the whole thing up to Imogen, who had sounded almost relieved by the news of Amira's death —not that Imogen had much intonation over the phone other than distracted.

"I figured if we were going to be able to tell what Bell's power was up to in me, I should probably be freshly stocked," Josie said with a slight blush, collecting their stares fully fastened to her.

"He just...you know, juices you up like that?" Rosa asked, eyes wide.

"Ew." Josie shook her head, eyes squeezed shut. "Uh, I—He...I think he thinks it's fun when I summon him for sex magic. It's like...flirting for him or something." She shrugged. "Demons."

June wanted so badly to look at Imogen at that moment. Had Imogen also "flirted" with a demon this way? She doubted it. Whatever reason Imogen had called her demon for, it had been solely for power, not pleasure.

"We always end up making it more about us after anyways," Josie murmured a moment later, sending a dreamy little glance out Rosa's window.

Right. Because right through the garden and over the hedge was Grimsby House where the demons all lived.

Rosa met June's gaze over Josie's shoulder, eyes blinking and mouth forming a silent 'wow.' Was she amazed at this soft and smitten Josie? June couldn't remember the dizzy delight of sexual satisfaction—she wasn't sure she'd ever had that with Brett, if she was honest, and now thinking of him only left her with a grimy, tired feeling in her chest.

"Well, the more power you have, the easier it will be to get a gauge, I think," June said, drawing Josie's attention back to their coven.

"Come on, we can get settled in the living room," Rosa said.

The living room was located through an archway decorated with vines, painted a rosy peach, with used furniture draped in vivid patterns and weavings from Rosa's grandmother. June hurried to take a seat in the armchair beneath the massive, abstract print that reminded June of the Hierophant tarot card. It was a dark, austere image in a house full of vibrance and playful color, but June knew the artist meant something to Rosa and she found a kind of calm under the shadow of the print.

"What do you need from me?" Josie asked, stealing an oversized cushion from a pile in the corner and making herself a seat on the floor as Rosa pushed a coffee table to the side.

"Just output," June said, adding when Josie and Rosa both blinked at her, "Find that power and imagine pushing it out."

"Don't push," Imogen said, settling on her knees on the worn carpet. June didn't miss the flinch in Josie's eyes as Imogen scooted closer. "Visualize it and picture it flowing out through your fingertips to start with. If we need more, we'll talk about pushing."

"How do we tell how corrupted it is?" Josie asked.

June and Imogen exchanged a glance. They would be able to read it, taste it on the air, but Rosa and Josie didn't have their training, even though June thought they both had fairly decent potential.

"Rosa, you can get a read on your plants?" June asked, and Rosa frowned and nodded. "If Josie directs the power into a plant, you'd have a sense of its quality?"

"Would it kill the plant?"

"Only if it was toxic, and I..."

Imogen picked up from June's hesitation. "We would probably be able to tell if Josie was carrying power that dangerous around."

"Really? 'Cause you seem concerned a couple weeks ago," Josie snapped.

Imogen didn't look the least bit daunted by Josie's glare, and June's teeth gritted in her jaw. Imogen hadn't reached out to Josie at all to apologize, even though she had promised.

"I overreacted," Imogen said.

Josie's chin butted up, and her stare turned back to Rosa, who sighed and stood from her couch. "I'll grab one of the babies."

"I was trying to—"

Josie let out a sigh. "I know what you were trying to do, Imogen. What I needed was for you to not be a bitch about it."

June's fingers tensed, digging into the arms of her chair, but Imogen's lips just twitched.

"Fair. I'm sorry I was a bitch."

June let out a slow breath as Josie nodded, and then choked on it as Rosa returned. She was carrying not a small potted plant but a massive one in her arms, with deep green leaves stretched up to tangle in her curls.

"Is that a baby?" June asked.

Rosa huffed a laugh, and Josie scooted back to make room for the plant. "No, but she's feeling especially hearty today so I figured she could handle a little experimentation. Fingers in the dirt, girl."

Josie glanced at June, who nodded, and then rested both hands on the soil in the pot, dipping her fingertips in and closing her eyes.

"Just let it bubble up," Imogen said. "I can already feel it simmering."

"Bell always gives me too much," Josie muttered.

June was aware of the hungry quality in Imogen's stare, the almost jealous glare of her gaze. Even June had a little nibble of craving in her chest. To be so easily—so pleasurably, by Josie's own claim—stocked with power like that?

And it wasn't Beleth who came to mind. He was too

much the king. Josie could bite back at a wolf with her sharp teeth, but June—

She shooed away the thoughts of demons and sex and power, especially where they all tangled together on one particular subject.

"Feels..." Rosa laughed. "Like sugar actually."

Josie's nose wrinkled, and Imogen shook her head at Rosa before commanding softly, "Focus."

June slid down from the chair cushion to the floor. Rosa was right—the little traces of magic bleeding from Josie and not going directly into the potted plant did taste sweet. Rich too, maybe a little sharper than usual, but more in a lively zesty way than like the blade it would've been coming from the demon himself.

"More," Imogen said, eyes sharp on Josie's face.

Josie's brow furrowed, and Rosa shifted, head tipping, gasping as the leaves rustled. "Um, Josie—"

"Is it poisonous?" Imogen bit out, and Rosa shook her head. "Then let her keep going."

"But—"

"It's important," Imogen said.

June wasn't sure it *was* important, but she was as curious as Imogen, especially when little buds sprouted, swelling fat and tipping to sharp points, before faint lines of pink appeared.

"Keep going," June said, her own hand reaching out to hover near Josie before June remembered herself and tucked both fists beneath her legs.

Imogen just laughed, watching the buds begin to blossom, unfurling heavy, broad flowering heads with bubbling stamens, until June recognized what was in front of her, the brilliant pink of the massive crinkled petals now mirrored on Josie's cheeks with her effort. Hibiscus. Enormous soft vibrant blossoms now swollen and weighing on their branches.

"Are they healthy?" June asked Rosa.

"Very," Rosa breathed out. She wasn't flushed like Josie, or staring hungrily at the flowers—the power that had been used to create them—like Imogen and June. Rosa looked frightened. As she should. This was more than their coven's usual brand of magic. Rosa looked every bit as nervous by the beautiful work as she had when they summoned Vine in Imogen's basement.

"Enough," June said to Josie, remembering that magic was supposed to have limits and she had just crossed one.

"Oh fuck, wow," Josie said, eyes bugging as she took in the results of her borrowed power. "Wow. So..."

"It's safe," Imogen said.

"It's not *corrupted*," June corrected, sending a warning glance to her sister. "Rosa, you should probably keep an eye on this to make sure Josie didn't strain it with the sudden growth."

Rosa nodded and swallowed hard.

"How much did that take?" Imogen asked, leaning into Josie's space, but she didn't wait for the answer. "You still have plenty. Getting power like that is like pulling teeth from demons. You have to be so specific, it's like measuring voltage and—"

"Imogen," June snapped.

"I'll go get the pastries," Josie offered after a quick, wary look between the sisters.

"I'll get plates," Rosa rushed out, chasing after Josie toward the kitchen.

"I didn't mean for me, Junie," Imogen said with a giggle, but she was too alive, too wired with excitement. And how awful was it that June started to worry when her little sister looked *happy*?

Because the things that make Imogen happy come at a cost.

"The only thing we needed to know was that Josie wasn't in danger, or wasn't going to put anyone else in danger."

"But if she could—"

"No."

Imogen's eyes narrowed, lips pursing, and June recognized the expression as an imitation of her own. "Demonic power is an incredible tool, and Josie has *uncorrupted* access to a limitless amount. We could protect Sweet Pea, we could—"

"No, Gin," June said again.

"As far as I know, Bell hasn't turned me into a toy for his advantage. I'm not going to do that to him either. I'm not crossing whatever line we're on, not that far, even for Sweet Pea," Josie said in the narrow doorway of the kitchen, the heavy tray of treats in her arms.

June held Imogen's gaze. Josie wouldn't have to agree. Imogen could steal the power, maybe. Or she could use manipulative magic to force Josie to demand more, to hoard it away from the demon.

"No," June whispered.

It was a mistake to let Imogen examine Josie in this way. It was like bringing a kilo of heroin to an addict and telling them they should keep it hidden, untouched.

The electricity of Imogen's clear gaze settled, feral tension in her face softening, and she let out a slow, thin breath. "Fine."

It wasn't the declaration of 'You're right, June. It isn't worth the cost,' that June was always secretly hoping to hear, but it would have to do.

Josie walked warily back into the room carrying two

plates laden with what June considered 'nibbles,' sweet bites so brief, they were barely worth the chewing. June's stare zeroed in on the platter Rosa had in her hands. Quiche and tartlets and croissants. That was more like it.

"So what did you find out about the accident?" Josie asked, settling her plates on the coffee table and dragging it back to sit between the circle of the four of them.

Imogen sat up straighter, a chocolate covered madeleine already pinched between her fingers. "You're asking about the accident?"

"I wanted to know if it was the storm or..." June shrugged, and her gaze skidded away from her sister's over to Josie. "Mark said they were investigating a dent at the back of her car in case it was a hit and run, and they were going to reach out to her ex. I assume Brett."

"But if it was a hit and run, why did you feel magic at the scene?" Rosa asked, offering the platter to June before resting it on the table.

June stacked a croissant on top of a raspberry chocolate tart on top of a slice of quiche and puzzled her answer out as she made her plan of attack on the food.

"That's what I don't know and can't really ask Mark. I don't even know if Brett found out about her coming to me, or if she said something about getting the hexes off but—"

"People die, Junie," Imogen said. "Accidents happen."

"Seriously? And the magic was...what? Her attempt to save herself?" Josie's nose wrinkled, and she shook her head. "That doesn't really add up, Imogen. But for it to have killed her... I mean, that's big magic, right?"

"There are energies, spirits, that can be called on who wouldn't leave the kind of trace science would pick up," June said carefully, avoiding her sister's eyes.

Who could tear two grown adults to pieces, leaving an unrecognizable, violent abstract behind in the woods.

"There are also icy patches on mountain roads in the winter," Imogen said.

"If he was able to do something to her without a proxy... Either way, it's big magic, yes," June finished to Josie.

"And she's dead," Rosa whispered, gaze vacant.

"Bell wasn't with me until late that night, but..." Josie shook her head. "Never mind. I'm going to be unbiased. You thought it wasn't Ashtaroth when you were with him, but could it have been one of the others?" Josie asked, nibbling the powdered sugar off another madeleine.

"You were with Ashtaroth?" Imogen snapped.

June had neglected to tell her sister about getting that ride home. Imogen had no room to judge, and yet...

"I hate to be their alibi, but I saw the demons in their backyard by a bonfire that night," Rosa said with a shrug.

"Dark rites?" Josie asked hopefully.

"Drinking beer and sitting around. Kinda just dude stuff."

"Ugh, demons are dull." Josie huffed and blushed. "Not that I, you know, want them committing murder."

"Ashtaroth gave me the impression that the wards have them fairly stuck on what they can accomplish," June admitted softly. "They would've had to have been outside at the same time Amira was."

"Ha, that's right! Take that, horny fuckers." Rosa laughed and then sobered again. "Sorry, we were talking about a young woman's murder, weren't we?"

"Why are you consulting demons?" Imogen snapped across the sea of pastries on the coffee table.

"I'm not consulting. My car wasn't going to make it down the mountain. He was on the road too, checking the wards in the woods, and he drove me home." Even to June's ears, the excuse sounded strange and weak. Perhaps because there had been a kind of...not just peace, but union between her and the demon at the accident.

"Bell got prickly about the murder. He wanted to make sure there wasn't a connection to me. Thought it might've been someone targeting witches specifically," Josie said, tipping her head to June. "I didn't tell him about you, but Ash might have."

June nodded stiffly. Ash had more or less asked her if she'd had anything to do with Amira's accident.

"There's no connection now," Imogen said, and there was a magnetic, uncomfortable tug in her direction, forcing them all to turn to her. "She died, for one reason or another. If we dig into it, we're only going to draw attention we don't want. June, it's done. He's not in our lives. Don't bring him back."

June's tongue was dry in her mouth. That impatient, battering animal squatting inside her, desperate to break free, was burning with anger. At Imogen? Or the rest of the world? It wasn't clear. It was like she was carrying a monster inside of her that she couldn't properly see or hear or touch. Only echoes of the creature's rage rattling her until her whole body ached.

"I absolutely understand why you both want to put this man well and truly behind you, but we're talking about murder right now," Rosa said, reaching a hand toward Imogen. Her fingers twitched, hand flexing, and she withdrew it with a gasp of breath.

"We don't know that for certain," Imogen said.

"Seems pretty fuckin' obvious to me," Josie muttered.

"They're right," June whispered. Why did it feel as though she was sitting in front of her father, small and nervous and too afraid to try one of his experiments? Everyone said June and Imogen looked like twins, but June saw her mother in the mirror and her father in her sister.

"No, Junie. It was just one little sliver of him back in our lives, and now it's pulled out. Let the wound close."

June frowned and shook her head slowly, trying to keep her voice soft, calm. "It's been eight years, and it hasn't closed yet, Imogen. Why would it now?"

Rosa and Josie were stiff and quiet on either side of her, but they were like solid walls, keeping her upright as Imogen's disapproval tried to pin her back down again.

"And how will you stop him, Junie? How will you fight him and the dark things *we* taught him? How do you think he knew how to kill a girl from miles away?" Imogen unraveled the words, a little whispering spell of their own, twining around June and squeezing until her heart pinched in her chest. "Will you let me use Josie's demonic power? I could probably squash him with a good hit of that."

Josie went pale, rearing back.

"Would you really undo all the work you put in on me? Wasn't that the whole point of this coven, to try and keep me clean? Oh sure, a little white light circle on Saturdays is nice, especially if you can funnel it into me and try and burn out all the grime and rot," Imogen hissed. Her eyes flicked to Josie and Rosa. "That's the truth, and you both already knew it. You're not here to learn, you're not here to be *friends*. You're my leash. A slow detoxification where I'm allowed to play with scraps of magic in the hopes it distracts me from tapping into the actual wells of power. The ones we would really need if we were going to take down Brett fucking Lohman!"

"Enough!" June shouted, the room spinning around her

as she found herself suddenly on her feet. But it was too late. Really, what more could Imogen possibly say?

Josie's face was turned away from Imogen, tilted down, but June could see the furrow of anger on her brow, the clench of her fists. And Rosa... Rosa's shoulders were up to her ears, lips tipped in a frown, fingers picking nervously at a bit of fringe on her skirt.

"I think we're done for the night," Rosa murmured, all her bright green energy twining around herself protectively.

Josie nodded, but neither of them so much as twitched to move.

"You should go," Rosa added, chin lifting and eyes meeting June's.

June's stomach turned queasily. That was pain there, a hurt friend. Imogen had spoken the truth, June had cultivated the coven to try and keep Imogen in line, but...

It had been a little bit selfish too. A place to remind herself that not all magic was so painful. A place to be a witch and safely explore her power.

Imogen tucked the satisfaction behind her usual empty mask, untangling her legs and rising, pastries in hand.

Find your own way home, June thought. And also, *Go fuck yourself, Imogen.*

But she didn't say either. It was clear that the invitation to leave was only intended for the Byrne sisters. That Josie and Rosa would stay here together, dissecting them, comforting one another. All while June carted her sister back up the mountains to the dark cabin she would rather never visit again.

Imogen followed June quietly, stuffed her mouth with a treat, and put on her coat. Their boots crunched on the thin shoveled pathway through the snow out to the road where they'd parked. June's car was cold, and she thought wistfully for a moment of that massive beast of a vehicle with its heated seats, fat, reliable tires, and blinding headlights.

She took the shortest, steepest route up, wondering at every skid of her tires if they would go careening backwards.

"What is wrong with you?" June whispered, their breath still fogging in the cold car. It was a question she had often swallowed, wishing she could pretend that Imogen was whole, not a creature she ought to be afraid of.

Imogen didn't stir from where her head was pressed to the windowpane. "You know what."

"No. No, Gin. You can't blame them for this. Not this time."

Their parents could take the credit for a great many things, but not for what Imogen had just done to their coven. June wasn't even sure if Imogen understood how thoroughly she might've broken their circle.

"We're safe, Junie. Stay away from Brett."

The beast buried in June roared and rattled the walls of its cage.

9    BACKUP

"And I told him—and it really is true, you know—'Lord, Edgar, I swear you wouldn't know what to put between the bread if I didn't tell you.'"

"You could always *stop* making his sandwiches for him," one younger woman muttered under her breath.

Mrs. Montgomery and her ilk all continued to laugh and snort as if they hadn't heard the girl.

Ashtaroth forced a chuckle out and tried to pretend he wasn't watching his little stitch witch rattling behind her desk as if she were standing out in the swirling snow instead of in her warm, cozy shop.

June Bryne's stitches were slipping, thin runs appearing in the fabric of her, form unraveling. And all the while, she sat with her needles click click clicking along, her gaze absent on an intricate lace pi shawl spreading gradually out of the ring like a spider's web. The gleaming glittering cage around her flickered, her fingers pausing, eyes going wide and horrified while focused on nothing, and then there was a shuddering glow and back she went to work.

He had tried for months now to crack that cage,

studying it, studying the woman inside, and he had never seen it so close to shattering.

"You're awfully quiet, Mr. Ash," Mrs. Montgomery declared in a lemon drop tone—sugary but tart.

Ash didn't mind playing the clown for these women if it gave him time to keep an eye on June, but there was something more appetizing on the menu tonight. Not to mention that June looked about one squeak of the rocking chair away from screaming and turning over all the furniture. What a glorious sight that would be.

"I heard a funny story today," Ash said, deciding tonight was as good a night as he had yet for picking at June's locks.

The women all turned expectantly toward him, even June's eyes shifting and narrowing in his direction, some of the chaos stirring inside of her settling as she focused on him.

"There was a tourist over in Jamesville last month. Rare winter month visitor. The locals saw him every day in and out of shops. Really friendly guy, sort of average, middle aged. Ate in all the restaurants, bought a little something in every store. But no one could figure out where he was staying. Thought maybe he had a camper up in the woods." Ash spun the tale patiently, yarn wrapping, needles picking, the dense texture of his sweater weighing down his hands. The sound of knitting was hypnotic, measured and whispering, and it added to the spell of the story.

"At the same time, funny little coincidences started popping up. Folks finding wet footprints in their house. Missing change off the table. Lost food," Ash continued with a little shrug, the first hint of unease passing around the circle of women listening with rapt attention. "One woman, single mom with three kids, heard her television running in the night."

Ash chuckled and eyed Mrs. Montgomery, whose rocking chair had finally stopped creaking. "Another single woman found the toilet seat up. Eventually, the little puzzle became clear. They caught him on a nature cam, just sliding into the unlocked backdoor of a house late at night. Turns out that tourist wasn't staying anywhere but with them. The very friendly locals unknowingly accommodated the stranger in their own homes. Easier to hide when he picked a different place each night."

And here was the final touch, the last little brick on the unsteady balance of Ash's story, complete with the threads of magic his stitch witch's wards would let him use, her grip a little looser when his end goal was to offer a break from the crowd.

"What they can't figure out is where this guy went. He vanished pretty much the second they figured out what he'd been up to. They don't know if he's still there, just too good at hiding, or if he found his way to a new town."

One of the women chuckled nervously, but the sound died abruptly.

"Well," Mrs. Montgomery said, eyes drifting to her purse at her feet. "Well, I don't think Sweet Pea has seen any..."

Ash spared a glance for June, surprised she'd let him get away with this gentle version of terrorizing her customers. Her head was tipped thoughtfully, the storm in her cage swirling tirelessly as she observed the scene.

"I should get back. Help Nick put the kids to bed," one of the younger women said, gathering up her things.

"It does look like the roads are getting messy. Should probably—"

One by one, they bundled up their bags and made their excuses, Mrs. Montgomery rising up from her throne with a glint of paranoia in her wide eyes as she glanced at Ash.

"What town did you say again?"

"Jamesville," he answered.

She swallowed. "Would make more sense for him to go to Peabody next."

Ash shrugged. "You know the area better than me."

Another minute, and they were gone, June's wards settling calmly into place as the door swung shut behind the women, a little dust of snow on the floor.

"What were you trying to accomplish?"

Ash stretched up from the small fold out chair that barely accommodated his form and waggled his eyebrows at June as he moved to the rocking chair. No squeaks were heard.

"Come on, starling, you know you like it better when it's just the two of us." Ash waited, but June only stared at him from behind her desk. "Would you have preferred they were here when I asked why you look like you're about two minutes from a meltdown?"

Just like that, the cage flashed and the chaos started up again, an expression of pure terror cracking through her calm façade. She stood, hand fisted around a twisted hank of yarn. He spared a little more power, tried to catch at the hard casing that contained the witch. She stepped around the desk, and he wasn't sure if it was his influence or her own determination.

"Stay out of it, beast," June muttered, stumbling her way to the yarn swift on the edge of the table.

Ash grinned. If she thought that word bothered him, she was sorely mistaken. He stood up from the rocking chair and crossed to her, the windows of the shop fogging up and obscuring the view of his slow transformation. June was staring at their reflection in the mirror, watching him grow taller, broader, his grin turn into a snarling snout, his shoulders and legs growing new twisted joints.

And through it all—the new heat in the room, the scent of a struck match, his low growls—she untwisted the hank of yarn, deftly placing it onto the swift and stretching them both taut, loosening the strings that kept the hank tidy. She turned to him, breath short with fear, but she had already told Ash. She was always frightened, a fact which baffled and disturbed him. If she was afraid, she would be cautious, and cautious people were always harder to catch.

It wasn't just fear in her eyes though, flicking rapidly over his demonic face, up and down his massive form. There was curiosity too, thorough study.

"You're ripe with chaos," he snarled, and the fine pale hairs on June's skin rose with the depth of his voice. "I can't tell if you're about to implode or explode, but if it's the latter, I think you could take this whole precious town with you."

June paled at that, bottom lip trembling, but still, she wouldn't speak.

"Who was the woman in the car accident?" Ash pressed, looming over June Byrne.

"She was from my ex's coven," June breathed out, one hand resting over her no doubt hammering heart.

Ash blinked and sagged back into his human form. Well. That wasn't what he'd expected.

"This is...guy problems?" he asked stiffly.

A ragged, anxious laugh broke out of June's lips, and then another, her whole body starting to shake, hands trembling as she reached for the loose end of the hank and began to twist it around three fingers.

"Fuck," June whispered, shoulders dropping. Ash nearly opened his mouth to push again, but he didn't have to. "Brett showed up after my parents died. I was in foster care, and he was the only connection I had to magic. And he made it feel...positive, not safe but not terrifying anymore. I was sixteen. He was twenty-eight."

Ash watched the yarn as it twisted through June's fingers. She was putting the story into the wool as she wrapped it around her hand. The magic was surprisingly dense and bitter. Ages meant very little to demons. There was only so much to pack into a lifetime, human or otherwise, before the measuring system of years became meaningless. What Ash did understand was the energy of a predator.

"Imogen was also sixteen when he started pursuing her, although I didn't realize it at the time," June said with an eerie kind of lightness as anger and desire burrowed into the yarn. She folded the loops around her fingers and began the ball, around and around and around as the words fell free, poison in every ply of the wool.

"When I did realize, Imogen and I left the coven. It's not really young girls he wants, I think. Or it's that too. But it's easier if we're young. He wants power, and we were not as hard to control."

"How did you leave?" Ash asked. "Without hexes like the other girl."

"I've always been good at wards. I put them in place before we left. The others... They always tried to *talk* to him," June said, frowning and nose wrinkling. "They were just warning him. Imogen and I are better at pretending."

June looked up at him, suddenly remembering him there, that she was spilling secrets—her secrets—to a demon, and Ash assumed she would throw him out in that moment.

"We're a little like you, beast," she said, the corner of her lip curling up. "Trying and failing to pretend we're like everyone else. That we think like everyone else. I warded us, Imogen hexed him enough to warn him off, and we left. And then she came." June frowned again and turned back to her yarn. "No, then...then it was bad for a while. I was... Brett was very good at seducing us, and I really wanted to believe in him. And then one day, I just...didn't care."

Because your sister had a demon help her bind your emotions, Ash thought, an uncomfortable slithering in his head to pair with the slightly snowy chill that was gathering around June. Frost on the cage surrounding her.

"I put the coven together for Imogen. Everything was fine. Everything was fine for *years*, and then she came."

"Did you kill her, starling?" Ash asked, voice low and soft, slipping the words into her ear to search for the truth.

"No, I wanted to help her. Not come forward, not like she asked. I promised Imogen we would never have to see him again. But I would've taken the hexes off," June said, the yarn ball growing steadily between her fingers as she wrapped.

Ash realized that his own power was getting caught up in the stream June fed to the yarn, that she had somehow ensnared him rather than the other way around, and she was putting his strength into whatever project she was preparing to knit. It wasn't anger, but a warm kind of pride that filled him at the understanding. Clever stitch witch.

"Brett killed her. Or someone from his coven."

Ash nodded and offered her a little more power just because he was curious what she might do with it. Around and around the yarn twisted on itself.

"You and your little detective coven at it again?" he guessed.

June's face crumpled, and the ball slipped suddenly from her fingers. Ash caught it before it could hit the ground and break the spell.

"No. Fuck. No, I don't even know if there's still a—I promised Imogen we would never see him again, but..."

June was trembling, the pretty bars of that infuriating cage rattling. Ash helped himself to one of her hands, almost surprised that he was able to touch her with the way she was ringing like an alarm. He passed the yarn ball back into her clammy palm and rested both his hands on her shoulders. It didn't take much, just a little hint of demonic power and the cage strengthened, calming and numbing the woman inside. He would've rather broken it altogether to see what came out, but only the sister and Dante could do that and he... He *wasn't* unsettled by the stitch witch's distress, he told himself. He was just curious to hear the rest of the story.

June let out a slow sigh, her body leaning into the press of Ash's hands until he held her upright. She blinked at him, drugged and tired.

"I want to destroy him," she whispered, brow furrowing. "And at the same time, I don't care that he's done this. I'm angry and I'm nothing. I want to know why."

Had she ever felt the cage around her before now? Ash wondered. She was building an awareness now as the trapped pieces of her fought for their own freedom to rage.

"You're going to confront him," Ash guessed.

June paled but nodded. "Imogen can't know. And the coven...I don't know if there's still a coven. But don't think for a second, beast, that that means you and your men will be able to hurt Sweet Pea. I can handle you on my own."

Maybe she could. Either way, it was cute that she would hiss at him like a baby animal warning off a predator.

"You need backup," Ash said, head bowing over hers, shadowing her face from the glare of the lamps above him.

"Backup," June echoed.

"For your witch ex who's been siphoning the power of young girls. That was the gist, wasn't it?"

June nodded, eyes narrowing.

"I think we can make a bargain, stitch witch," Ash murmured, leaning a little closer. Close enough that her eyes had to bounce between his and he could catch the black tea and mint on her breath. "Whatever warding you have..." He knew even better than she did what warding she had. "...whatever power, add me into the mix and this perverted little hustler won't stand a chance." Not unless this Brett asshole had more than just young women under his thumb, but June seemed like she would've known as much.

"Oh," June said.

It wasn't the slight curve of her smile that surprised Ash, but the obvious craving in her eyes. She'd never given him that look before, not even when he'd caught whiffs of curiosity and desire from her on the drive home. No, this was a craving for exactly what he'd offered—a demonic compact. His power in exchange for... Well, he hadn't set those terms yet.

"You must think I'm stupid, beast," June said, blinking, smile growing.

Ash swallowed the defeat gamely. He hadn't expected to win, right? Only for a moment there.

"Sign over Sweet Pea for your help in a problem that doesn't even touch this town?" June shook her head, the humor wilting as she turned away and began to wind the yarn off the swift again. She didn't steal any of his power this time, and when he tried to sneak some in, her walls were up again.

"I can handle myself, Ashtaroth," she said.

His name on her tongue was dry and teasing, cold too, and he itched to hear it again.

"Nice trick with the spooky story," she added, ignoring the reflection in the window of him standing at her back, encompassing her slight form within his larger one. "Way to clear the room."

"Do you want to know if it's true?" Ash asked, mostly to see if he could get her to look at him again.

"I don't care. I keep my doors locked. Speaking of, think you could pack it up early since you scared off everyone else?"

She still had half the hank left to wind, she wasn't going anywhere, but he had been thoroughly dismissed. Ash laughed under his breath and went to grab his knitting bag, a beat-up old leather satchel he'd found at the antique store that Vinny thought was funny to call a purse. Like Ash gave a fuck.

"You know how to find me if you change your mind, starling," Ash said, heading for the door. June raised a skeptical brow at Ash, and he added, "Or is your sister the only one doing the demon summoning?"

It didn't land the way he hoped—continuing their antagonistic ease together. June paled and her chaos started up again, burning through the power he'd put into calming her. The door to the shop swung open, and June abandoned her yarn winding briefly, twisting her fingers and pushing them toward him. The net of magic caught, tangling around him like iron and throwing him out into the snow.

Fuck, she was fascinating. Ash let out a bellow of laughter as the door slammed shut in his face. So efficient and exact with her magic, so unassuming he often forgot what she was really capable of. She *could* hold Sweet Pea together, coven or no coven behind her.

Speaking of which.

Ash pushed through the snow, leaping over the small

mountains that gathered at the curb from the plows, and jogged across the street to the Inferno. There was a couple in one of the booths having dinner, but otherwise it was dead. As usual, no big deal. Morningstar would back the endeavor as long as the mission took, although a little capitalistic revenue never hurt the cause.

Ash joined the others at the bar. "Trouble with the coven," he announced.

Dante had been rolling his eyes at Vinny, Pie working on the rather mundane task of paying bills on a tablet Cornelius had found for them, Bell and Aim drinking with Barbie for company. But these words drew all the demonic attention right to Ash.

"What?" Bell asked, his gaze twitching out the bar windows, a small frown burrowing lines onto his forehead.

"Don't know the exact details," Ash said with a shrug. *But I bet you could talk them out of that little kitchen witch you're pretending we don't all know about.* Ash wasn't sure if Bell was approaching her as part of the mission like he was with June, or if he was having a bit of fun on the side. Didn't really care either. "Just that they're up in the air at the moment."

"So the wards are..." Pie trailed off, staring at him over the rim of his glasses.

"The wards are solid and probably will stay that way with her behind them," Ash said, tipping his head in June's direction. The lights in her shop were still on, and Ash would bet anything she'd remain there late, enjoying having the place to herself. "Could really use a slip on that binding, Dante."

Dante's face hardened, a hand coming up to comb through thick locks. "Can't get within a hundred yards of basement witch. She's gotta call on me," he said. "Why don't you just spill the beans on your end?"

"It's more fun watching her realize it on her own," Ash said, and the words had the faintest sour flavor of a lie. Did he have to tell them the rest? The ex-boyfriend and the murder and that his stitch witch was a secret nervous wreck in a tentatively explosive structure? No. No, she was his angle to work. He'd call for help if he needed it.

June, on the other hand, might let herself go up in flames if he didn't keep an eye on her.

10 EARLY EDUCATION

Brett's thighs were framing hers, his whole body warm around her back, his breath brushing over her shoulder.

"Good, keep your eyes closed, keep focusing," Brett whispered, his hands resting on June's waist, making it more impossible than ever to focus.

She took in a deep breath, her grip on the threads of energy tenuous at first, but growing steady until they were more than a current, almost tangible in her fingers. Like little bursts of static.

"God, that's amazing, June. Keep going."

Her cheeks were hot, her skin too alive, almost getting tangled in the magic she was trying to work. Aside from Casey—her foster brother at Dana's—she'd never been this close to a guy, and Casey didn't even begin to compete. Casey was a boy, prickle of wishful beard notwithstanding. Brett was a man.

"Oh, careful you're—That's it. That's amazing." His chin rested on her shoulder, and June tried to maintain her breath, but she was pretty sure she was panting like a dog in summer.

She twisted her fingers, tangling the threads, looping them through one another. Cat's cradle. It was the game her father had taught her for practice and she'd invented her own variations with the string, but none she'd shown anyone. None she'd actually tried with magic, too afraid of what might come out. Not until Brett had encouraged her, offered her the safety of his working with her.

June finished the pattern, one she had practiced on yarn, written out in careful graphs, and Brett gasped, fingers squeezing her body, making her tummy jump anxiously.

"Holy shit. Wow, wow, can I—?" June's eyes opened to find one of his hands leaving her side and reaching for the working. She thought she saw it flash, and then was too busy twisting to see the amazement on Brett's face. "Ha! June, this is incredible. This is like one of the best wards I've ever felt." His eyes met hers, and June's throat swelled up so tight she couldn't breathe. "You okay?"

She couldn't answer, so she just nodded and his head tipped, that understanding of her he always seemed to possess coming through the warm brown of his gaze.

"Seriously, you okay?"

"I'm okay," June whispered. "It's good?"

Brett laughed, and her whole heart flipped in her chest. "Shit, June, you are so...This magic is... You are..." He trailed off, eyes scanning her face. His hand retreated from the ward back to her waist, and this time his fingers slipped under the hem of her shirt, resting right on her skin. "You're so young, June," he murmured, head tipping down to rest his forehead to hers, the tips of their noses brushing.

He didn't make it sound like a bad thing.

It was still such a pretty memory, even with all the ugliness of time and perspective behind it. She'd just turned seventeen. Just started meeting with Brett's coven. Her crush was an entire animal of its own.

And he had just begun to carefully validate her feelings. The praise, the gentle offerings of what kind of potential she had, what kind of witch she could become, that had always been there. Now there were touches, little expressions beyond her power and into how it made him feel, how she made him feel.

In another month, she would kiss him first and then flee in embarrassment, which he would smooth away with the sweetest and most carefully neutral comfort. A month after, his seduction would be in messages first, words. By Yule, he would have her pressed to a wall, whispering what he wanted to do with her in her ear, never actually following through. By Imbolc, kisses.

By Beltane—of course Beltane, could he have chosen a less sexual holiday?—she'd lose her virginity. All before graduation. He had just turned thirty.

She thought she was special.

June's fingers drummed on her steering wheel as she examined those old emotions with a numb distance. She stared at the old school building that Brett had converted for the coven from across the street, parked in the local playground's parking lot. If Amira had succeeded, Brett would've been chased out of that red brick behemoth by the town, wouldn't he? A registered sex offender living so close to a playground? It wouldn't fly.

She and Imogen had moved in there after she graduated. They'd had their own room, although she spent more time in Brett's—the principal's old office, of course, how clever. It had been like having a family for the first time, or at least the one June had wished for. She knew some of the others were jealous of her—those older girls, recently discarded—but she couldn't blame them and they all cooperated regardless. The coven house had been home until it wasn't.

Brett had groomed her and used her for her wards.

She'd hidden things for him without asking what or why. She'd made a more secure environment for him to work in. And then she'd brought him Imogen. He promised June safety. He promised Imogen power.

You came here. Now what are you going to do about it? The thought sounded so much like Josie that June had to catch her breath.

She hadn't reached out to the others. They hadn't reached out to her. Would Josie have come if she'd asked?

Not for the first time, June regretted not taking the demon up on his offer of a bargain. Imogen would've helped her find her way out of it eventually, and June was overdue a fuckup.

The front door to the coven house opened, and June's pulse pounded so hard it drummed in her ears. Long brown hair down to her waist, heart shaped face, loose dress to her shoes. Christine.

As if she'd thought her name too loud, Christine's eyes darted to June's car. Fuck. Time to run or go through with this. June pushed open her door and stepped out, and Christine, walking down the stairs and just stepping onto the sidewalk, froze.

Christine had been twenty-five when June joined the coven. Not Brett's latest, a little too high on the shelf for him. She had tried to warn June. She probably tried to warn them all. And when she failed, she'd been kind to June, made June feel welcome where the other ex-girlfriends refused.

A cold whip of wind ran up the street of Millersville, obscuring Christine's face, but the two women walked slowly towards one another to the edge of the sidewalks. Christine raised a hand up, sweeping her hair back, and shook her head at June.

Don't come back.

But there were faces in the windows of the schoolhouse already. Another minute, and Brett would hear about her. Better to march in than run scared. June could channel Josie's bravery, even if she couldn't have it here with her now.

Christine turned back to the schoolhouse, to the street, up and down the sidewalk as June crossed the road. Was she searching for an escape route or for someone to come help?

"You can't come back, June. You left the coven." Christine swallowed and winced against the bite of the wind. "You can't."

June was inclined to agree with her. She didn't *want* to be here again. Or did she? It was all getting muddled. She turned her cheek into the cold and stared at the coven house out of the corner of her eye, the great drafty old box of a building.

"Those are my wards on the door, Christine," June said, and Christine stepped aside as she moved forward. "He can't keep me out."

"You're making a mistake," Christine muttered, and she pushed herself through the wind, down the road to the town. Probably running errands for him. Christine had always been a bit of a lapdog, loyal to the point of blindness.

June's boots crunched over the rock salt on the stairs. The only feature of the brick building that appeared to be changed was the set of front doors. They'd finally replaced the old glass double set with good oak and a classic lion's head knocker. June ignored the growling maw, taking the cold handle and pushing in. The latch clicked, and her wards greeted her with hungry little fingers, begging to be refreshed and cared for. Brett was such a lazy witch.

It wasn't as warm inside as she expected, the old furnace

failing to keep up with the mid mountain winter, or Brett not keeping up with the bills. Some of the coven had already gathered, a few familiar faces with a good number of new, all staring openly at her. A young boy huddled against the hip of one of the unfamiliar women, and June recognized his eyes immediately. Shit. Brett had always been careful with *that* before.

"June?"

Ella.

June's shoulders rose to her ears, falling back twenty years to when she was a girl again and she'd first met the older woman in front of her now, been terrified of her.

Ella—a beautiful hedge witch from June's family's old coven, close with her father and often around testing her and Imogen—stepped up from the basement. Her hair had gone elegantly grey, chopped short around her chin, and she was dressed in heavy layers. June remembered her magic and it reminded her of Imogen, just a little too inclined to dangerous workings. But Ella was ambitious, and June was surprised she was still in a coven like Brett's—whose only ambition seemed to be collecting witches.

"Where is he?" June blurted out. Social niceties were not her strength, it was true, and Ella made her nervous.

Ella's lips pursed, but June thought she looked a little amused. At June's expense or Brett's?

"In the labs. Greg can show—"

"I remember the way," June said, waving a hand in the direction of the young black man who'd stepped forward from the upper landing. He moved back to the wall, face showing no understanding that he'd been brushed aside by magic. New then, or just poorly trained.

"Have fun catching up," Elle called, a chuckle in her tone.

June ignored it and marched for the short set of stairs that would take her up to the first floor, eager to escape the older woman's study. The school labs were in the far right corner of the building, over the old gymnasium that had served as an indoor garden and space for ceremonies. June had liked the commune quality of the coven, found it strangely reassuring to be able to hear everyone moving around, talking through the air vents, after her childhood in the isolation of the mountain cabin.

The coven whispered around her as she jogged up the steps and moved familiarly down the hall, past the class-rooms turned bedrooms. The library was to the left, and she itched to go there. Brett had inherited quite the collection from her parents, and even as toxic as the material was, it was the one thing she wished she'd rescued when she and Imogen fled.

Another familiar face, Josh, sat up from a cot in the bedroom directly ahead of her, his eyes wide on her approach. He'd always reminded June of a less impressive Brett, although now, with the advantage of age, she realized he was handsome—a little bulkier than Brett's slim frame, and with a wild curly blond mane.

"Is...is she with you?" Josh asked, scrambling up from the cot.

Imogen. She had hexed him after catching him rifling through their things. In retrospect, that had likely been under Brett's orders, but at the time June had assumed Josh was just a perv after her sister and had warded their private room to the very corners.

June ignored him and turned left into the last corner room. It had been a science lab in the school's previous life, with a small wash station and the hotplates still left behind. The coven had transformed it into a space to brew tinctures and distill ingredients. Today's scent, layered on top of over a decade's worth of others, was star anise, and it coated June's lungs with its overpowering and nostalgic spice, her eyes watering.

The tears blurred her first sight of him in nine years, and she blinked them quickly away, finding Brett Lohman with his back to her, the smaller figure of a woman—probably a girl—tucked against his side. He had one hand on the back of her neck, fingers under curly red hair, and his head was bowed to speak low in her ear. Acclimating her to his touch.

It didn't take long for him to realize they were being interrupted, but June took a bitter kind of pleasure in the stricken expression that passed over his face briefly as he found her and not one of his coven. How old was he now? Almost forty? And the girl, who blushed from neck to forehead and stumbled back as she saw someone else in the room, was certainly not legal yet. Perhaps she was the one who had replaced Amira and made her finally realize what was happening all along?

There was no jealousy, no heartbreak in meeting Brett's eyes for the first time in nine years. He straightened, and June searched for the tremble of her own heart, the prickle of awareness on her skin, but all she really felt was queasy. Queasy, and that buried, boiling over warning inside of her.

Brett was tall, still slim, although June remembered him being a little more...carved? Muscular? His brown hair had started to thin and recede, but he was still good-looking in a way. The cheekbones, the dimple on his chin. Those eyes full of color.

"June."

One throb, one echo of a long-lost pain. That was all.

Brett took a step forward and the wall went up, unconscious and reflexive, stopping him in his tracks and making his lips twitch.

"Jess, would you mind giving me a minute to catch up with June?" Brett said, no qualms about reaching to the young girl, squeezing his hand around her shoulder as she looked up at him with big green doe eyes and nodded.

June got an airy flavor from the girl, Jess. A psychic maybe? That would explain the star anise. She reached curious tendrils toward June as she slipped through June's barrier. June caught one with a knot and stole it, tucked it away to examine later.

She still hadn't convinced her tongue to speak.

"It's been a long time," Brett said conversationally as his eyes glinted warmly on June. "To be honest, I really wasn't expecting to see you again."

"That was the plan," June said, too quiet.

"So what changed, Junie?"

June's fingernails dug into her palms. He had picked up the nickname from Imogen, and she wanted to rip it right out of his mouth. "Amira came to see me."

Brett's smile grew, eyebrows raising. "Who's Amira?"

June blinked, frost lacing in her veins. "Don't play pretend with me. There's no point now, I'm not one of your girls."

Brett eyed her out of the corner of his eye. "You are. You always will be. You all are. So is—"

"Amira came to me for help. How did you know?"

"June, what are you going to do here?" Brett pushed at the wall. No, it wasn't seeing him again that brought the past back. It was remembering his magic. Heady and comforting, seductive. That was his real gift, she supposed, magic that you wanted to sink into, allowing you to confuse it with the man.

"I don't think you were the one who killed her, if I'm honest," June said softly.

Brett froze, and his power retracted like the snap of a rubber band, making it easier to think as she stood in front of him.

"I don't think you *could*," June added, privately pleased with the sour clench of his jaw. "How old is Jess? How many of them are there between me and her? I suppose, when you add it up, the prison sentence for a serial statutory rape offender adds up. But *murder*? That's the icing on the cake."

"You just said I couldn't have done it," Brett said with a laugh. "And you're right. The police already came to speak to me. I was busy the night of the accident. I didn't hit her. She must've hit my car on her way out." He shrugged softly, spilling more info than he even knew, and June realized he was wearing the sweater she'd knitted for him. Bastard. She would curse him with moths.

"I never said I thought the hit and run was real," June said. "I was there that night. I tasted the magic on the air."

Brett paused, a knot on his brow, and June wanted to reach out and dig into the line, carve out his secrets. "You know anyone can leave at any time. Amira left two weeks ago, and I haven't seen her since, June. It's that simple."

"Nothing is simple. Magic fucks Occam's razor," June said. It was a quote from her father, actually, but for once, it served her. "You should've let her run."

"Like I let you run? Like I let you take Imogen with you?" Brett asked, lines digging deeper into his forehead, lips flattening.

"You couldn't have stopped us."

"I could have. I let you leave as a favor to your father."

Brett's frown deepened as June let out an abrupt and uncomfortable laugh. As if their father would've cared. Brett might've been a disappointment, but he was more impressive than her little Sweet Pea coven's white light workings.

But that's not all you do now, June reminded herself.

"You haven't changed your wards, you haven't found anyone better at hexes, based on what Amira was sporting. I came here to remind you that your coven isn't the only one around. You can't throw witches off of mountains, Brett. Not without answering to someone."

"And you really thought it was a good idea to come here to tell me that?" Brett's head tipped, eyebrow arching. "Let's say I am in some way responsible—entirely unprovable, but let's pretend—for Amira's death? Was coming here to see me the right choice, June? Was it the safe choice?"

"Touch me," June whispered.

Touch me, Brett, please.

Brett frowned, and June shrugged. "Go on. Touch me, right now. *Try.*"

He couldn't. He couldn't even raise his arms from his sides, although he was only just realizing it. June was very delicate when she wanted to be, and the threads she'd twisted with the yarn fisted in her palm were very gentle. But not gentle enough to let him move.

"I will find a way to prove what you've done. Or I will bind you. Banish you. Take the magic you've been hoarding away from young women," June said, watching the vein in Brett's throat tic with anger as he fought and failed against her bindings. They would only hold for a little while, but she had already started working on the knitted net to trap him for good.

"How is Imogen? The cabin off Old Pine Road, up in the mountains?" Brett hissed and grunted as June pulled hard on the loop around her index finger.

For a moment, June's heart leapt into her throat,

slammed and fought to go flying out of her. And then a stiff and uncomfortable calm returned, and she forced a smile on her lips.

"I dare you to find Imogen, Brett," June said. "She wouldn't be half as friendly as I've been. And I think you know a little of what she's capable of, but I never did manage to burn Pearce's influence out of her. So sure, go up to the cabin. See how well that goes."

June turned away, the animal in her roaring too loud to hear her own voice.

"June!" Brett barked, stuck behind her wall, caught in her web. "June! Be honest with yourself. You came back to *see* me. To remember me. Do you still miss me, Junie? I miss y—"

The door to the lab snapped shut on the words, and June let out a slow sigh, aware of the eyes watching her from doorways and communal room cots. She walked calmly back to the stairs, down to the front door.

The little redhead, Jess, was coming back up from the basement level, curls tucked back and curious eyes on June.

"See you soon," she murmured, frowning slightly.

June caught a breath as she yanked open the front door. Definitely a psychic. And not good news.

She snared the wards in her hands as she hurried for the steps, yanking the fine threads of her own work until they tore and split, leaving the schoolhouse with a gaping hole in its security. She left little bugs dangling at the frayed ends, little wisps of hungry magic, bad programming, to eat away at the rest of her power.

Brett Lohman could figure out how to cover his own ass. It was past time she stole back her own shields.

11 UNRAVELING

Contrary to popular belief, Imogen Bryne did have an income. It was modest, moving directly back into the account with the rest of her inheritance that she lived off of, but it helped stall the slow leak of her funds.

"Shadow work is pretty in right now. We could move you up to a daily article on the website if you could upload to our—"

"Weekly is fine," Imogen answered over the phone to her literary agent.

"Are you sure? If the magazine pushes for more, you may get passed over for someone else."

Imogen stared out the window. It was barely five pm and dark as night on the eastern side of the mountain. Diane, in California, was no doubt still sitting in the sunshine if her office had any, or under fluorescent lighting.

"The signal for internet on the mountain isn't that reliable," Imogen said. Not her real reason for refusing. Shadow work wasn't something you churned out like a moon-charging fluff piece or a daily tarot tip. Weekly articles may not pay her full winter monthly heating bills, but at least they left her time to actually do the work she wrote about.

"Mm. I forget how removed you are," Diane mused. "It must be easier to work up there. Fewer distractions."

When I'm not on the phone with you, Imogen thought, making no effort to disguise the heavy sigh she released.

"Still. Keep it in mind. The magazine loves your work. Keep that relationship strong, and you'll have an easy landing with a publisher when you have a book ready. Have you given any thought to that?"

Diane wasn't the best at taking hints, but she made Imogen's life simpler. Imogen sent Diane her writing, Diane liaised the rest with her fifteen percent cut. She always wanted *more* from Imogen. Diane had done the same for Imogen's mother, although Celia Bryne *had* had the ambition for publishing books. Successful ones that still contributed royalties into Imogen's inheritance. Books that hardly skimmed the woman's interest in folk magics and shadow work.

Imogen was saved from answering by the beep of a call waiting. "Diane, there's someone on the other line. I'll email you the next piece on Tuesday."

"Oh! Okay, sounds good. Good catching up with y—"

Imogen pulled the phone away from her ear and swiped with a narrow-eyed glance at the caller ID.

"Ella."

"Imogen."

The cabin took on a sudden chill, and Imogen stood up from the couch by the window to pace over the dusty floor, waiting for the other woman to speak.

But Ella was patient. Imogen remembered her watching from the edges of the room as Imogen's father had tested her, lectured her, coached her. He lost his temper easily when Imogen failed to respond the way he hoped, but Ella had simply watched, curious and amused. Her father's face would get red, his muscles tight, his voice growing loud, and Ella would step forward as Imogen began to cower, setting a hand on his shoulder and guiding him out of the room. "Again," she would say, and back to the edges of the room she would go to watch Imogen practice.

But on her third pace from front door to opposite wall, Imogen's patience broke first. "What is it?"

There was no real sound to prove it, but Imogen was sure Ella was laughing at her. "June came to the coven yesterday."

Imogen's socks scuffed on the worn floor, her body swaying with its own momentum as her heart dropped like an anchor and she came to an abrupt stop. "What?"

"Mm. He isn't happy. She tore the wards down on her way out."

June, no. Imogen reached for the binding, the one that was meant to keep June safe, keep her from unraveling, to prevent her from *going back there*. And it was there, a little tense and taut, as it had been ever since the demons came to town, but not fractured, not ragged. So *why*?

"The coven has too much to lose, Imogen," Ella warned. "They'll stand with him, even if they hate him. Get June to back off, and I'll do what I can for you."

"He's not a threat," Imogen said. Which was mostly true. Brett wouldn't measure up, not to June and not to her. Not to Josie with a demon's power, if Imogen hadn't managed to piss her off so much.

"He's not alone. He has me too."

So this wasn't simply a courtesy call. Imogen blinked. The light in the cabin had changed, the fire damping down in the fireplace, shadows spreading deeper into the heart where she stood. Ella *did* scare her. Just a little. She knew too much.

"June won't be back," Imogen promised. Her throat was coated with cement as she tried to swallow, the drafts of the cabin were circling and closing in on her, her pulse drumming irregularly.

"Good. Thank you."

This time, it was Imogen's turn to be hung up on. She shivered in the room, eyes sliding to her feet as the shadows grew taller, looming closer. Her phone screen glowed in the dark, sending a hazy black outline of herself up the wall. She pulled up her contacts immediately, a dozen missed calls in red, and hit the top one, counting her breaths through the slow trill of the ringer.

"Gin, there you are."

"Come to the cabin," Imogen said over the phone. "We need to talk."

June was quiet for a minute on the other end of line, and Imogen was *certain* her sister knew exactly why she was calling.

"Okay. I'll bring dinner." There was soft resigned quality to the words, so familiar to Imogen.

The hour ticked by creepingly, the worry stacking up like bricks in her mind. Brett Lohman had been a toxic thorn in Imogen's side ever since her parents had died. June had only hated him after Imogen proved his true intentions, but Imogen had known from the start. He'd tried to steal June from her, leaving Imogen behind with the foster family, stealing June's focus.

June was the only person in the entire world who really loved Imogen—her parents had offered affection as a reward system, but even as a child, Imogen could tell the difference, could almost taste it in the air, as if it were another form of power to identify and manipulate. After Pearce and Celia were dead, Brett had tried to hook that love and reel it in for himself. It'd been easy enough to show June what that man was really made of. Uncomfortable for Imogen, but worth it in the long run. Lohman had his weaknesses, and Imogen, with all her power and potential and her *youth*, had been too tempting to ignore.

And then, even after they had left, even after June had loved her and protected her once again, Brett was still a threat. June spent her days crying in bed or staring wistfully at her own hands. Imogen wanted her sister back, and she wanted June *without* Brett's claws embedded in her heart.

So she made a sacrifice. She would give up June's love in order to keep her sister from going back to the man who had corrupted it. She would bind June's emotions for her own good. Lock and bury them to magic's best ability, so that they couldn't rule June's actions.

And now here she was, encased in that binding, too calm, too removed to touch, to shake sense into, to keep away from Brett. Imogen watched as June meticulously rearranged and cleaned out her fridge, a stack of takeout boxes left on the counter untouched by them both.

"You promised me you'd stay away from him," Imogen said.

June was in the middle of excavating an accidental biosphere from the back of her fridge, and she paused in her work, face still twisted with annoyance.

"Imogen."

"Years ago, you promised."

June sighed and abandoned her task, shutting the fridge door and turning to lean against it. June had turned the lights in the cabin on, and for once, Imogen didn't mind the harsh glare. A moth fluttered around the ceiling lamp, and

June's eyes slid up, watching it for a moment before stepping forward and rising to her tiptoes, catching it gently in her palms.

"Years ago, no one had been murdered," June said wearily.

"What do you care?" Imogen asked, shrugging as June stared at her with wide eyes. "Seriously, June, who was she to you?"

"She was me, Imogen. Or I was her. She only did what we did, or maybe she wanted to do what we *should* have done," June said, head shaking, eyes on her cupped palms where the moth waited restless. "How did you find out?"

"Why didn't *you* tell me?! You should have. You should've taken me." June scoffed a laugh and shook her head, heading for the front door. "Where are you going?"

"To put the moth out."

"It's the dead of winter, it won't survive."

"Neither will the sweaters you steal if you keep it in the house." June shooed the moth out and locked the door again as she shut it, turning to face Imogen. "What is going on, Gin? I don't just mean about this, I mean... You attacked Josie, the coven. You hate Brett. You can't be protecting him."

"Of course I'm not protecting him, I'm protecting you!" Imogen cried out, the words cracking with rare volume. She didn't like to shout, didn't even like to speak, but it was as if she were eleven again and her sister was slipping through her fingers, the only person Imogen *mattered* to. "That's what we do, we protect one another. No one else."

June blinked, reaching a hand up and twisting long blonde hair around her fist absently. "This isn't right, Imogen, you know that."

"It doesn't matter!"

"It should! It *should* matter, I know it should." June's brow was furrowed, her voice cracking, and she tugged on her own hair. "It's like there's this anger inside of me and I can't actually feel it, but I *should*. You should too. We should've been burning Brett and the coven to the ground when we left, Gin, so why didn't we? Why is it that I know I should be angry and upset, but I'm not?"

Imogen could beg or she could scream or she could cry, but...but June's emotions were locked away and none of that would shake June. Had the binding been a mistake? Imogen held her breath as June brightened in the shadow by the door, the power shimmering over her, containing the fury inside.

"You broke your promise to me," Imogen whispered, brow furrowing.

Had she miscalculated all those years ago when she'd put the spell on June? She'd wanted to protect her, keep her from drowning in sorrow, keep her from going back to Brett. But it failed now. June had stuck her nose back into that rat trap, even with the binding in place. Because she couldn't feel that pain, couldn't remember how much that man had hurt her. How much Imogen had hurt her too. Maybe that was the real reason Imogen had called on Dantalion. She had saved June from Brett Lohman, yes, but she had harmed her sister in the process too by sleeping with him.

June sighed and leaned back against the door, eyes falling shut. "Maybe it was a promise that needed to break. I don't know. Something isn't right, Imogen. With *me*. I want to fix it. And the murder of a young woman shouldn't go unpunished. The coaching and sexualization of us as children shouldn't either. You know that."

But June couldn't fix it. Only Imogen could. And in doing so, she might break June for real this time. Or maybe just June's last little straw of love for her, however deep it was buried.

"I'm not hungry," Imogen whispered, staring at her sister, trying to memorize June, in case she lost her in what came next. "I don't want you here."

"Gin—"

"Leave, June. I'm..." *I'm so sorry.* "I'm too angry with you."

June's gaze shifted to the left, a little huff of irritation escaping her. "You don't have to be involved, but I've had enough of you trying to manipulate people to keep me out of this. I'm going to talk to the others."

"Get out. Go home," Imogen hissed. She couldn't take her eyes off June, tall and pale and glowing, the little storm inside of her that Imogen had so diligently tried to placate, to soothe. June would never forgive her.

That's overdue, Imogen thought numbly. *And deserved.*

"Fine. Fine, keep the food, Gin. I'll call you tomorrow," June said, yanking her coat off the hook and swinging her small purse over her shoulder.

Imogen's palms itched to reach for her sister. She rarely wanted to be touched, but it might not happen again. She could remember sneaking into June's bed when she was a little girl, combing fingers through June's silky hair, tying little knots in midnight boredom. Imogen gripped the countertop until her hands hurt, barely distracting from the tearing in her chest, watching June wrap up to leave the cabin.

June paused, hand on the door handle, eyes casting vaguely over her shoulder in Imogen's direction. "I think you need to grow up a little, Gin. We're not the only people in the world who matter, regardless of what Dad tried to tell you."

"Out!" Imogen snapped, because if June didn't leave soon, Imogen might not go through with her plan.

June shook her head and flipped the latch with an audible and brittle *snap* before swinging open the door and stepping into the night, slamming it shut behind her.

Imogen let out a long moan of a breath, sinking down to the floor on her knees. Her forehead pressed to the cabinet door and rested there for a moment, listening to the sound of June's car starting, tires crunching over the snow—was she imagining the pressure of them driving right over her? —as she turned around.

The binding had to go. If June's lack of feeling was what made it easier to dig into Brett, it needed to be destroyed. And if it wasn't...June would need her anger to go up against him.

Her anger at Brett, at their parents, at Imogen. Anger at being bound, when she realized. Anger with Imogen for fucking Brett to make June see what an ass he was and for the death of their parents. It would be a reckoning, and Imogen wasn't sure June would invite her back on the other side.

Maybe it had been another selfish mistake in a long list of them, a way of anchoring June to Imogen for a little longer.

It was time to cut the rope, and Imogen was sure she would be the one left drowning.

DANTALION APPEARED in a rush of feathers and heady whiff of roses and mint. He wore his human disguise, nearly the same one he'd worn the first time she'd met him—months after she and June had left Brett's coven and June wouldn't leave her bed. He was a little rougher around the edges now, with a dense beard and tattoos to match his biker persona, but his smile was every bit as dangerously charming as it had been years ago.

"Well, I love to see a repeat customer," he purred, head cocking and eyes scanning the small cellar room. "Same basement, same witch. And here I thought you might've moved on to other demonic pastures."

Imogen frowned at him.

She'd been just eighteen the first time she'd summoned a demon and Dantalion had sounded fairly harmless, but it hadn't stopped her from nearly swallowing her own tongue at the sight of his naked beauty when he appeared. Tall, bronzed, shockingly handsome, and deceptively human in appearance. Now, older, she understood better. He was a vain asshole. But he'd served his purpose at the time.

"I'm not going to compliment you further than necessary," Imogen said plainly.

Dante's eyes narrowed, and his smile hardened. His lips still looked soft, although she'd never felt them. She considered it, that first time, but sex magic didn't require softness. And he had been decadent enough without her taking the opportunity to kiss his mouth.

"What do you need, basement witch?" He glanced down at his bare cock and raised his eyebrows at her. She resisted the impulse to look.

It was...it was almost a shame that she *didn't* need to fuck him this time. It had felt good at the time. Dantalion was... thorough. And fun, almost. She shook a dusty old memory of his laugh out of her thoughts.

"That won't be necessary," she said, and he shrugged. "I want you to dissolve the binding."

"The binding," he repeated, face smoothing into something too even to be anything other than a disguise.

"On my sister," Imogen said, annoyed that she had clarified it for him when they both knew full well what she was referring to. "Will it... What will happen to her?"

Dante arched an eyebrow. "She will *feel*."

"But will it hurt her?" Imogen pressed, trying to make the *right* decision. Just once.

"Does it change your command?"

Her lips parted to say *yes, of course it would*, but... No. June needed the binding removed. Imogen shook her head. Maybe it would be better not to know what June would go through. Her sister was stronger than anyone, Imogen knew that.

"There will be a cost, witch," Dante warned, chin tilting down and golden eyes fixing harshly to hers.

"I know how bargains work, demon," Imogen answered, a cold pit forming in the base of her belly.

12  WEATHERING

June glared at the dismal contents of her fridge. She'd wasted a perfectly good meal on Imogen, one that would end up moldering at the back of Imogen's fridge until the next time June was there to clear it out.

Now she simmered with annoyance and stifled anger, *and* she was hungry.

June shut the door, sighing and leaning forward to rest her forehead against the cool surface, imagining that if she opened it again, she might find new contents.

Weirdly, and worse, she was craving those disgustingly—tasty—messy wings from the Inferno, but it was closed tonight.

She should've refused when Imogen kicked her out. They were long overdue for a talk, a *real* one, but June was so used to Imogen rebuffing her efforts that she hardly put up a fight anymore.

It was too much now—Imogen's treatment of the coven, her reaction over Brett. June had let Imogen push back too many times, and now she had to learn how to reshape the boundaries instead of letting Imogen have her way.

With a last wish, June wrapped her fingers around the handle of the fridge, preparing to make some frankenstein of a meal.

A shiver stroked up her spine and June paused, eyes widening. It was like someone was poking at one of her wards except this was...foreign, not pulling in her head, only tickling outside of her.

The Sweet Pea wards, maybe?

June stepped back and turned, and a pang struck her heart like an arrow, drawing a gasp from her. She pressed her lips tight and let her vision blur, and then nearly lost her focus at the strange glow of angular lines now breaking around her.

You're a prism.

An ancient memory from childhood—the dark and cold of the basement, June's hands searching through nothing for comfort—slammed into her, and June tried to bury the whimper in her throat at the sudden *terror* that struck her veins.

Another followed, her heart slamming in her chest in time with young June's as she shyly pulled her dress over her head in front of Brett, his gaze narrowed with hungry examination. Nerves, excitement, the background wondering if she was *ready*.

June stumbled out of her kitchen, scrambling toward her purse. She needed help. Were her wards breaking, or was it—

Shame, sticky and rotten, dropped June to her knees on her sheepskin rug, and she moaned into her fists, shuddering in the spot, waiting for this rising inside of her to *end*. She rolled to the side and winced, trying to push her own magic out, to grab at the plates of shimmering light that were cracking around her. Trying to thread them back together, to hold the storm in, as they chipped away into nothing. The flavor of the prism was demonic but also...

Imogen.

Love and hate were tangled like thorns in silk. Imogen, her baby sister. Imogen, her competitor. The sister she protected, and the one she resented. Imogen, who had saved her from Brett. Imogen, who had fucked the man she loved and let her see it firsthand.

June tried to scream for help but the sound was mangled with tears.

"CAN YOU NOT DO THAT HERE?" Vinny snarled.

Ashtaroth blinked, glancing around the kitchen, searching for the source of Vinny's irritation—just in case they needed any help making it worse—before realizing he was the demon to credit. Well, him and his knitting.

"How is this bothering you?" Ash asked.

"The clicking."

Ash blinked at Vinny, holding the other man's stare, and added a scratch and slide to the friction of his knitting. Vinny's face went a satisfying and unfortunate shade of red the longer he continued.

"Fuck you," Vinny growled.

"You should find a hobby too," Ash suggested.

"Might keep you out of everyone else's ass," Aim agreed, entering the kitchen, rubbing his growling stomach. "I keep forgetting to feed this thing."

"I don't," Ash said, patting his slightly rounded body with a grin. It was winter, it was good to have a little extra padding on hand.

"The only ass I'm in is—"

Ash, Aim, and Bell—who entered from outside—all let out a unanimous 'Boo' of disinterest before Vinny could finish. He glowered and was interrupted from any further bitching by Paimon following Bell in.

"Dantalion was summoned an hour ago. He's on his way back through the woods."

"My, my, we *are* busy around here, aren't we?" Ash asked, brows bouncing. First Vinny a couple weeks ago, now Dante?

"Starting to feel left out," Aim said, sliding into the seat next to Ash, his shadow, Barbie, finally appearing to stand behind him.

"Are we really working against the witches if we keep doing their bidding?" Ash asked, grinning at Bell.

Bell scowled and took a seat at the island counter, arms crossed over his chest. *Hitting a little too close to home*, Ash thought curiously. He wasn't sure how many of the others were aware, but Bell was definitely up to *something* with the kitchen witch from town, and Ash was less and less convinced it was for the benefit of their mission.

Before he could take that train of thought any further, Dantalion appeared out in the yard, black wings dusted with snow and chest bared.

Paimon leaned his head out the backdoor. "Put those away before someone sees you."

Ash and Pie both glanced toward the green witch's carriage house just over the hedge, but the lights were off. Dante's wings vanished into shadows, a simple white T-shirt shining on his chest as he stepped inside, feet still bare and leaving wet marks on the tile.

"Imogen Bryne called me," he announced, and Ash perked up in his seat, pulling his stitches onto the circular needle's cord and bundling the sweater sleeve in his lap.

"The dark witch?" Bell asked, leaning forward.

Dante nodded and shrugged at the same time. "Dark*ish*, I think. She wanted the binding removed."

At that, Dante's stare turned to Ash. Not just his, but the others' too.

"And your bargain with her?" Paimon asked.

Dante's jaw tightened at that. "Not relevant to our mission. She will pay her cost. Now's your chance, Ash."

Ash's fingers drummed against his thigh. June's binding was off. She must be... His eyes flicked to Bell, then Pie, and back again, unsure of who his superior really was in this moment.

"Permission to go meddle?" he asked, trying to keep his tone light.

"Like he said, now's your chance," Bell repeated.

Ashtaroth noted that whatever possible attachment Bell had to Josie Benoit, it didn't extend to June. That was for the best for Ash. He couldn't finish the job if there was a chance the Warlord King would try and stop him.

Ash swept the sweater sleeve up into safekeeping in his bedroom and drew out his jacket. He was finding wiggle room in the wards recently. He simply had to shift his motivation away from the mission and personal interest. Keeping the sleeve safe for his own sake didn't work, but keeping it safe because June respected the yarn did. Grabbing his jacket to 'check on her' was also available.

It was so easy to make the mental shift it almost made him nervous.

"I'll be back," he said, heading for the backdoor.

"Good hunting," Pie said, eyeing him.

Ash pulled a long scarf from his bedroom too as he greeted the bitter cold outside, sliding around the back of Grimsby House. He considered taking the Humvee, but it would take a few minutes, and meanwhile June and her pesky little diamond shell would be shattering.

He had to stamp down the excitement in his chest, go back to that wary, tentative sensation he'd met on the last knit night while watching June vibrate with secret tension.

He was going to check on her. He was traveling for *her* sake. He was—

Ash stepped crossways into darkness and then back out into the alleyway behind the knit shop. Easy enough.

One step, and he could taste her. Electricity snapped on the air, etching a clear and direct path to her door, an unassuming little narrow piece of metal that Ash would have to stand sideways and duck to fit through. The handle burned against his palm as he reached for it. The rest of the alley was empty, dark, and upstairs...

June's wards were rioting, overwhelmed by their own maker's crisis. Ash still had to wait, to pluck and rearrange their threads to make room for himself before the door would finally unlock and swing in.

She tasted like a heat storm in summer. Like a power grid collapsing. A sea of gasoline at the touch of a match.

Ash ran up the stairs, fought another terrified netting of wards, and made it inside at last.

There, on the floor, was the most beautiful thing he'd ever seen.

June Byrne was *exploding*.

ONE AFTER ANOTHER, they carved her open. Disgust like the bile at the back of her throat. Loneliness like the weight on her chest pinning her to the floor. Humiliation as hot as the fire licking up her neck and over her cheeks. Betrayal like the lightning strike drumming in her bones. Worthlessness twisting her up and shrinking her in her own skin.

The walls of the small apartment groaned in time with June. Her eyes were wide and electric blue, hands clutching over her chest as she fought for air, lungs burning and tight. Her feet curled and pushed against the floorboards, body arching and bones aching, muscles screaming. She tried to thread magic around her like a cocoon, to trap the sudden flood, but it never dug deep enough. It pulsed and pounded, glittered and stung in the tear tracks running over her cheeks and down to her ears.

A panic attack of a witch's power.

A shadow moved out of the corner of her eyes, and June gasped and tried to grasp at it like a lifeline.

"H-h-help," she squeezed out, forcing her head to turn.

The lamps flashed in warning, revealing the mountain of demon approaching her cautiously. Ashtaroth, massive and dark and shining, watching her with cold, calm focus. She didn't care it was him, too busy drowning under every other emotion she'd been missing for the past nine years. He was solid. He was strong. Would he save her? A whistle sounded, a train coming or a tornado. June choked and twisted, and the whistle grew louder, the scream inside of her building.

"P-p-please!" Her nails clawed at her chest, snagging a thread of her sweater and leaving a painful trail on the skin of her breast bone.

Ash's boots thunked against the floor as he approached, eyes closing, lips curling, and face lifting as if he were bracing against a storm. Sparks of her own rage kissed his cheeks, and June savored a glimpse of his hunger. Her anger spiraled around him like a windstorm, and he snared her in his curiosity. Sorrow beat down in an attempt to drown him in an intangible sea, and she was buoyed with his delight.

He was strong enough, and the empty twisting pit in June's belly ached for him. The magic and the emotion that had been buried for so long would kill her. She couldn't breathe, her heart wasn't beating or it was beating too fast, but Ashtaroth would weather her.

"Please."

Ash's eyes opened at the note of the whimper. One of June's hands reached out, catching him by his pant leg, tugging. Her lips gaped, her throat choked, lungs frozen in her chest.

The anger was eating her from the inside out, dragging its claws through her blood, shredding her muscles as she struggled to move, burrowing into her bones, and Ashtaroth just observed her from above. Briefly, his gaze blazed with anger too, and he knelt on the floor. June's fingers snatched and grasped and begged at him as if he were the only boat in the middle of the ocean. She gasped and gasped and gasped and never caught a real breath, vision wavering, black spots appearing, and felt something like relief at the idea that maybe this would just *end*. Warm, large hands slipped under her shoulders as she twisted, hauling her up from the floor and into a broad chest, the first rush of air reaching her lungs.

June's hands clawed into Ash's back, wet breaths puffing, her magic lashing like a whipcrack over his skin, stealing his calm to help steady herself. Ash wrapped his arms around her, settling her on his lap, her legs draped over his, her face pressed into his bristly chin. She clung to him, moaning and shaking, trying to remember how to breathe as a decade's worth of emotion clawed its way back into her veins, her thoughts, her heart.

Suddenly, pressure—slow and steady and gentle—pushed back at her magic, leaned into the anger rattling her whole body, a wad of cotton on the open wound. A wall of sandbags stemming the tide, Astaroth braced himself into June to take the beating with her. June shuddered and sagged, trembles softening.

"The bargain," she whispered, leaning back in Ash's arms. His eyes were narrowed, lips flat, the most solemn expression she'd ever seen on his face. "Give me a bargain, beast. Put it back. Put the binding back."

It was the reason he was here, surely. Had he known the whole time? Her veins went cold. Had it been *his* power Imogen had called on. No, no that was Dantalion, according to Josie. Even in the unwound mess of emotions in her, she had room for a little relief at that.

"Just put it back," she begged, eyes stinging, breath hiccuping and punching her chest.

Ash's hand slipped up to the back of June's neck, her pulse thrumming like bird wings under the tip of his finger, his skin scorching against hers, and she held her breath, waiting for the walls to erect again.

"No," Ash said.

June's storm stopped for a moment, so shocked by the statement, and Ash tucked her face back into his throat, his swallow caressing her cheek as silence rang like a bell in her ears.

"Beast," June gasped, and Ash flinched against her. "Put it back."

"No."

It was an impossible answer. A refusal that stabbed into the already wounded heart of hers. And yet...

Her breath caught, and then again, and the tears rushed down Ash's throat where he held her in place. One hand slapped against his back, but the fingers only fisted in his coat, June pushing herself deeper into his chest.

"Why?" she whispered, the word broken with a new rise of weeping slamming up from her lungs—a new wave, another year of sorrow, rising up in her like a tide. Ash welcomed it into himself, so entirely open, she knew the answer before he said it.

"Curiosity."

It wasn't a real answer, but with this communication of magic between them, June knew it was the truth. Ashtaroth wanted to see who she was, now that she was out of her cage. He was fascinated by every bit of her that beat at him now, even fascinated by her suffering. June wanted to add a punch for that answer, but her strength was gone. So instead she let him hold her, let her tears soak into the collar of his shirt, her silky blonde hairs tangle into his beard, her little dull nails scratch at his jacket as they weathered her storm together.

And gradually, one ache and one tear and one barely caught breath at a time, the roaring winds and striking lightning and rumbling thunder and weeping rain settled until there was only a trickle of memories and of sorrows passing through her.

June stretched and arched in Ash's arms, waiting patiently for him to twist and find her staring up at him. She was studying him, still hiccuping but as aware as he was of the strangeness of their embrace. And aware of more than that too. She'd always known he was handsome and often found herself attracted, but this was *more*. It hadn't just been rage and heartbreak buried in Imogen's working. Arousal reared its hazy head now as she stared at Ash's full mouth. Maybe it was because sexual interest was such a relief compared to everything else she was feeling, or maybe it had been buried too long.

Either way, it only took a simple tilt of Ash's head, a lock of hair falling to brush against his brow, and she was surging up, her hands on his face, drawing him down to her starving mouth that caught and hooked his lips. June shook in the kiss, arms twining tight around his neck, teeth digging into his bottom lip, not caring if he responded or caring too much as she feasted on his mouth. Her eyes were squeezed shut, her own forehead tangled, and the air was a fractious mix of desire and anger.

THE KISS WAS STRANGE, one-sided, flavored with June's panic and desperation, her hunger for distraction, and the combination was sweet. So were June's tears as he licked at her lips and found her ready for battle. She sucked on his tongue and caught a shaking breath as Ash's hands slid up her back, following curiosity to a new road map of touch. June's hands fisted into the collar of his coat and wrestled it down, teeth nipping his lips as she trapped his arms at his sides, squirming on his lap, warm and broken but full of strength and demand too.

Ash pulled his arms free, and June gasped as he tipped her backwards to the floor, severing the kiss. Her hair fanned out around her face, a brighter shade of gold than it had been while she'd still been bound, cheeks flushed with crying and arousal, lips bitten brilliantly pink. Vivid blue eyes, surrounded by weary red, blinked up at him as Ash stretched himself above her. She was beautiful, in her catastrophe as well as in body. Shaking hands reached up and fisted in the sweater he wore, a fresh batch of tears starting to glimmer in puffy eyes.

"Please...anything," June whispered, the shaking getting worse again. "Anything to make it stop."

A bargain. The distraction of sex. Anything on offer. He'd already refused one, as much to his surprise as hers. And he found himself strangely reluctant to accept this too.

That's not a challenge, Ash told himself, as if it were an excuse for refusing.

He lowered himself unhurriedly, watching June sigh as he pressed himself on top of her, his resolve wavering at the fit of her beneath him, the flavor of her still on his lips. Her shaking stopped at last by the force of his weight, and she softened, welcoming his body further. His nose touched hers, and June turned enough to let their mouths slide together. It wasn't just her tears. He liked the taste of her, so bitter and alive, sweet and begging. He stroked his tongue against hers, stealing the emotions that bled out of her and replacing them with calm.

June relaxed as he kissed her, sighed as he sank into her, even moaned a little and stretched her throat as his mouth traveled there, pausing over her pulse and waiting for it to slow, for exhaustion to take over.

"Oh," she breathed, finally realizing he was putting her to sleep.

When she was limp and still, little tears still finding their way out of the corner of her eyes, Ash lifted himself enough to draw her back up into his arms. The bedroom was down the hall to the left, a tiny bed pushed up against the far wall, a room filled to the brim with bookshelves stuffed with yarn and crumbling texts.

"You tricked me," June mumbled, her forehead on his shoulder.

That wasn't true. He'd...spared her. At least for the night. He'd intended to conquer June Byrne before accepting her surrender. Tonight's defeat wasn't by his hands.

And tonight's defeat was so thorough, he found it as mesmerizing as it was...moving. Like exceptional art or shared tragedy.

He carried her to the bed, huffing and trying not to smile as her hands clawed into his sweater, catching somewhere new every time he tried to pluck them free.

"Just...just stay, beast. Don't leave."

This was turning into one mistake after another. Or...or maybe his grip on her would be more secure if he stayed, played the part she was casting him in, held her a little while longer and caught that new whiff of cotton and cream and blackberries in her hair.

"You'll owe me, starling," he whispered, and June hummed and shivered, forehead wrinkling as something new tried to scratch its way to the surface.

Ash captured it in his fist and crushed it to nothing, and June sighed as he forced his way onto the mattress beside her. The bed was absurdly small. Even alone on his back, Ash would've spilled over the edges. He stretched the length, listening to the wood frame groan, and then the width too until he knew he wouldn't roll out. June either didn't notice or didn't care. Ash wondered if she'd been sleeping on her back with her arms at her side like a cadaver in a coffin this whole time.

He'd missed the moment he'd been waiting for since he'd caught sight of the witch in the pretty glass cage. Crack her open. Wait until she crumbled. Make her turn to him. Make a bargain.

No, not missed. He'd refused it. Not only that, he'd used

his demonic power to soothe June without a second thought.

Now she was balled up against his side, facing the wall. He scooped his arm beneath her shoulders and rolled her to face him, and a moment later she was clinging to his chest, leg hooked over his hip and fingers digging into his sweater right down to his skin. She tapped one finger over his chest.

"You need a heartbeat," she murmured, voice still watery.

Ash made himself a heart to beat for her and watched with confusion as the sound of it lulled her to sleep.

HE LOST track of time in the night, slipping in and out of the witch's thoughts, her guard broken and mind open to him. June's dreams were full of blood, the same horrific scene playing on repeat for an hour, until even Ash's stomach was turning. There were other ones, ones that must've involved the ex because it looked tender but filled June with rage that he gobbled up so she could continue resting.

The worst of it settled before dawn, and Ash suddenly remembered why he had come. And also how completely disinterested he was in following through. If June's life, so full of these awful flavors, hadn't broken her yet, then she deserved a little peace. Which meant he ought to leave.

She stretched in sleep to fill the space as he vacated it, her face turning into the pillow where his head had rested. He drew a blanket up out of a stack at the foot of the bed and spread it over her. Another too, for good measure. He ran warm, and she had been using him as a heater for most of the night.

The bed looked too big for her now, and Ash scowled and scuffed his hand over his beard.

You...fucked up, he told himself, but mainly he was annoyed at the questions he would have to answer when he got back to Grimsby house.

Stuffing his hands into his pockets, he tread quietly back out to the living room, his coat abandoned on the floor after June had finished tearing it off him. He wanted her little claws back on him, her mouth demanding more from him, her body sinking softly and sighing beneath him. Human cravings, made more exquisite by June's sudden rebirth of passion.

The new heart in his chest pounded unevenly.

Ash headed for the door before he found himself accidentally turning back to the bedroom again. He hurried down the stairs and came out into the alley.

This time, he wasn't alone.

Bell was walking leisurely toward him, breath fogging in the air, the door to another apartment clicking shut. Bell's steps paused, and Ash froze outside of June's door, the pair of demons studying one another. It was Bell who closed the distance, eyes narrowed slightly.

"Did you make a bargain?" Bell asked.

Ash hesitated and then offered the truth. "No."

Bell sighed, shoulders dropping and one hand rising to push his hair back from his face, eyes rolling. "Yeah. Neither did I."

Which more or less answered Ash's question about the kitchen witch.

"You don't even want to now, do you?" Bell asked him, smirking slightly.

Trapping June in a bargain sounded dull to Ash. She'd been bound for nine years, wouldn't it be more fun to watch those wings unfurl? But it wasn't just that, there wasn't logic or argument to the problem. Bell was right.

"No," Ash repeated, frowning, waiting for Bell to clap him in irons or banish him from the mission or try and barge into June's apartment to finish the deed he hadn't bothered with.

Bell nodded and shrugged. "Fuckin' witches."

Ash tugged on his beard and glanced between Bell and the door he'd just closed. Bell laughed and started to walk again.

"Yeah, I know that look on your face. Come on. Let's get back before the others are up. I'll tell Pie you made progress," Bell said.

"But I..."

Bell looked over his shoulder, eyebrow raised. "Unless you'd rather tell him you're compromised."

Are you compromised? Ash wanted to ask, but the answer was obvious, wasn't it? Bell smelled like sugar and chocolate and spice, and he was walking with a notable swagger. Ash wondered if he should've fucked June instead of cuddling, but it all seemed...not quite right that way.

Shit. He was compromised, wasn't he? When had that happened?

He liked the stitch witch. He liked her better than... anyone else.

"You coming?"

Ash blinked and found Bell at the end of the alley, waiting and watching him, a smug satisfaction in the twist of his lips. Bastard was probably glad not to be the only one.

Ash followed reluctantly, a little too aware of the distance that grew at every step, between him and the woman asleep in the apartment above.

13 PERSONAL RENOVATION

The world was on a higher volume. *June* was on a higher volume. Waking up without the binding was like being hungover and hyper hormonal at the same time. The sunlight scratched her tear sore eyes. She cried at the mulberry red yarn stashed on a high shelf—the color was so beautiful—at the two blankets Ashtaroth had placed on her, at the sight of the rug where she'd collapsed the night before, and also at the relief of drinking coffee once she'd finally been able to get around to making any.

Her magic was now swollen and heavy too, with a hair-trigger, and it had taken her three tries to put a familiar charm on a cup of tea just to even out the rollercoaster of emotions she was riding.

Also, and somehow worst of all, she was horny. It simmered warmly under her skin, stole her breath as the water pressure of her shower caressed her back. She'd been missing the dizzy distraction of desire for *years,* and the sudden arrival—and what she'd tried to do with it the night before—was sending her further into the tailspin.

June had kissed a demon. A demon had kissed her back.

By a miracle, June made it down to the shop on time, and the peace of a place so familiar righted the uneven world a bit. She stared blankly at the hank of yarn in her hand, remembering the stroke of full lips on hers, the impossible span of Ash's hands on her back. The kiss had been somehow intimate and also impersonal, the pair of them mindlessly hungry for the other's touch. Or had that just been her?

June swallowed hard at the thought that she might've molested an unwilling demon.

He tucked me into bed.

She wanted to speak to Josie, who had experience with this sort of situation. But speaking to Josie would bring up Imogen and—

A thin moan rose up June's throat, and she rested her forehead against the shelf in front of her, breathing in through her nose and out through her mouth, counting to four each time as the internet had advised her that morning.

Imogen. Imogen had bound her. And then, after what June had assumed was a run-of-the-mill argument, had unbound her. June wondered if she'd known it was there. Known but not wanted to examine, because in all honesty, being bound was easier than living with the wreckage after leaving Brett and—

June gagged and spun, shoving the yarn into the cubby and staring wildly out of her frosted shop windows, trying to catch her breath. Too much had resurfaced all at once. She'd spent nine years in a reliable and numb fog. She'd forgotten how afraid of Imogen she was. How heartbroken Brett had left her. And in the years that passed, she had missed even more, like the bond between Josie and Rosa, which had seemed practical before but was now precious and fractured. Imogen's binding had denied her the experience of friendship, and then Imogen had gone and ruined it before June could even enjoy the possibility.

Perversely, the only remotely easy thing to process was Ash.

And that was a complicated clusterfuck of confusion.

Looks like I got myself into a bit of a pickle, June thought in Ash's low rumble, a hysterical giggle rising and dying on her tongue.

If a customer walked into the shop to find June clinging to the shelves, eyes wild and on the brink of a panic attack, the whole town would hear about her breakdown before sunset. She needed to get herself under control. Or close the shop... *That* was a tempting thought. She could go back up to her apartment and dive back into those sheets that smelled like a match tip and gasoline and—

Something was wrong.

June straightened as her wards throbbed in the shop, the pressure of their warning a punch to the gut. She gasped, eyes widening, landing across the street on the glowing open sign of The Inferno, and then at Flora Fresca, before another strike came, this one rattling the hangers with her carefully knitted samples.

Had the Sweet Pea wards fractured last night when Imogen's binding was torn away? And if they had, what did that mean for how likely her shop wards were to hold?

Fuck. Brett. She'd marched her ass back to him, accused him of murder and expected him to, what? Not respond?

And now she had no one.

Imogen would— No, the thought of Imogen made her stomach riot again, but the anger that followed, burning through her veins and tensing her muscles, was necessary fuel.

June rushed for the windows, tracing fingers at the corners, catching at the little threads that ruled the frost, and tugging them together to send brittle lace rushing over the surface of the glass, concealing her work from the street.

Brett hadn't even been able to replace her wards at the coven house. If she was quick, there'd be no way he'd break in.

Another hammer of magic pounded at the shop, trying to reach her, rattling the doors and windows, making the yarn bounce on the shelf, making the bile rise in June's throat. Demonic energy.

June's breaths came in short pants. In through her nose, out through her mouth, fuck the count of four, that wasn't working. She ran for the display wall, where an intricately woven lace was throbbing on the special pin board she'd made. She pulled it down to the floor, grabbing the nearest spool of yarn—black, good, that would help—and ripping the lace free of the pins.

Let the wards hold, let them hold, she thought. They would, wouldn't they? Unless the energy belonged to—

June's fingers slipped and fumbled as she tried to loop around a nail, begin a new warding, her free hand swiping at the wall for a crochet hook to work with.

Ash. Ash could break her wards. They were too used to him.

And she didn't have the best defenses against him at the moment, the taste of him still on her mouth, his scent in her bed and her hair.

The shop shook, and June's teeth ground in her jaw, heart rioting in her chest. The door banged open, and even under attack, even with demonic energy hammering at her wards, there was the idiotic moment of relief to see Ashtaroth in the doorway.

"They summoned Vine," Ash barked, slamming the door shut behind him, palm swiping upwards and the lock clicking. "Get to work, stitch witch!"

What the hell are you doing here? she wanted to ask. But then again, what the hell had she been doing hoping he would come?

He *had* come.

June's hands worked fast, twisting, looping, hooking, the pattern forming on the board half-memorized and half-improvised against the now toothy pinch of the attack trying to burrow its way through her wards to reach her. And with the threads burning through her fingers, she caught the ones in the air, the ones that shone so much brighter now than they had the day before. A shadow fell over her, over her work, and warmth pressed to her back.

"Bottom right—"

"I know!" June snapped, swinging the yarn down, tweaking and looping it around nails, snagging at the corners of her shop and locking them to her working to ground the ward, adding in her apartment for good measure.

Ash chuckled at her spite, his arms reaching down to hold the board steady as she worked faster, daggers of electric pain striking her temples.

"I'm not—"

Ash shushed her, his beard on her shoulder, that heartbeat she'd requested drumming steadily against her back. "Focus, I'll push back."

She had dozens of questions for him, ones that tried to distract her from the work. And then a warm shiver shrouded her from head to toe, sharp juniper burning on her tongue, and the pain in her bones and temples vanished. Ash's breath puffed against her shoulder, a little heavier than before, and June's fingers flew, the threads of old wards drifting hopefully closer to her, wanting to be included, shimmering at the corner of her eyes.

"Where did you learn this?"

"My father taught me to see them," June said of the glittering strands that crossed and connected everything around her. "It's...almost like crossing your eyes a little to see them. Manipulating focus. I taught myself to use them."

By playing with those cat's cradle strings when she was bored and her parents were busy with Imogen. Under Brett's encouragement too, although he could never follow her patterns.

"Cross your threads," Ash whispered.

June's brow furrowed with annoyance. She *knew* that, but she was busy working the base, and anyway, what the hell did he know?

"Cross them, starling," Ash bit out, more of a bark in his tone.

"Fine, half finished it is," she snapped back, plucking fiercely at the spiraled weave she'd fashioned in the center of the board, criss-crossing and stretching threads to new pins until they were woven and locked together.

Irritatingly enough, the demon was right. The threads of power gleamed and the rattling of the shop quieted, glass windows still groaning, and Ash sagged a little of his weight onto her back. He was warm, heavy, broad, and June had no interest in shaking him off.

"Now you can fin—"

"Yeah, I get it," June grumbled.

Ash laughed, and his breath ruffled her hair, his hands moving from the board to hold her waist. "Don't think I'm not impressed," he said gently.

June pursed her lips to keep from smiling, focusing on

adding the curls of flourishes that stretched to the corners of the board. They would stabilize the ward, but Ash was right —the crosses had locked out Vine's power.

Ash settled back, grunting, and then guided her into his lap, June squeaking as she brought the board with her to finish the piece.

"Why warn me?" she whispered.

Ash didn't answer, just rested his massive chin on her shoulder. June's fingers flew until the friction of the wool made the tips numb and sore.

"Why come last night for that matter?" she asked. Ash was warm and solid and terrifyingly comfortable. He surrounded her almost entirely, just as he had practically smothered her beneath him last night. "Why not take the bargain—"

"I don't know, starling."

June blinked, weaving the yarn back and forth through the pins to the last corner. "Why 'starling'?"

That question had been bothering her for weeks. She liked starlings, the dark birds who flew together in swarms, even when others thought they were pests.

"Suits you. Suits your magic," he added, reaching out to tap the edge of the board. "Making something powerful by the pattern of pieces, movements. Plain little birds that shine when you look closer."

June's eyes narrowed, fingers fussing with the strings, trying to decide if she was complimented or offended.

"Do you really want to be put back in a cage?" he asked.

June swallowed. The attack had retreated or— "Will the summoner know they were unsuccessful?"

"Probably, but they spent the energy and Bell's got Vine on a leash," Ash said, body brushing against hers with his shrug. "That's the second time he's been summoned."

June's eyes widened. So it was Vinny's power that attacked Amira too? She stopped the warding lace at last, turning her head to catch Ash's eye. He was so close. And fuck, he *was* handsome. Devastatingly big and beautiful and warm, and she knew how he tasted—

Ash raised his eyebrow, and June cleared her throat. "Why did Bell give that order?"

Ash's expression went blank, his eyes studying her thoroughly. "I think you might know more about that than I do."

Josie. Bell didn't want Josie getting hurt. Or he'd vowed to her that she was safe and was keeping his word.

"No, I don't think I want a new cage," June admitted finally.

Ash nodded slowly, a slight twitch of his lips starting. "If someone's going to bind you up, it's going to be me, starling."

June lifted her chin, glaring at the broad and powerful lines of Ash's face. "You had your chance, beast. I won't ask again."

"I don't mean with a bargain." Ash grinned as June's belly flipped and her heart stammered in her chest. His head cocked, and his hands on her waist twisted her to the side. "What do you want?"

June blinked back at him and shook her head.

"No bargain, just tell me," he said, his thumbs sliding down to press over her hip bones.

Did she even know? How was she supposed to untangle the mess of worries and regurgitated emotions that had been buried for years, in order to find what she *wanted*? But Ash was patient. He'd been patient this whole time, watching her, studying her, picking gently to see what threads she'd let him pull. So she unraveled a few of her thoughts until she found an answer for him.

"I want to pretend you're not waiting for the opportunity to break this town, and I want to pretend that I'm not a pile of emotional rubble." *And I want you to kiss me again, but not to try and put me to sleep. I want to feel something good again,* she thought.

Ash's gaze went distant, brow furrowing. June decided to give into the insanity of the moment, reaching one hand up and digging her fingers into his beard, fascinated as his eyelids fluttered briefly and his face grew weightier in her hand. His eyes opened fully again, locking with June's and holding her stare.

"Honestly, I don't give a fuck about this town," Ash rumbled. June frowned at that, and he shook his head, continuing, "I don't care if it goes on shining like a sugary sunshine beacon of goodness. I don't care if it burns down."

"I'm not letting that happen," June said, pulling at his beard in warning.

Ash smiled faintly and nodded. "That's what I figure too."

"So what do you want?" June asked.

The frost was starting to melt on the windows, the shop was quiet and still, and she was still sitting on Ash's lap on a cold winter morning, her fingers aching and a new ward thrumming at her side.

Ash took the hand she'd placed on his jaw and drew it down to his chest. "I want to know why this felt like I was going to explode when I found out that Vine had offered up his power for another witch to attack you."

Under her palm, Ash's heart picked up its pace, his dark gaze holding hers, brow tangled and waiting for the answer. She didn't have one for him that made any sense to her. Just as she didn't have one for herself as to why Ash seemed...*safe*. Safer than anything or anyone she'd known in a long time. If ever.

"I think I have really bad taste in men," June murmured without thinking.

Ash's frown deepened at that. "If you're comparing me to that human predator, starling..." He trailed off, mouth hanging open.

Brett had disguised his real personality, but there was no confusion for June on what Ash was. Or was there more confusion? He was a demon. One who had refused her soul when she'd offered it up for some mental peace. One who had tucked her into bed. Who'd raced to her when her life was under attack. Who sat on the floor of a yarn store and held her in his lap as they shared uncomfortable confessions.

"Let's pretend, beast," June whispered, deciding that a terrible decision was better than no decision.

Ash blinked at her and watched as she leaned in, slower this time than the sudden way she'd thrown herself at him the night before. His head tilted in her direction, enough for their noses to graze, their foreheads to meet, and his lips were parted for her as she found her way easefully into the kiss.

Fuck. It felt so good to *touch* someone, without the foggy cotton layer of the binding she'd ignored for years. Ash's fingers were calloused, catching on the cashmere and silk of her sweater. His beard was soft and ticklish against her cheeks, tongue smooth and slipping a heady flavor into her mouth.

The world wobbled, which seemed right with lips like those on hers and hands that big gripping her hips, but then June caught her breath, eyes fluttering open, and realized that Ash had lifted them from the floor. Her arms were wrapped around his shoulders, legs around his hips, and his cheek pressed to hers as he carried her through the shop.

"You're not putting me to sleep again," she warned. If she got rejected twice by a demon, she was throwing in the towel.

"We're not doing this in full view of the town," Ash answered. "Never mind the others across the street."

June's head warred with the two important pieces of information in that declaration—he didn't want demons to know, and more significantly— "What's the '*this*' that we're doing?"

He only took them around the corner, to the doorway of her inventory closet, and pressed her back to the frame, pushing himself into her and latching soft lips to her throat. June's heartbeat expanded into her swallow, her veins, right down to her long neglected core, and she moaned at the sweet pressure of his mouth over her pulse.

This was good, she decided. Or it was wonderfully wrong.

She combed her fingers into his hair, squeezing her legs around his hips, the answer of how he would feel there arriving at last. He was a giant, and it was an almost painful stretch in her thighs, a satisfying ache that she wanted to share with every other neglected muscle in her body.

"Ash," she whispered, because it had been such a long time since she'd said a lover's name this way, and this time it brought a grin to her lips. A grin she hadn't worn in *years*.

Ash growled, head lifting, and her smile vanished as he demanded a kiss from her, her head pressing hard to the wooden doorframe as he ravaged her mouth with teeth and tongue. Heavy hands stroked the back of her thighs, the skirt of her dress rucking up with every pass until his fingers stopped abruptly at the discovery of the bare skin above her stockings.

June gasped as his grip dug in, her body bucking against his and then groaning with the sudden revelation of *friction*.

Suddenly, the dubious lid she'd put on the resurgence of arousal was knocked away by the boiling over of heat and *need* in her blood.

"Ash, please," she gasped, rocking indecently into the solid mass of him. There wasn't anywhere he touched her that didn't sing in response, his chest holding steady as hers rubbed against him, the burn of his jeans on the tender insides of her thighs, the semi-stiff ridge of him digging into her covered core. Even the scratch of his eyes watching her tremble and beg with her body.

Ash's hands squeezed once more on June's thighs, before lowering her feet down to the ground. "It's been a long time since I enjoyed sins of the flesh, starling," Ash murmured, and June tried not to whimper as he stepped back. "But I've always been good with my hands."

"Prove it," June gasped out, but Ash was too quick to tease.

One hand grabbed the back of her neck, squeezing lightly, arching June for Ash's consuming kiss, and the other reappeared beneath her skirts, stroking up one thigh to rub the crease at her hip. June moaned into his mouth, clutched at Ash's collar—damnit, he was wearing that coat again. She was already oddly attached to the texture and weight of the leather in her grip.

His touch followed the same path up the other thigh as Ash's tongue stroked against her. She liked the hand at the back of her neck, the authority of him, possessive and controlling, simplifying her choices. Her previous experience—she decided not to think his name—had been so gentle, it left her uncertain. Ash's touch was determined and familiar, he teased but only to prepare her, up and down her legs until she started to shake with the wanting, hips kicking as he cupped her through her underwear, pressing and holding her in place.

"God, Ash, please!"

He laughed, and June opened her eyes to glare at him, ruffled by the ease of his smile. It was more powerful than ever, and now without the binding in place, it drew a laugh out of her too until they were both grinning at one another. Ash's fingers smoothed up—just greeting her clit through fabric—and down beneath her underwear, skin on skin. June's grin faltered and fell open on a moan as Ash petted her, simple and gentle and divinely thorough, stroking through her folds. He made a sound like a growl as he spread her own arousal over her sex, hand and body crowding closer to touch more, claim more, push her a little further out of her own head.

And damn, but that was a relief that was more than physical. June softened, pinned and supported by Ash's hand on her neck, her sex, his thigh between her legs, sinking into the call and response between sensitive skin and a tired brain.

"I knew you were going to give our mission trouble, but I didn't think I'd make this easy for you," Ash said, but he didn't look mad and June couldn't care less because one slightly rough and very thick finger was wiggling its way inside of her, stealing her breath.

"Do you want an apology?" June gasped out, trying to find a grip on the moment, even as her eyes fell shut, Ash's other fingers still nuzzling and nudging and brushing over every sensitive inch of her.

"I want you to take me with you when you push back at

your ex's coven," Ash said, voice going quiet, finger pumping in and out of her slowly.

"Why?" June asked, squirming into his touch, taking him deeper. Ash was rubbing his cheek against hers, and she clung to his shoulders as he let her ride his hand.

"So you don't get killed, starling," he whispered.

It was dangerous territory, and it gave her too many questions, so June turned her head, finding his mouth again and begging with nips and licks for him to kiss her. He gave in easily, abandoning her neck to wrap that arm around her waist and hold her close. A second finger joined the one inside her, the stretch sudden and insistent. Ash swallowed her cry, thumb focusing on her clit, working her into a tense and trembling frenzy.

The door of the shop rattled, and June broke away before Ash could hesitate. "Don't stop!"

He chuckled, biting at her jaw, and June curled a leg around his hip, until they were too tangled together to do more than kiss, more than the steady play of his hand on her pussy.

It occurred to her, very briefly, that he'd probably forgotten as much about how an orgasm felt as she had, and then everything started to narrow into a fine point of pressure that threatened to make her scream. Someone was knocking on the door, calling for her, and June was panting into Ash's throat, his mouth pressing kisses in her hair, his fingers curling and spiraling, summoning something greater and more painful and more exquisitely perfect than she'd ever had before.

"Call me beast again," Ash rasped, the arm on her waist sliding lower, lifting her off her feet and pushing her harder onto his hand.

"Beast," June pleaded, and a wild, crazed, giddy smile

broke over her lips as the pressure cracked, and a dizzying glowing rushing ran through her, from cunt to head to toes and fingertips. The stroke and rub and play of Ash's touch drove her through each sweet wave until they grew bitter-sweet and overwhelming, her body trying to arch and shy away, shaking as he continued, mouth whining.

"June! June, are you in there? Are you okay?!"

Rosa.

Ash's hand slowed and stilled, his mouth covering hers as she panted and settled. Her toe touched down on the floor again, and June whimpered as Ash gently pulled his fingers free of her, an embarrassing rush and tremble running through her until embarrassment was replaced with fascination as he brought his fingers up to his lips, sucking them clean as he stared back at her.

"Don't leave the ward till I get back."

June opened her mouth to object and wondered why. If a demon wanted to guard her back without asking for anything in return, who was she to argue? And if Ash wanted to...

"You don't make any sense," she said, thoughts a little loose after the relief of the orgasm.

Ash nodded, a line appearing between his brows. "Yeah, I'm confused too. Now say you'll wait."

At least she wasn't the only one. "I'll wait."

Ash gave her mouth a long, disturbed study before the door of her shop rattled harder, Rosa's call growing urgent.

He stepped back, and June held herself firmly to the wall, ignoring that impulse to sway closer as Ash retreated, heading for the backdoor.

Her whole body was still humming, little trembles of relief running through her as she reassembled her skirt and underwear, checked that her tall socks were still in place, and headed for the front door. The back one clicked shut, and there was a soft pulse of power as Ash warded that too.

The lock was sticky, and June's fingers paused over the spot, surprised and inappropriately softened by how determined Ash had been when he flipped it shut.

"June!" Rosa barked from the other side.

The real world came back with the rush of cold wind, June guarding herself behind the door as she let Rosa in. The shop was untidy, yarn needing to be escorted back into the cubbies, the new ward left haphazardly on the floor, the old one discarded in a wad to the side. Rosa ignored it all, grabbing June by the shoulders, searching her face.

"What the hell happened? Are you okay? I totally felt something super nasty headed right for you, and then it was like... June?"

"I'm okay," she murmured.

"You don't look okay!"

June reached a hand up to her cheek. They were warm, and shit, she was still smiling like an idiot, which was probably going to freak Rosa out more than anything.

"I got a ward up before anything serious happened," June said, combing her fingers through her hair, pleased with the whiff of that fresh match scent of Ash's.

"June, there's all sorts of fuzzy stuff going on in here," Rosa said, squinting and staring around the room.

"That's just the yarn," June said quickly and then let out a wild giggle as Rosa glared at her. "No, you're right. Um, demonic power, I think like what hit Amira."

Rosa's eyes widened, big and dark and pretty. Wow, Rosa was so *pretty*. June hadn't ever really seen her before, and her friend was all colors and long lashes and red lips and soft curls.

"You're so pretty!" June echoed her own thoughts.

Rosa paled. "Oh, June, what happened to you?"

And because that question drew up everything, from beginning to end, from her parents to Ash's kisses in the corner of her shop, from Brett's manipulation to Imogen's binding, June burst into tears.

Again.

14

UNDECIDED

"Vinny is grounded," Bell muttered at Ash's side. "Got him bound up in Grimsby's basement. Barbie is pissed at him over something to do with Danny, so no arguments."

Ash grunted. His back was to the windows of the Inferno, eyes focusing on the quick switch of stitches building the cabled neckline of the sweater he'd been working on, a good twisty braid to keep—

He blinked at his work. The sweater was nearly finished, sized to fit him, and here he was, imagining the sleeves hanging down to pale thighs, blonde hair brushing the collar warded with stitches to keep the wearer safe. His chest ached for the five hundredth time that day, and he resisted the urge to reach a hand up and rub over the spot.

Had he fashioned himself a broken organ? Was that the explanation for all this clenching and pounding and panging?

"Are you even listening?" Bell asked, a little sharper.

"No," Ash admitted.

Bell huffed, and then the huff turned into a laugh. "Yeah. Fair enough. Why not just go?"

Ash's eyes flicked up and glanced around the bar. "Where's Pie?"

"Why are you worried about Pie?"

"Why aren't you?"

Paimon wasn't like Bell. Beleth was a demon of the battlefield, immediate and active, a creature of strategy, sure, but also not the man to keep the law in line. Paimon was a being of shadows, trimming out the untidy edges in the Bowels, reminding everyone to keep their place. Surely Ash couldn't *defect* from the mission without consequences, and since those clearly weren't coming from Bell, Paimon was the one he needed to watch.

So that's it? You've decided? he asked himself. *No, but it's better to be prepared for the possibility.*

Ash's body was twisting toward the window, and only the sight of Bell's smirk reminded him to straighten up and *ignore* the view across the street.

"This whole thing sounds like a her problem not a Sweet Pea problem," Bell said.

Ash glared at him and tipped his head in thought. "So it...doesn't matter if I..." *help her?*

It did matter. Saving June's life mattered. And he didn't mean that for himself.

If Vinny's power had made it through June's wards and she'd been killed, the wards on Sweet Pea would fail. Their demonic powers would work to their fullest again. Vinny could cause car crashes and Aim could start fires and Barbie's perpetually sour mood might actually infect someone else for once.

"You know that's bullshit, you just don't care," Ash said, staring firmly back at Bell, watching the Warlord King squirm in the booth seat. "Look, I've got no illusions about what it means if I—What it *already* means that I failed last night. That I stepped in this morning. The only thing that puts me back on Hell's side is if I make a U-turn real fast on that witch. There's no straddling the line, Bell. You realize that, don't you?"

Bell scowled, glaring across the bar at nothing, swigging hard from his beer. "So you've made your choice?"

"No," Ash said, frowning at himself, staring at the sweater in his hands.

He'd started winning trust from June, which meant he now had something he could use against her. He could hand her over to that ex of hers, clear the way for the mission. He could feed little doses of poison into her ear now that her head was vulnerable without the cage. He could take her to bed, make her beg him, wring a bargain out of her at her most desperate moment.

"No, not yet. But I'll make one soon," Ash said. "Are you sure you haven't made one already?"

Bell blinked, expression stricken, and Ash rose from the booth, giving in to the urge at last to check on June's shop over his shoulders.

The lights inside had dimmed, but he caught one glimpse of her shadow passing, prepping the shop to close, and the tension he'd been carrying in that new heart of his eased at the sight.

"I'll be back at the house later."

Bell grunted in acknowledgement, and Ash resisted the urge to tell Bell another uncomfortable truth, especially when it was one that might've been equally true of him.

He grabbed his knitting bag, tucking the sweater inside, and headed for the door.

"Where are you going?" Dante asked, arriving with

Cornell and Thurman in tow. Ash didn't know if Dante was with them for the sake of the mission or because the older couple was funny and enjoyed flirting with Dante, feeding an already swollen ego.

"Stitch markers," Ash lied.

Cornell scoffed and gave Ash a knowing look out of the corner of his eye, but the three of them stepped out of Ash's way. He jogged across the street, deciding he liked winter, liked the *zing!* of cold in his lungs and the brilliant glitter of the stars in a clear sky at night.

June met him at the door. Her cheeks were pink, but so were her eyes. She'd been crying again, and his heart did that stupid aching clench. She ducked back into the shadows of the shop without a word, her shoulders softening as he locked the door behind him.

"What happened?"

"Nothing. I need therapy. I'm fine," June said, waving a shaky hand through the air.

The conversation with the green witch then. Ash wanted to ask if the coven was broken, as she'd claimed before, but it felt too closely related to the mission he was ignoring for the moment.

"Vinny's on lockdown, but it's no guarantee that—"

"That Brett or his coven won't just summon another demon," June said, nodding and turning to face him. Her arms were crossed over her chest, holding her sides, and Ash wanted to unfold her, drape her around him again and watch her give in to the rush of her own pleasure. "It could be you next time."

"I get summoned for art and science and maniacal architecture, starling, not for murder," Ash said.

Her arms loosened, and a soft laugh escaped. That pesky animal in his chest thumped in triumph.

"But the seven of us aren't the only ones," Ash continued, nodding. "Your apartment is stronger, but we'd better check it out."

June stared back at him. She was more sober than the craze of the morning, more like the woman he'd known for months, contained and calm, or maybe only feigning calm. He stepped forward, intrigued by the little swipe of her tongue over her bottom lip as she looked him up and down, but she didn't surrender so easily. Her guard was up. At least this one was really hers.

"What's your game with me?" she asked softly.

"Curiosity," he answered without hesitation, using the same excuse from last night. Her head tipped, and she waited. "Do you feel like the same person you were yesterday morning?"

June's eyes narrowed, and she didn't move or speak for a moment but finally relented, shaking her head a little. "No, but yes. I feel...more than I was."

Ash smiled at that and nodded. "I want to know the rest of you. Are you still afraid?"

"More than ever."

When she'd first told him, he'd been amused. Now June's fear brought a growl up his throat he fought and failed to stifle. "I like you," he admitted with slow reluctance. "I've got dibs."

"On my destruction?" June asked, arching an eyebrow.

No, he thought, but he answered, "Maybe. I haven't decided that yet."

Oddly, wrongly even, June relaxed at that, nodding her head. "At least you're honest. Thank you. Let me grab my things."

He didn't want to destroy her. He was starting to get a

general idea of what he did want, but it was so *impossible* there shouldn't have been a word for it.

June finished turning the lights off, and Ash followed her through the dark, watching her layer another sweater on under a coat, all just to run outside and then back into her apartment. She grabbed her own bag of knitting, a curiously familiar pulse inside, and pulled a jingling set of keys out of her pocket.

"I'm not in any shape to deal with Brett tonight," June murmured, exiting the back of the shop. Ash was quick to slide around her, scouting the energy in the back alley. Innocent, the only hints were a few sugary wisps of Bell's witch and the residue of the magic they'd fought off earlier. "I need to have my head on straight."

"You look steady to me," Ash said, thinking of the spectacular display of her undoing the night before. June scoffed, and something occurred to him. "It's a woman summoning Vine, by the way."

June's key scratched over the lock as she whipped her stare to Ash, blue eyes wide and lit by the streetlamp at the end of the alley. "A woman. Just one?" Ash nodded, and June's lips pursed. "My sister?"

"It didn't happen inside your wards," Ash said. "You think your sister would've attacked you like today?"

June frowned and shook her head, unlocking the door and stepping in, swinging it back for him as if it was a given he would follow her. His feet were already moving, so it must've been.

"Vinny said she was wearing a shroud so he couldn't see her."

"Not Imogen then. She wouldn't care," June mused quietly, her back to him as she padded up the stairs to her apartment door. His steps made the wood groan. "Do you know if it was the same woman?"

"He thinks so. He knew it was heading for you too." Ash could've strangled Vinny if he hadn't been more interested in running for the knit shop. That said enough about the state of his decision, didn't it?

"That narrows this down. Alone..."

Ash joined June on the landing, resting his hand over hers on the doorknob. "Let me go in first." Bell had given him the story of Josie finding the murderer in her apartment. Human homes were spectacularly vulnerable.

June's hand didn't move beneath his, and she turned to lean against the wall, staring up at him. "Are you really coming in just to put up a ward, Ashtaroth?" Her lips were curling up, eyes narrowing, and he got the impression she was laughing at him.

He understood the question. Was that all he wanted? Or would he take her up on another physical offer like earlier? He'd claimed a taste of her at the end and regretted not spending more time on his knees in front of her at the time, but now...

Time alone with June Byrne was risky. Time away from her was uncomfortable.

You should've let her die, a dark voice whispered in his thoughts. He flipped it off. June wouldn't have died. She was too strong. Maybe she would've been wiped out, maybe it would've been a close call, but she would've survived. He only made the battle a little easier for her.

"You haven't decided," she said, hand slipping out from under his, the warm imprint of her still against his palm, hell, still on his fingers.

His fucking heart tripped unevenly in his chest, and he blinked before entering the apartment. It was quiet, empty, a few of the woven wards on her walls hanging crookedly but holding. June didn't wait for him to call her in, shutting the door behind them both and flipping on the light.

"You really think I wouldn't have known if my place was compromised today?"

...No.

"What do you eat?"

Ash was losing his footing the longer he was around June. He'd understood the trapped version of her, mysterious as she was. This new freed woman was unpredictable.

It's just food, he thought, laughing at himself.

"Nothing, anything," he said, shrugging.

"Well, I know how to boil noodles. Take your coat off."

He wasn't going to stay, was he? Apparently he was, his coat was half off his shoulders. June was bustling through her apartment, tossing off her own coat, carrying her heavier sweater into her bedroom, leaving her knitting on the floor by the couch. Ash went to steal a peek, flipping the bag open.

"What are you using the yarn with my power in it for?" he asked as June breezed by him again, heading for her kitchen.

She was drawing her hair up high on her head, revealing a long neck and a bruise mark from *his* mouth. His own knitting thumped down to the floor next to hers.

"A banishing net," she said, rifling through her cupboards.

"For Brett?"

"Actually, I started it for you."

Ash laughed, and June's cheek turned in his direction. That smile of hers kept growing, getting closer and closer to the one she'd worn when she came on his fingers.

"Clever, starling. Would've been an effective trap. Why just me? What about the others?"

June filled a pot up with water from the sink, her gaze shy as she turned to place it on the stove. "I wasn't as afraid of them."

The heart in his chest—the one he'd made for her—twisted uncomfortably until she glanced up, something flirtatious and soft in the flick of her eyes.

"If it isn't a direct attack from Brett, it could still be under his orders. But him not being in the room for the summoning is strange," June said, sliding back into the real reason they were together. Or at least what was supposed to be the real reason.

"Do you know enough about his coven to guess who it was?"

June wobbled a hand in the air. "Ella maybe. She was part of my father's coven too, and she would have the knowledge."

Ash thought of the scene from June's nightmares, the one colored by flashing police lights, the gruesome jigsaw of her parents' bodies in the woods.

"Is she responsible for what happened to your parents?" Ash asked.

June's eyes widened, cheeks paling, and he regretted the question. "No. No...Imogen is," June whispered and then shook her head. "Not... She was only eleven at the time. And my parents carry more of the blame than she does. I don't— What happened to them isn't relevant."

There were tears welling up in her eyes, her shoulders rising up to her ears, and the box of pasta in her hand was rattling with her tremors. Ash rounded the half wall into the kitchen, surprised and relieved when June let him draw her into his chest. Some of that wild, chaotic power from the night before was swelling, and Ash spread his hand flat on her back, not pushing it in to trap it there but leech it out of her until June softened.

"Better?" he asked.

June sighed into his shirt, nodding, and then turned, still leaning against him. "I don't like Ella, but I don't think she'd try and kill me. She knows Imogen would go off the rails, and I think in a weird way she likes Imogen. Or is afraid of her. Probably both."

"Have you spoken to—"

"No." June shook her head and dumped the pasta into the now boiling water. "I'm not sure I want to face her. I'm too angry."

As far as Ash could tell, it sounded like Imogen needed someone to be angry at her. But he wasn't sure it would do June any good to be that person.

"Aside from Ella...there are a few women who are devoted enough to take me as a threat," June said, wrinkling her nose. "I wish it'd just been him."

"Why?"

"Because I hate him. Because finding a way to put him in jail would've been really satisfying. Now I've got another murderer to worry about."

I can think of better places to send a pedophile than jail, Ash thought, but kept his mouth shut for once.

"You make dinner. I'll add to your wards," he said instead. "We'll work on that banishing net after."

June shot him a slightly baffled smile and then stirred the pot of noodles as Ash left her in the kitchen.

A YOUNG JUNE *wandering through the halls of an enormous old building full of other witches, an odd tension in the air, eyes darting away from hers. A loosely locked door, one that was supposed to be left open. June's simple flick of power breaking through the light ward.*

A young girl in a T-shirt, lying face down on a mattress, a man on top of her, his hands stuffed in the shirt beneath her chest, his moans dying off at the interruption of June's arrival. The girl, Imogen's face, turning to stare directly back at her sister.

June whimpered and twisted, Ash quick to snatch the dream out of her head, allowing her to settle again. He'd only let it play out of curiosity.

June had fallen asleep on the couch after an oddly peaceful evening of dinner and knitting, her head on Ash's lap. He'd gathered little threads of information about her, about her family's history of dark folk magic, well beyond the simple constraints of Christianity and its supposed counterparts in Satanism. This was *old* magic they were playing with. She wouldn't speak about her sister now, something frozen passing over her face anytime they got too close.

There was still a sour expression on her face, and Ash set the circular shawl—the banishing net—aside, reaching one hand down to comb her hair back over her shoulder, revealing that mark on her throat again. He wanted to nibble on it.

Aligning himself with June Byrne would create waves. Paimon—Bell, if he was bothering to do his job—would be after him. He might get sent right back to the Bowels. Maybe Hell would even send a new demon to take his place. Ash could fight that, June could bind him on this plane, to her, and they could battle it out with Hell's Bells or the Bowels. He could puzzle over this new heart in his chest and its demands while untangling June's story, watching her build the new unbound version of herself.

But the obvious thing, the simplest maneuver, would be to betray June.

Simple was right. It was what he *ought* to do. If only Ash weren't the kind of demon who preferred a challenge.

 15 DUALITY

"It doesn't make sense," June said, sitting upright out of a dead sleep, a half-formed thought bubbling from her dreams.

She was in bed, alone, the dark sky cluttered with storm clouds giving her bedroom a shadowy and ominous tone. The last thing she remembered was testing Ash's thigh as a pillow—supportive if not quite squishy enough—and discussing the merits of adding a traveling vine section to the banishing shawl.

Ash was missing, which didn't surprise her as much as the fact that he'd tucked her into her bed for the second night in a row.

The bubble she'd woken up with—something to do with Brett and Amira—was floating away, replaced with the heavy groggy quality of waking up. June reached for her phone to check the time, wondering how Josie would feel to be called and quizzed on demon dating etiquette.

If that was what was happening with Ash. It was hard to say.

4 missed calls from

Imogen

June tossed her phone quickly facedown onto the bed.

Of course Imogen would wait until their relationship was imploded into catastrophic rubble before being the sister to reach out.

Maybe it's time to let Imogen go, a gentle voice cautioned June. Perhaps it was the other way around. Imogen had released June's binding. June had always thought she'd been the one holding onto her younger sister, but now, without the magic in place, Imogen was the one topic on which she was numb.

She loved Imogen. She hated her too. She was afraid for Imogen and afraid of her. Maybe it was their childhood, their parents, maybe it was what happened with Brett, but everything that held the sisters together was poisoned.

And June was too tired to fight or to try and keep Imogen afloat anymore. Not while she was at risk of sinking herself.

She left her phone facedown and went to start the coffee maker and grab a shower before the building's hot water tank ran short.

On her couch, thrumming with power—Ash's yes, but also hers amplified by anger and a newfound focus—was the shawl, the banishing net, fine and delicate and the most intricate pattern she'd ever seen. Ash had taken liberties, and June was annoyed with how quickly he'd finished an applied lace edging, something that would've involved days of tediously repetitive work for her.

Her annoyance vanished when she noticed he'd woven the ends in too. That was weirdly arousing.

Worry and dread joined the other wild tangle of emotions—she'd forgotten how many one brain could hold and how queasy and headachey it all got after awhile.

Ash had finished the shawl, which meant her reason for stalling a counter-attack against Brett and his coven was now gone.

She really hoped he would keep his word on backing her up, otherwise he was planning on throwing her to the wolves alone. *Maybe even intentionally*, she warned herself.

"Coffee before panic," June decided out loud.

"I'M SORRY. For everything. For the coven and for Imogen and for *me* and—" June stopped, licking chocolate from the corner of her mouth, watching Josie and Rosa glance at one another—that frustrating *unity* between them that June wanted in on.

They'd arrived to the knit shop together too, a rugged bouquet from Rosa and a box of bakery samples from Josie. It was strange to be given presents when you were the one who owed the apology.

"Imogen was being ugly the night we tested Bell's energy," Josie said, leaning back in the chair at the knitting table in the heart of the shop, where they'd gathered together. "I was—*am* angry, but I already knew some of what she said was true. It didn't make the coven less important to me as a tool and a community, knowing that it was meant for her."

Rosa's eyes dropped. She and June—mostly June—had talked for hours yesterday with a lot of crying and a fair amount of cursing on Rosa's part. Josie might've been practical and sharp and seen right through June, but Rosa had trusted her.

"I don't think you're entirely to blame for being unavailable as a real friend all these years," Rosa said cautiously.

It was forgiveness, but it stung too, reminding June of

her failure. Prompted by the binding maybe, but she knew she was at least a little complicit in that.

"What I want to know is what this will change," Rosa said, squaring her shoulders and lifting her chin in challenge.

"What do you guys want to change?" June asked immediately. They glanced at one another again, and this time June took the leap. "I don't want the coven to break up. Sweet Pea needs us and I...I want us to be *friends*, but I can't work with my sister."

Josie's eyebrows rose. "You're sure?"

June nodded and then sagged in her chair, fingers itching to reach for another treat. She'd always liked Josie's food, but it was richer and sweeter and more decadent than ever today and she was not too proud to stress eat. "At least for now. And until you're both comfortable too, of course. If you're comfortable with the coven at all."

"I mean...we do still have Sweet Pea to protect," Rosa said, fussing with the greenery she'd brought.

Josie rolled her eyes, shooting June a sly sideways smile. "I *like* working magic with you both. Speaking of, what are you going to do about this attack?"

"The police were already looking at Brett because of the paint match on Amira's car dent," June said, frowning and tracing her fingers over some of the lace on the banishing net.

"Bell made Merryweather fess up to the police. I could ask him to—"

"Ashtaroth is coming with me to confront him," June rushed out.

Josie's eyes narrowed on June at the same moment that Rosa's widened.

"Now you have a demon too?!" Rosa cried out.

June should've scoffed or denied it, but instead she thought of Ash's eyes staring down at her as he licked her release off his fingers. Her cheeks flamed, and she shifted on the chair.

"I don't know. I don't have a vow like Josie, just...a general tendency of him being helpful," June said in a small voice. "He says he's curious about me."

Josie frowned and crossed her arms over her chest. "I'm the last person to caution you on interpersonal relationships with demons, but are you sure you want him to be at your back in a situation like that?"

It was surprisingly easy to nod. "He was there for the attack. He was...he was there when the binding came off of me too. I *begged* for him to put it back on, and he wouldn't," June said. "It's not that he couldn't turn on me, I know that. But...he could've already. Even he doesn't understand why he hasn't yet. Even if I don't."

Josie took in a deep breath and then nodded, arms loosening and falling to the table. "Okay, good. And if you want us too, we're there."

June bit her lip, eyes watering and a quavering smile rising as Rosa nodded in agreement. "Thank you. I'm grateful and a little tempted. But Brett's not alone in his coven. Even if this goes smoothly, someone from the coven might want to strike back at me later. I'd rather I was their only target. The advantage of taking Ash is that he's pretty impervious."

"Not to mention powerful," Josie said.

"Not to mention stacked with muscles and nice to look at," Rosa added with a nod. She shook her head, curls bouncing around her twitching grin. "Someone needs to study the catnip-like effect of witches on demons. Or is it just you two? I'm starting to feel left out."

"Rosa Velasco, you keep your cute little button nose out of those other demons' business, you hear me?" Josie snapped, pointing a finger in Rosa's face.

"She's right—I wouldn't trust any of the others. And to be honest, I wouldn't trust Ash if it were you he was helping and not me. Maybe that doesn't make sense."

"No, I get it. Bell's got my back. I'm sure of that. But I doubt he'd lift a finger for anyone else," Josie said, grimacing and letting out a long, heavy sigh. "What a mess. You sure we shouldn't use that banishing net on the whole lot of them?"

June's fingers tightened, slipping through the eyelets of lace. She wasn't sure. But she wasn't ready to send Ashtaroth packing yet either.

THE DEMON regularly occupying her thoughts was waiting for her outside of the backdoor of her shop after closing.

"You could've come in," June said, locking the door behind her.

"No one knows I'm going with you tonight."

June blinked at the door of her shop and hoped the dark covered the blush on her cheeks. Josie and Rosa knew, but Ash didn't need to know that. She was covering her own ass, that was all.

"Tonight?" she asked, turning to face him.

Ash raised an eyebrow, pushing off the wall of the alley. June's fingers tightened at the sight of that familiar leather jacket, already wanting to reach out and grab on.

"You wanna wait for them to strike again, starling?"

June sighed and shook her head. "I'm not sure I'm ready."

"That's why you have me," Ash said, shrugging.

June swallowed, a kernel of suspicion popping in her chest. Would Ash push her to act prematurely just to watch her fail, after everything? Now with the binding off, the sting of that kind of betrayal would be so much fiercer.

Ash's head tipped, lips twitching, reading her with a scroll of his gaze. "We go in, lock the building with your ward. You call him out, I make him confess. You do your thing with the banishing net while I keep you safe. Simple."

Simple was not going up against a coven. Especially not one like Brett's. Not for June, at least.

"A lot of that plan relies on you protecting me. Have you made a decision about me yet?" June asked. She was suddenly and viciously jealous of Josie and her vow from Bell. If Ash would give her one too, she could deal with Brett confidently. Except a vow sounded like a binding, and she didn't want to *force* Ash to be her ally.

Ash laughed, pulling one bare hand out of his jean pocket and reaching across the cold feet of space between them to her. "I'll tell you my decision after we're done. Come on."

She had told Josie and Rosa that she trusted Ash. Trust had never proven fruitful for June, and placing hers in a demon, of all people, now seemed wildly idiotic.

Ash must've caught the doubt on her face because he stepped forward until that burn of him, warm and steady, struck her cheeks. Her head tilted back to stare up at him, those teasing smiles gone from his lips.

"Yes, I made my decision. Have you?"

No, June thought with a sigh. She slipped her hand into his, and the ground was solid beneath her as Ash huffed and turned to lead the way.

He'd parked the enormous monster of a vehicle at the

far end of the alley, out of sight of the bar and the other businesses on main street. It was idling, roaring like a wild animal at the curb, and Ash opened the passenger door for her, lifting her up onto the seat like a doll, reminding her of the night he'd picked her up in the storm.

"Please have my back," June whispered, alone in the cab. "I need someone to have my back."

Ash looked up as he rounded the front of the truck, meeting her eyes through the windshield as if he'd heard her.

Josie and Rosa had her back, June reminded herself. And maybe if she'd spent less time focusing on keeping the coven harmless and gentle, they would've been prepared to go to battle against Brett with her. For all Ash's promise of how simple it would be, bindings and banishments and forced confessions weren't the kind of work she'd practiced with them.

Ash joined her in the warm cab, and June wrestled the seatbelt on as he watched her with an arched eyebrow.

The demon would have to do. Worst case scenario, if it looked like he was going to turn on her, she could still use the banishing net against him.

"I can hear your heart hammering from here," Ash said as the car roared with a tap of the gas pedal, rumbling quickly down the street, turning to head out of town.

"So can I," June muttered, the drum of anxiety loud in her own ears.

16

A KIND OF MONSTER

I*'m not ready. But I never will be*, June decided, staring up at the old school, her former home. On second thought, several things weren't right.

Ash was quiet this evening, watchful, studying her again. That wasn't so new, he'd done that since the beginning. Now, she realized the examination took place like he was on the other side of a glass wall. Before, that wall had been her binding. This one was of his own making. He was the observer, and it faltered her faith in him. Would he break the barrier down to save her ass again or just watch from the other side?

More importantly, though, this view didn't feel right.

"That magic is yours," Ash said, glaring at the dark brick, dressed in ragged threads of old power.

"They never replaced my wards," June said. "I tore them after coming back last week."

They were leaning against the truck, watching the building from across the street, and Ash was only inches away. Close, but still, June wanted to lean into his side until their hips were touching like they had been while they ate noodles on her couch the night before.

"They didn't have anyone put up new ones?" Ash asked.

June shrugged and frowned. "Brett always preferred flashier magic. He let others worry about stability."

"Should keep a secure house first," Ash muttered. June was inclined to agree.

This was a coven that was summoning demons. Committing murders. Led by a man luring in and grooming underage women. Not having any defenses up was...sloppy. Stupid.

June was tempted to see if she could just wait in the car. Couldn't Ash waltz right in and find the fucker himself? Save her the trouble, surely. But she had a feeling she needed to see this through too, to make that asshole beg for forgiveness and then to refuse it. Petty perhaps, but satisfying.

June started forward, but Ash stopped her with a hand on her shoulder. "Don't say my name in there. I can cover my tracks and watch your back at the same time. One of them finds out I'm a demon and—"

"There are laws they could manipulate to use you against me," June said, nodding. "I understand, beast."

He smiled, and some of June's unease vanished, especially as the hand on her shoulder slid to the back of her neck, squeezing there and dragging her in for a firm, long kiss. Here was her demon. Humorous, powerful, curious. Deliciously demanding and hungry in the embrace.

"All right, starling, your show now," he murmured against her lips.

He stepped away, and June stared back at him for a moment, common sense and caution and hope all waging a war in her opinion of him.

Save it for afterwards, she decided, turning on her heel and marching for the road, barely remembering to check for traffic in her momentum. It didn't matter. It was late for winter in the mountains, and the town was quiet.

"We're spotted," Ash murmured at her back.

June nodded, glancing up at the faces in the windows. Even if they did see her coming, the coven couldn't do anything about it. Without wards, it wasn't like they could *stop* her from coming in.

She was expecting to meet a locked door, but it opened before she could reach the handle, Ash's hand warm on her back, his body close. There was no matchstick whiff from him and less of an oppressive energy than usual, but his body heat was reassuring enough.

Ella stood in the doorway, dressed in plentiful layers, with narrowed eyes and smirking lips.

"Ella," June greeted, reminding herself that she wasn't nine years old and Ella couldn't whisper disapproval in her father's ear.

"June. I hoped Imogen would've been able to talk sense into you," Ella said, gaze flicking over June's shoulder at the massive figure of Ash.

Imogen. June's gut dropped. Ella was the one to report to Imogen then.

"Listening's not my strong suit," June said, a bit breathless.

Ella huffed and then sighed, stepping back. "I told him to fix the wards. Come in, I suppose."

"You could've put new ones up," June said softly, reaching back long enough to reassure herself that Ash was there before walking inside.

Ella hummed agreement, sly smile turning up the staircase on the right. "It's dull work. I'm a teacher, not a grunt."

The insult cut deeper than June expected. Her wards were exquisite, thank you very much, Ella. The older woman was dressed with little hints of other witches' magic, and June thought Ella was a leech more than she was a teacher. She was also the only one June knew for certain had the knowledge on summoning a demon for the kind of work it would've taken to attack her and Amira.

"June!"

Christine again, at the top of the stairs, hair twisted into a braid, sweet face pale at the sight of her. Ash's hand slid around to the side of June's waist, taking a firm grip, and June wondered if they should've come up with a more elegant plan. She was warded, he was covered, but how many more of the coven would appear before June got to Brett? Their numbers had grown, and surely there was some kind of limit to what Ash could take on her behalf.

"You can't be here!" Christine cried.

June looked to Ella instead, who had edged cautiously away from Ash, leaning against the stairwell and watching June.

"You know why I came."

Ella shrugged and glanced at the bag resting against June's hip. "I can guess. He's in the cafeteria. It's dinner time. Are you sure you're ready for this fight, Junie?"

"Are you?" Ash growled over June's shoulder.

Ella's lips twitched as she took another long examining glance at Ash. "You'd be surprised."

Christine turned tail and headed for the cafeteria at the same moment that Ash nudged June forward to the stairs. She didn't feel ready for the confrontation, and Ella's ominous statement didn't help.

You have a demon, and they don't even have wards, June reminded herself. As long as Ash proved reliable, she would be safe and Brett would end up locked up somewhere for a long time.

Christine's long braid whipped around the corners as they followed her. She'd always been a bit of a lapdog to Brett, which June had found curious, considering that she'd also tried to consistently warn June away from the coven. Did Christine think she could win Brett if she dug her teeth in long enough, or did she have nowhere else to go like the others?

"Your old room," Ash murmured as they passed the corner classroom she'd shared with Imogen.

"How did you know?" June asked, but Ash only shook his head and the sound of the dinner conversation in the cafeteria pushed his comments aside.

Brett was at the center of the room, just as he'd always been. The young redhead, Jess, was at his side, frowning up at Christine as she bent to whisper in Brett's ear. June's steps stopped at the sudden impact of the blow to her heart. Her emotions were still bound the last time she'd seen him, but they rioted now. June's nails dug into the palms of her hands as rage exploded inside of her, flooded her like scalding lava, quickly followed by the cold chill of heartbreak. It hurt to see him. It brought back all the shame, all the sense of insignificance, all the feelings of failure. And with that came the new determination to destroy this man as she'd nearly allowed him to destroy her.

"Steady, starling," Ash whispered, stroking his hand up to the back of her neck and then down again, stealing some of the burn and the drowning tightness in her chest.

June nodded, squaring her shoulders and leaning into that steadiness behind her. She buried the aching sorrow and the shame too, but saved the heat of anger in her veins for her working. Brett stood a moment later, finding June in the door, frowning at the sight of Ash behind her.

There were maybe two dozen other witches in the room, maybe a few more, and most of them were familiar, old faces she'd thought of as family without really *knowing* them. Brett didn't want her having real connections with the rest of the coven, they were all meant to be dependent on *him*.

"Any threats?" Ash asked.

"Ella, maybe the table in the back corner," June answered, catching sight of a familiar few older women, ones who'd been fascinated with Imogen when June brought her in.

"June, it's family dinner. It isn't the time or place for you to disrupt our coven. You made your choice to leave, give us our peace," Brett called, drawing the entire room's attention to her position.

Making her out to be the villain, disruptive, threatening. And in a way, he was right—tearing Brett out of this coven would likely unravel it completely. Some of these people wouldn't have anywhere else to go if the homestead was taken away.

Their comfort isn't worth more than Amira's life.

June's heart was in her throat, pounding so loud, it drummed in her ears. Her fingers twitched against her palm, ready and waiting to cast, tingling with the threads of magic floating through the air, rich from the activity of the coven house. She stepped forward with Ash at her back, the pair of them looming over the diners, a few witches sliding on benches out of their way.

"I want you to confess to what you did to Amira." June's voice was tight, quiet, but no one else was speaking and it floated up to the rafters.

Brett huffed a laugh and combed a hand through thinning hair, eyes rolling but checking his coven for their responses too. "I told you, what happened to her was terrible but I had nothing to do with it. The police have my alibi," he said, eyes flicking in Jess' direction. "This isn't any of your business, June."

"I don't believe you," June said, trying to stand taller, to draw up the woman she was rather than the girl Brett had known. "You didn't have to be there, I tasted the magic at the accident."

"Whose magic?" Brett asked, laughing.

"Demonic," June answered, and a flurry of whispers whipped around the tables, other witches rising from their seat.

"Demonic?" Ella repeated from behind her, footsteps approaching, the older woman's eyes wide with surprise.

Genuine surprise, which meant that it wasn't Ella who'd summoned Vinny. But it could've been any woman in the room, any of them who might've gone to extreme lengths to protect their coven leader, or their lover, or...

June glanced at Jess. She was startled, surprised, a little frightened as she gazed up at Brett. *Would I have summoned a demon to protect Brett when I was that age*? June wondered. Probably not, not after what had happened with Imogen and the Lich. But she might've hexed Amira for him.

"June, I think we both know that's not my wheelhouse. I can only think of...one witch who would be inclined toward that kind of work," Brett said. His voice was low, but he was making sure it carried, his arms open at his side as he rounded his table, walking slowly out to meet June.

He was trying to turn it all around, push it back to her, to Imogen. And for all of Imogen's crimes—and there were *many*—June didn't think her sister would intentionally try to kill another witch. Not after the accident.

"You're upset. You've always cared so much about other people, June," Brett said, voice soothing and saccharine. "But Amira was *our* covenmate. Can't you see the hurt you're causing by coming here and accusing me of something I didn't do?"

June glanced around the room, but she didn't see *hurt* on these people's faces. Suspicion, yes, but not just directed at her. This wasn't a family. She'd mistaken it for one because she'd never known what that word meant. It was barely even a coven either. Brett's control was complete, all of their connections were forged to be with him rather than each other. Little alliances popped up amongst the older women, but nothing obvious and open.

June's regret for dismantling this whole tangled wrong mess of people evaporated as her anger rose, pounding and boiling in her veins. Ash's hand spread over the base of her back and a drum of power tingled at the tips of her fingers.

"What is your wheelhouse, Brett?" June asked, voice rising from her murmur to ring into every ear in the room. "Because I think your wheelhouse is seducing and grooming underage women. Coaching them in magic and then in sex, belittling them until they rely on you, and then using them to make your coven stronger when you're bored with *fucking* them. And I think as soon as Amira realized that, she planned on doing something about it. I don't know if she told you herself, because she was brave, or someone she trusted, but you made sure she couldn't speak to anyone about what you were doing."

Josh, the little Brett in training asshole, stood from the table nearest June and marched forward until Ash shifted and he seemed to think better of approaching. "We protected coven secrets, nothing more."

"This coven's only secret is what Brett likes to do after hours," June shot back, voice rising, growing steady at last. She whipped her stare back to Brett, whose jaw was clenching. "What happened? Did someone tell you she came to me, or were you just stalking her and figured it out for yourself?"

"He didn't hurt her!" Jess cried, jumping up, eyes full of tears.

"Then you told someone else to," June said directly to Brett.

Brett's hands fisted at his sides. "Enough, June."

"It really isn't." June shook her head. "It won't be. Say it."

"I have nothing to confess to."

"Say it! You had her killed! It doesn't matter if you weren't in the room, you provide these people with their home and their food and you convince them that they need you. How much work did it take for you to convince them that they'd be in danger if Amira landed you in jail?"

At last, energy exploded in the room, but it wasn't from Brett.

Christine barreled forward, skidding to a stop as Ash stepped out, his shoulder slightly in front of June's as a shield. "It's been ten years, why did you come back here? I warned you not to join this coven, I warned Amira too! But you made your choice. You can't attack us now, it's too late!"

Christine's eyes were wild, tired, her body thinner than June remembered, withering to bones in her service of a man who couldn't care less about her.

"Why are you still here?" June hissed. "You know what he is!"

Christine paled, lips pressing roughly together, and

when Brett snapped his fingers at his side, she flinched and retreated backwards. Like a trained dog.

"Do you have evidence?" Ella asked, arms over her chest.

June's breaths were heaving, and the only thing keeping her upright and the room from spinning was the gravity of Ash's touch. "No. Nothing I can take to the police."

"Then what are you doing here?" Ella asked, frowning.

"I'm here to bind and banish Brett," June said, voice small but eyes focused on Brett's as his widened.

"And I'm here to get the confession he'll take to the police station," Ash echoed at her side.

"What?! You can't—you can't *make* me confess," Brett spluttered. "June, who the fuck is this guy? You brought someone to *beat* me—" His voice choked, eyes bugging and face going red. Ash's scent finally appeared heavy and crackling like a live wire with his power until Brett began to spit out words. "I was stalking Amira Mehan. I was angry with her. She was going to report me for years of statutory rape with the women I live with—"

"No! No it's isn't true. He was with *me*," Jess shouted, running for Brett, whose confession ran on in a strained tone.

"—I was following her to Sweet Pea the night of the accident. She realized I was behind her and tried to speed away—"

"Is this really how you want to do this, June?" Ella asked, but she was surprisingly calm.

Christine stood with her hand clapped over her mouth, the other faces of the coven staring horrified at Brett as he spat out the words June had prepared for him.

"Someone do something!" Josh snapped, eyes whipping between June and Brett.

A woman stepped forward, a little older than Amira,

with short brown hair and a round face. She raised her hand toward June, arm shaking, and June's eyes widened as her own heart picked up speed. A blood witch? That was rare, a shining trophy for Brett's collection.

"June," Ash growled, heading for the witch, but June stopped him, stretching out her arm and relieved when he let her stop him.

She caught the blood witch's magic, slippery and hot against her fingers, and pulled them free of her chest, her pulse alive and drumming in her wrist as the young witch gaped at her. It was a relief to have something to work with in her hands, and June toyed with the magic for a moment, twisting and braiding it into a jury mast knot, one of her old favorites that looked almost decorative. She cast one loop around Josh, another around Christine, and the final around Brett, before yanking, all three witches grunting and grasping at their hearts.

"Impressive," Ella murmured, and June scowled at the soft bubble of triumph that rose up in her.

"Please," Brett gasped out, eyes widening. "I was protecting myself. My reputation. She had to die."

The confession wasn't true. She knew that. But the truth was messy and full of magic, and nothing but this hex of Ash's, forcing Brett to constantly spew out guilt for Amira's murder would stand in court.

"I hit her back bumper. I wanted her to drive off the side of the mountain or to crash into it. I wanted her to die. You can't *do this*," Brett gasped out after the finish, but then his mouth started gaping again, no sound for a moment, a record skipping, and then, "I was following her the night of the accident."

"No, stop! No, I have proof," Jess shouted, running toward June.

June pulled the shawl out of her bag with one hand, oddly numb, eerily calm, and snagged the old traces of her wards with the other, tossing up a protective bubble around her and Ash with a few quick knots. Jess' feet stumbled and stopped abruptly, striking against the temporary ward.

"I have proof we were together," Jess cried, weeping and hiccuping.

June's fingers twisted over the lace edging of the shawl, heavy with Ash's magic. Brett was responsible for Amira's death, she reminded herself. He was responsible for the counts of sexual assault against numerous young women. He had broken her heart in a cold and calculated way, doing his best to try and sever her relationship with Imogen, who had put equal effort in cutting June off from him. She was *sick* of being manipulated and steered.

Was that why her stomach was churning uncomfortably now? Because what they were doing required so much force? Brett would lie, over and over, accepting the blame he deserved but not actually revealing the truth.

"Are you ready, starling?" Ash asked her, low and patient.

The coven was gathering around Brett, their hands linking, preparing to try and cast a ward for their leader. One June would be able to untangle in a moment. But not all of them joined together. Ella was still watching quietly, as were a few of the other women. They glared at their coven leader, sat with impassive and angry stares.

"Brett Lohman, by stitch and seed and thread and power, I bind you from me," June said, walking steadily forward, carrying her wards with her like the thin and sticky strands of a spider's web.

The linked hands served next to nothing, there was a protective chant on a few handfuls of loyal lips, but June's specialty was wards. Building them, breaking them.

"By ground and sky and flame and rain, I bind you from your magic," June continued, turning the shawl in her fingers, counting the eyelets around the edge, spreading it wide and tracing the words into the intricate loops of the piece. "By heart and blood and mind and flesh, I bind you from your passion. By thought and word and grasp and claim, I bind you from your control."

Ash's demonic power cut through the coven's magic like a hot blade. Jess was sobbing, the protective chant stumbling on her lips, and June wanted to reach out and draw the younger girl into her arms, reassure her with June's own certainty that being separated from a man like Brett Lohman would be a relief someday.

"By my own magic, my own mind, my own heart, and my own blood, I bind you to my will, Brett Lohman," June murmured.

The shawl was burning her own skin. She was only feet away from Brett, blocked by the trembling forms of strangers and former covenmates. Ash stepped around her, and Josh yelped as he was pushed to the side.

Brett's body jerked, an impulse to run buried beneath June's control with the blood witch's knot. He was sweating, flushed cheeks and throat, white pale around his eyes. "I killed her before she could expose me for—"

"Make him stop," June murmured, and Ash nodded, the words dying on Brett's lips.

That was...not better, but her stomach didn't feel like it was about to riot now. The banishing net was right. He deserved this, she was certain. He deserved to be cut off from his magic and from his predatory interest in manipulating young women, his influence over them. She deserved this chance to punish him, her own heart pounding as if she were still cursed.

"You sought me out. You made me trust you, and you tied that trust into my magic, made it about *you*. My power is my own, not yours. My body is my own. My sister was not yours to take!"

Brett was shaking, his mouth sealed without Ash's words on his tongue. His eyes were wide, horrified, and his throat flexed, sweat dripping down his temples.

"You've had this coming for a long time," June said, reminding herself, reassuring herself.

She raised the shawl in her hands, draping it around his shoulders, over his head. Red lace marked her hands from the heat of the magic, and Brett howled behind closed lips as it burned into his skin.

"It's a shame about the yarn though," Ash murmured.

June had to clap a hand over her lips to keep the frantic laugh trapped, Ash's eyes narrowing in that secret smile of his. *It was a shame*, she agreed privately as the yarn vanished with the magic, seeping into Brett's twitching body, tightening and leaving its mark, forcing the binding into place.

June stumbled back a step and so did Brett, but he kept going, back and back and back, until his legs hit an abandoned table and his torso leaned away from her.

The banishing at work, a dark satisfaction roaring in June's chest as Brett scrambled to escape her.

Behind her, hiccuping and tearful, Jess moaned out, "You know it wasn't him. I know it wasn't him. I can show the police the proof. I will."

June turned to answer her, but found Ella drawing Jess into her arms. "You'd better go, June. It's done."

Christine was joining Ella, stroking up and down Jess' back, the young girl moaning and shuddering at the touch.

Ash's hand slipped into June's, soothing away the ache of the magic left there and tugging her toward the door.

Anger was bleeding away, leaving cold behind. "He'll be running for the police station before the morning," Ash said.

"I can show them the video. We were together that night. And there's pictures too," Jess said through her hiccups.

"Show me," Christine whispered, watching June retreat out of the corner of her narrowed eyes. "You can show me."

June was dizzy, lightheaded from the use of magic and from the eerie feeling of knowing *for sure* she would never see Brett again. He would be running from her for the rest of his life, and she let herself forget him long before he found peace. She turned back once more for a last look. Brett was pale, shaking, searching the exits of the room for escape as his coven tried to calm him. The net was buried in his blood now. There was no escape.

It was cruel and thorough. It was just too. He'd never have magic again. Never be aroused or interested in another being. She wasn't sure there would be much of a man left in the body she'd bound. Certainly not the one she'd known. *This makes me a kind of monster*, June admitted to herself without regret, turning away.

Ash's hand anchored her, and she followed him in her uncomfortable floating, all the way out to the car.

17 SOLID VOWS AND BROKEN BEDS

His stitch witch was silent on the drive home, and he didn't like the sour, chalky flavor of her thoughts as he waited for her to speak. The confrontation had been easy —half that coven hated their leader as much if not more than June—and June was beautifully fearsome, turning other witches' magic on them, a queen of vengeance. But he wasn't blind to June's...lack of satisfaction. Maybe she'd wanted more of a challenge, or maybe...

Maybe he'd expected June to be relieved, and the fact that she obviously wasn't made him want to turn the vehicle around and go for a second round, burn that bastard right down to the hellhole that was waiting for him.

They were nearly back to Sweet Pea before he gave in to his curiosity.

"You have regrets?"

June remained staring out the passenger window so long that Ash almost repeated the question. Then she sat up straight and twisted to face him. "I don't know. Maybe. I... Do you think it matters that he wasn't the one to summon Vinny?"

"Like you said, it wouldn't have taken much for him to convince the right person to do the work for him," Ash said with a shrug. "His soul is not in good shape."

Ash had caught whiffs of thoughts from the crowd, especially the women. Brett had secrets he could use against them. Like those pictures the little redhead had been crying over, prepared to share with the police for that asshole's protection.

"The binding will work. I can..." Ash frowned at the offer in his head and then went ahead with the words. "I can take the murder confession out and he can still turn himself in for statutory rape."

June's eyes widened. "Really?"

He nodded.

"You believe him then?"

Ash's hands flexed on the steering wheel. He had no qualms about Brett Lohman going to jail. Not after what June had told him, and especially not after some of her dreams he'd spied on.

"He didn't know about Amira being killed," Ash admitted reluctantly. "It doesn't mean he wasn't what motivated the summoner."

"Could you tell who it was?" June asked, shifting closer.

Ash shook his head. "It wasn't my priority. I checked the girl, the young one, but it wasn't her. I can go back and—"

"No. No, I don't want to go back," June murmured. "None of this makes sense, and I... Take the murder confession out. He's guilty, but it makes me feel even guiltier if we force him to lie."

Ash nodded, one hand falling from the steering wheel to the seat, waiting. A quiet moment later, June's fingers linked with his.

"You chose me."

Ash's smile quirked up in the corners at her words, and he turned onto the main road that would lead them into Sweet Pea. "You're more interesting than warfare, starling."

June hummed, and he caught the start of her smile. "That's because my wards don't let you do anything fun."

Ash laughed and pulled into a parking spot at the corner by June's alley entrance. It was late, the Inferno would be closed, and like she said, he'd already made his choice.

He turned the car off and twisted to face her, dipping his head toward hers. "June Byrne, you have my vo—"

June's eyes widened, and her hand slapped over his mouth, his eyebrows bouncing in surprise.

"Don't. Don't do that."

Ash's heart, the one hell-bent on belonging solely to the woman silencing him, clamped and ached in his chest.

June's hand slid cautiously away. "I want this to be your choice."

"It is my choice, that's the point," Ash said, tipping his head and frowning.

"Tonight it is," June agreed, nodding. "But if tomorrow—"

"June."

"If tomorrow you change your mind, then I don't want there to be something binding you to me," June whispered, eyes wide and clear, holding fast to his. "Trust isn't something I should be handing out after everything that's happened, but I'm giving you mine. No vow, Ash. Just choose me. I'm a big girl. If you change your mind, I'll get through it."

"If I change my mind, you make another banishing net. An even stronger one," Ash said, uncomfortable with her refusal. Shouldn't she *want* the security of the vow? He wanted to give that to her, and it seemed wildly unfair she would refuse it.

June nodded solemnly, and Ash let out a soft growl. Tricky little witch. The open door out was practically a challenge to stay.

Smart, starling.

He ducked, and June's chin tipped up to his. Trust. Surrender too. And they were his.

June tasted like magic, her clear and intricate lace of ice that she worked with was sharp on his tongue. Sweet too as she sighed into his kiss, arched toward him, hands fisting in the collar of his coat. Her apartment was outside and around the corner, but that was a long way to walk when the car was warm and she was wiggling up onto her knees to crawl closer.

"Hungry little stitch witch," Ash growled out, scooping June up and onto his lap, latching his lips to the mark on her throat that had already started to fade.

June moaned, and then Ash gathered a little extra boost of power, shifting them sideways through ether and then out again into June's dark apartment.

"Argh! Ash, the hell was that?" June cried, pushing at his chest, her chin bumping his forehead as she looked around. "Don't do that!"

"But it's convenient," he said, grinning up at her. "I was very careful."

A little rushed, but certainly not about to risk her safety.

"Then why aren't my shoes on?" June asked, scowling down at him.

He twisted to look at her feet. Oops. He'd left her socks behind too. "Because you won't need them," he said.

It was too dark in here, and it washed June out when he wanted to see her clearly, see all the flushes he put on her cheeks and chest, the color of her lips after he'd kissed her until she ran out of breath.

June's frown deepened as her lights all flicked on at once, her eyes wincing shut. "Beast!"

Ash let out a playful snarl. The floor? The couch? No, definitely the tiny bed. She'd have nowhere to move but to wrap herself around him. He turned and headed for the bedroom, and June's legs squeezed tighter around his hips.

"Ash." He looked up to see the little line of worry between her brows. "What do we do about the actual murderer?"

That was true. Whoever the murderer was, she had tried to kill June too for threatening Brett.

"Your wards will hold. I'm here," Ash said.

June bit her lip, and Ash leaned in to steal it back from her, sucking on the full swell and indulging in a lick. She was still tense, and he pulled away, crossing over to her bed and settling there with her on his lap, long and leggy and made of elegant sensual curves, but small in comparison to him.

"I don't think they know about the coven...and Imogen *should* be able to handle herself," June said slowly.

Ah. She was worried about the other witches. "Wait here," Ash said, kissing her mouth and then tossing her off his lap and into the pillows, a startled cry of laughter catching his ear before he vanished.

Bell was in the kitchen of Grimsby House with the others as he appeared.

"Where the fuck have you been?" Dante asked.

"Sniffing around on that summoner. Something is up with the witches," Ash said. True and true, but with a great deal of missing information. Bell stiffened and narrowed his eyes. "I've got the stitch witch, but...Dante, keep an eye on basement? Bell—"

"The kitchen witch, sure," Bell said, doing a terrible job of looking casual, his eyes on the door.

"The green witch is next door, so maybe, Barbie—" Ash started, although he doubted Barbie would actually *do* anything if June's friend needed help. Maybe he should've just warded her place?

"I'll watch her."

Bell and Ash both turned to Paimon, who was straightening his glasses on his nose and combing fingers through his beard.

"You think they're moving against us?" Paimon asked.

Ash stalled there. Bell was easy, he would protect June's friend. Dante was a bit of a gamble, but if nothing else, his lurking would put Imogen on her guard. But Paimon... Paimon might pose more of a risk to the green witch than no one watching at all.

"I think someone may be moving against them," Ash said.

Paimon blinked and tilted his head. "Yes. Yes, that is interesting. I'll watch."

Hesitating for a moment, Ash nodded and then slipped through ether again, pausing outside of Rosa's colorful carriage house to set up an alarm before reappearing in June's bedroom. He was starting to get a little winded after all the activity of the night. That was refreshing after so many months, years even, of twiddling his thumbs.

June was bundled on the bed, her arms around her bent knees, and she arched an eyebrow at him.

"They'll be safe," Ash said.

"Just like that?"

He wasn't sure telling her he'd sent *demons* to keep an eye on her witches would really reassure June, so he nodded and sat down at her side on the bed. "Just like that."

He tugged on one wrist, and June stretched, leaning back and wearing a shy smile. "Well. You do seem to come in handy."

"You'd be surprised."

"Have I said thank you? Specifically, thank you for weaving all my ends on my to be finished pile in the living room."

Ash grinned. He thought she'd like that. He shook his head and leaned in, balancing a hand on each side of her hips. "You've been spectacularly ungrateful, actually."

"How rude of me," June murmured. Her hands came up, clasping around his jaw, drawing him down to her mouth. "Thank you, beast."

In the Bowels, being 'whipped' was more of a literal state. Ash understood the human metaphor, but he preferred to consider himself an enthusiastic partner in a mutually beneficial arrangement. Still, as June grinned and giggled into the kiss while Ash crawled over her, the bed creaking ominously, he admitted—privately—that there might be no lengths to which he would not go to put a smile on this human woman's face.

She'd earned them, deserved them, after all the trouble in her life. And she made his life interesting. Allied with her for a handful of days, and he'd had more fun than the past decade in the Bowels.

Ash slid his hands underneath her, squeezing her ass in one and slipping the other beneath her shirt, up her smooth back to her bra clasp.

"Did you know I helped design these hooks?" Ash asked, tugging on the hooks and strap.

"Huh? Well, then you should be better at opening them," June mumbled, nuzzling into his cheek and throat, arching in his hold.

"That's the point—no one is good at it," Ash said.

"Ash, focus," June huffed out. One of her legs pushed insistently at his, wanting to spread and make room for him. He lifted his knee and slipped it between her thighs, raising up a few inches to watch her twist beneath him, rubbing herself on his thigh. That was certainly a view with potential.

"What do you want, starling?" Ash asked.

June's cheeks went pink, and she paused, shrinking a little, unsure of herself. He relaxed on top of her, dragged kisses down to her throat and shoulders, and she sighed, arching her neck for him.

"That. More of that. Everywhere." He slipped the bra hooks free as June's hands pushed at his coat. Ash sat up, shrugging his arms out of the sleeves and throwing it off the bed.

June's hands reached for her T-shirt hem next, wrestling herself out, her bra loose now and easily tucked out of the way by Ash's hands. June's eyes widened, back rising and lips parted on a moan as Ash stroked one hand over her breasts. Plush and soft with large nipples the same shade of peach as her lips. He rubbed a rough thumb back and forth over one, and June whined, eyes falling shut.

"Do you have horns, beast?" June gasped out.

Ash's touch paused, and her eyes opened, smile twitching in a sinful invitation. Ash shifted his human disguise around, revealing two large curving bull's horns sprouting behind his temples.

"I can," he said, grinning as June's eyes lit up. "Why?"

Her hands reached up, stroking up the sides of his horns before flashing him a wicked, toothy smile. "Because I think they'd make good handles."

Ash grunted as she yanked him down to her breasts. He

bellowed out a laugh against her chest before following the orders of her grip, sucking marks around a nipple before drawing it between his lips.

June slid her other leg out around his hips and then wrapped herself around him, exactly as he'd imagined. Controlling little thing. It hurt just enough when she pulled him roughly over to the other breast. He loved it, grunting and then kissing and biting his way over her tender skin as she moaned and writhed beneath him. Her hips were arching up, rubbing against his abs, and she released frustrated squeaks, trying to have him everywhere at once.

He wondered if he should suggest she ask for another set of arms on him too, and then decided he liked her impatience and desperation too much. Better to keep her wanting more from him.

"Ash, please!"

Her hands were starting to slip, losing focus on her direction, fingers sliding into his hair to hold him to her. Ash helped himself to the button of her jeans. He knew what she needed, wanted. He'd been thinking of it since yesterday morning after tasting her. June sighed as he drifted lower, mapping her ribs with his tongue, circling her belly button, kissing and marking her as his as he sipped on her sharp flavor.

He didn't need to make a vow. June already had her mark on him, it pounded in this flimsy human chest, a shockingly powerful motivator to make her smile, make her cry out his name in that torn voice, make her body soften with comfort or pleasure.

June's hips bucked, and Ash's hands pulled her jeans and underwear down over her ass, groaning at the dark lungful of her, aroused and lush. He sat up, and she pushed up onto her elbows, an objection ready on her lips before she realized he was pulling her legs out of her pants.

"Undress," she said, starting to curl in on herself again.

He was not having that. He stripped her pants off with a flourish that cracked a new smile on her face, and then his own clothes whipped away and to the floor with hers. June's mouth hung open. Ash glanced down. Had he accidentally brought some other demonic feature out with his horns?

"You really are a beast," June breathed out, eyes wide.

Ash twisted, checking the mirror across the room. Was this not what humans looked like anymore? He'd fact-checked himself according to their mission brief.

But when he turned back, June's shock was transforming into obvious sexual hunger, her gaze hooding, tongue wetting her own bottom lip.

"I want to feel you," she pleaded, sitting up and reaching out for him.

Oh good, because Ash was pretty sure the whole point of this pathetically soft flesh was—

He groaned, eyes shutting as June's hands mapped alternating paths up and down his chest, over his hips, shooting warmth and electric tingles through his body. One hand reached around to his back and pushed him forward, and Ash sank into her, that hot friction of skin on skin alarmingly *vivid* and consuming.

He didn't think through the next kiss, only claimed it out of need, his arms circling June, hauling her closer. Her legs looped around his hips again, and if Ash had room in his head to think beyond slippery heat, softness, and need, he would've appreciated that there was inarguable success to at least one thing to do with the human form.

Touching felt *good*. Amazing. Bewildering.

Divine, actually, and it had been a long time since he'd had anything to appreciate in that way.

June was soft and small beneath him, but somehow also perfectly arranged for him to be consumed by. Even her little teeth made him want to shout as they nipped at his earlobe.

His *earlobe*.

Ash groaned and copied her, and June hummed and rubbed her perfect squishy biteable breasts against his chest. Ohh, that was right. He wanted to—

June's hands found his horns again as he made his way down her body with kisses and nips and licks for tasting— her blood pounding and rising *just* to the surface, but he liked it inside of her too much to go any further.

Moving meant his cock couldn't rub up against her anymore, so he replaced that touch with his fingers, remembering the way he'd made her cling and drip onto his palm, wanting to do the same again. Wanting to taste her this time too.

"Ohh fuck!"

Ash grinned. June was tart on his tongue, a forbidden fruit indeed. He pushed a second finger inside of her, gaping at the way it stretched her opening and glancing down to compare it to his own size.

"Oh, that's what you meant by a beast," Ash said, grinning up the length of her.

June was rocking, fucking herself onto his hand, head tossing a little, and her smile flared as she nodded. "Keep going, Ash."

He stretched his fingers apart, appreciating the squeeze and resistance of her, and then lowered himself to his belly and stiff cock to enjoy his feast. June's flavor was as delicious as the sounds she made, magic buzzing on his tongue as he lapped at her clit.

It wasn't that he hadn't done all of this before, he'd been called to duty once or twice, and he had some foggy memory of angelic unions. But he couldn't recall an instance of sex taken purely for the sake of enjoying the other person.

June's hands clasped around his horns again, and Ash groaned as she arched and forced herself flat on his tongue, using him for her own pleasure. His stitch witch should always be so demanding.

"Fuck, Ash, *please*. Oh go—"

Ash burrowed a third finger inside of her, and June's praising thinned to a single, high, crystal note of pleading. He wrapped his lips around her swollen clit and sucked until June stiffened, her heels pressing down into his back as she came with a gasp. Her cunt squeezed around his fingers, fluttering as he twisted them and nudged them a little deeper. One hand slipped from a horn, nearly pulling him off of her, but Ash held fast, feasting on his shuddering starling until a low and ragged moan rose out of her and she tried to squirm away.

"You," June gasped. Ash leaned up to take a peek at her, pleased with her limp limbs now expanding out in invitation. "I want you, Ash."

He crooked his fingers, and June let out a strangled whimper, twitching on the bed as he slid up on top of her, licking her from his lips. "How do you want me, starling?"

June's eyes fluttered open, a little hint of aqua in the blue now. She was all pretty in pastels, creamy skin and peach blushes. His free hand reached for her hip, fingers digging shamelessly into the soft curves of flesh as he watched June soften and smile.

"Inside me, on top of me, all around me," she murmured, one leg rising up to hook over his hip, trying to draw him down.

He would crush her, steal her breath, pin her in place for his claiming. Ash grinned at the thought and drew two slickened fingers out of her, leaving one to help guide the way. June's lips parted on a strained 'O' as he started to press his way inside. And wasn't that an addictive moment, that first scorching clasp of her around the head of his cock, kissing and sucking him in.

June's hands drifted to his back, fingertips tickling up his ribs to cup over his shoulder blades, drawing him down to her. He pulled his last finger free as he sank in, sipping on June's pants and whimpers, molding her body to his until their hips were fastened to one another, breaths nuzzling their chests together, lips sharing grazing kisses and the air barely passed between them.

I could just stay like this, Ash thought, distantly and buried under the five thousand newly fascinating sensations of touch and sex. Chasing the release would be fun, but it was equally satisfying to simply possess the woman in his arms, to seal her to him.

June nibbled on his bottom lip, impatiently rocking herself beneath him, the friction a little dizzying.

"Tell me, starling," Ash whispered, kissing the corner of her mouth, leaving her own taste there, moving to nip her jaw.

"I want you, beast."

He growled into her skin, drawing back and studying the immediate pull on his cock, the demand of this body he'd invented to *return* to her, the pound of his heart that called him back to her like gravity. This was the vow, even if she didn't want one. This need between them would tie him to her, the simple request on her lips would be his bargain. No circle, no ceremony, no binding but the way she wrapped herself around him.

"Kiss me too," June said with a shy nudge of her cheek against his beard.

Ash smothered her smile with a ravaging kiss, drove into her and swallowed her cry, met the call of *fucking* and touching with a fresh urgency. It would end too soon, but that meant there'd be a new opportunity to start it all over again, and maybe next time, he could trick her into riding him.

The bed groaned in warning as June twined her legs and arms tight around him, gasping with every thrust. He would build her a new bed. Something ridiculous that would make her balk and glare in annoyance at him. An altar to worship her on, to sacrifice himself to her whims.

"Ashtaroth," June whispered into the kiss.

Ash shuddered, pressed one hand to the wall to brace himself, to keep from being too rough. And then June bit at his neck, and that caution vanished, a shocking bellow buried against her ear, their flesh clapping together, his grip on her ass surely leaving a bruise for him to admire in the morning.

She tightened on his length, bit off a scream against his throat, and Ash's whole body lit up in triumph and then in a sudden betrayal of ecstasy. He found her mouth again, their gasps tangling, hips grinding, his kicking her hard down into the mattress until there was a concerning *crack!* of wood they were both too consumed to note. The moment shattered into a hazy storm—soft and aching all at once, tender and crushing, and Ash's strength fled, leaving him a heap on an equally collapsed June.

She was petting him, hands running up and down his

back, and Ash suffered a brief moment of embarrassment at being so undone, he had to be *soothed*, then realized he was also absently stroking and touching her. Intimacy, that was the word. Affection.

"Air—" she gasped.

Ah, shit. He flipped them with a bit of power, and the bed creaked at his weight. June stole one great draw of breath before sinking back comfortably on top of his chest, her cheek over his pounding heart.

"Beast. You broke my bed."

Ash grinned at how pleased she sounded. He reached for her hair, smoothing it back through his fingers, twisting it around his fist and making a mental note as June shuddered and squeezed a little on his now oversensitive cock. It wanted to leave her heat and pressure, but Ash wasn't a quitter.

"How would you feel about a four-poster?"

"Why?" June asked, wiggling and propping her chin on his sternum. Her nose was wrinkled with disgust. He shook his head in answer and decided on a four-poster *with* a canopy. Her eyes narrowed and then fluttered shut as he combed his fingers through her hair again, but her brow remained furrowed.

Ash tapped the spot between her eyebrows. "You're thinking. I'm offended. I knew I was rusty—"

The tension vanished with June's laugh, a richly husky sound. They would wreck the bed for real if they had sex again, but Ash thought he could throw the mattress on the floor and have a grand time with June that way. He wanted to make the new bed properly by hand.

"You thoroughly distracted me, I promise," June said, kissing his chest and leaving a warm mark on the spot. "I just...started back up again with something that was bothering me on the drive back."

"Better tell me then, so I can destroy it."

June blinked at him, still smiling, and he wrapped his hands around her waist, pulling her up his body and off his cock before he could get hard again and keep distracting her.

June gasped and pressed her hands to his shoulders. "Mmm, okay. Why...why was there that effort to make Amira's death look like a hit and run?"

Ash frowned. He would have to try harder next time to wipe June's thoughts clear.

"If one of the coven was trying to protect Brett by killing Amira, why hit her car with his?"

"That could've been an accident," Ash said, but June was right.

"Then you'd make sure there wasn't any evidence that pointed to him." June scowled, but she leaned into Ash's hand as he tried to smooth the lines away. "I hate that I'm saying this, but I believe that Brett had no idea about the dent, which means..."

"Someone hit her car intentionally so the police would look directly at Brett." Ash grunted and then sat up, drawing June with him, his back to the cold wall and her cuddled on his lap.

She grabbed a blanket from the foot of the bed and covered them both, a little whisper of her magic in the stitches, something to help her sleep. Ash kissed the top of June's head and made a mental list at the back of his thoughts, ways to ensure June slept easy—eat her nightmares, wear her out before bed, act as a gravity blanket on top of her.

"Why go after you next?" Ash asked. As much as he

might've preferred to keep June soft and begging for more, he did like working out a puzzle with her. "You were after him, gaining information from the police. Why attack you instead of help you?"

June chewed on her bottom lip and then bit Ash's thumb as he tried to pull it free. "Because Brett had the alibi for the night Amira died. If I kept digging—I *did* keep digging and here I am, assuming that he's innocent."

"So kill you right after you've accused him again, and it looks like Brett's retaliated against two angry girlfriends," Ash reasoned and then shook his head. "It's sloppy."

"Desperate," June said. "Brett's alibi was an underage girl though, it might've fallen apart. Shit, Ash!" Ash tried to catch her as she scrambled up on her knees facing him, eyes wide. "She said it in front of everyone in that room. The whole coven. She said she had video and photographs for—"

Suddenly, the air in the room was too tight. A scorched scent appeared, and the pressure in Ash's head strengthened, another demon pushing at his wards on the apartment. A growl rose up in Ash's throat, the bed creaking in warning and June yelping in surprise as he scooped her up and jumped to his feet, placing her behind him.

"Ash, what's—"

There was a pop and crackle of static lighting the air, and Ash froze, crouched and prepared to attack—naked as can be.

"Ah, I've interrupted," Bell said, appearing in the open space of the room, arching an eyebrow at Ash.

Ash snarled, ready to wipe the slight smirk off Bell's face, as a small hand rested on his back. "What the fuck are you doing here?"

"Is it Josie?" June asked behind him, and he twisted for a

second to check on her, oddly pleased to see she was wrapped in the blanket and looking especially...rumpled.

"No," Bell said, dipping his head to June. "It's Vinny. He's being summoned again. I've got him on the leash, but—"

"Summoned? By the same witch? Ash—"

Ash nodded and relaxed, moving to grab his trousers. "Don't fucking bust in on me again."

"Josie is right—we should learn to text," Bell said shrugging.

"—Maybe if *we* could answer the summons, we could figure out who—"

Ash fastened his pants quickly and rounded on June, silencing her with a hard kiss. "No we, starling. Bell and I will go, I'll figure it out for you. We should send Vinny and follow," he said over his shoulder to Bell, who sighed.

"He's such a sour bastard though," Bell groaned.

"You can't go without me!" June barked, all her sweetness from the hour vanished, sharpening to the steel he liked every bit as much.

"Can too. I'm a big boy, I can take a witch," he said winking.

"That's not the point—"

"Especially one who tried to axe my favorite knitter." Ash leaned and pressed another kiss to June's twisted grimace.

"We should hurry before they aim for someone else," Bell said.

Ash nodded, finishing dressing, hip checking June when she tried to get out of the bed and sending the sheets to tangle around her.

"Hey! Stop. Ashtaroth, you are not fucking white knighting me. I'm going to—"

"Be good, starling," Ash said, slipping on his leather

jacket, watching June squirm and try to wrestle herself free. "Keep the bed warm."

"Okay, fuck yo—"

Bell grabbed Ash by the shoulder, and then they were sliding through ether. Ash was just excited to get back and let June chew his ear off.

Except as they followed Vinny's bitter trail through ether and out again, Ash suddenly realized the flaw in their rushed plan. By following Vinny's summons, he and Bell arrived—not at the shocked summoner's side—within a tiny and overly crowded summoning circle.

"What?!" the summoner cried.

"The fuck are you two doing here?" Vinny asked, naked and enormous and irate, seeming to finish the witch's cry.

Ash huffed a sigh and turned to Beleth, who was now equally enormous, with dark and feline features. But just past Bell, curled up on the floor in the corner, was the young girl from Brett's coven. His latest conquest. Jess. "We should've brought backup."

"Josie's going to give me so much shit for this," Bell sighed out.

18 · NANCY DREW AND THE RED HERRING WITCH

"That bastard," June huffed, worming her way out of her traitorous bedding. The next huff turned into a laugh and then a full blown cackle as she finally freed herself and rolled right off the bed, landing in a heap on the floor.

She scrambled away before her sheets could catch her and then stood, grinning at her now crooked bed. Ash was an asshole and an exceptional cuddler. She was sore in a way she'd forgotten, as well as somehow physically relaxed in a way she had never been before. And the man—demon —responsible had gone running off to deal with a problem —*her* problem—with a pat on the ass and the promise to take care of it, without her. It was annoying but also shamefully relieving to have someone else try to handle her issues.

Still, she was not staying naked on the bed and waiting for him to get back.

Ash had left everything in the truck, including her purse and cellphone—problematic at the moment—so June rushed to dress, digging through her drawers in the living area for the spare key while jumping into her boots. She needed backup. Backup other than Ash, who had just vanished, and that left less than a handful of others she could call. Considering who Ash had run off with, this time, the answer was simple.

June ducked her head outside of her apartment, bracing against the tunnel of wind the alley made and heading towards the truck, stopping at Josie's apartment door and buzzing hard.

A moment later, it opened, and a fully dressed Josie appeared with wide eyes.

"June, I've been trying to call. Something is—"

"Bell just popped in and took Ash. The murderer is summoning Vinny, and they're going to use the opportunity to find out who it is," June rushed out.

"Without us? Those stupid assholes, they're going to get caught in a summoning circle," Josie grumbled. "What do we do? Scry to find out where they are?"

"I'm pretty sure I know exactly where. Let me grab my car keys out of Ash's, and we can try and catch them there."

"I'm calling Rosa. And no offense, June, but if we're taking a car, let's make it that demon behemoth that could drive straight through a wall if we needed it to," Josie said.

June enjoyed a brief and vivid fantasy of plowing Ash's monster of a vehicle through the side of the old coven house as Josie locked her apartment, and then the pair of them were gusted back down the alley by the wind.

"Wait. So...did Bell interrupt anything?" Josie asked, glancing out of the corner of her eyes.

The Humvee was still at the curb, the doors unlocked, and since it was Sweet Pea, June's things were still waiting on the floor, the keys in the ignition of the car.

"He interrupted a conversation about the murderer," June said simply, but her emotions were unruly now, out of control, and a massive smile spread over her face until her cheeks hurt.

Josie arched an eyebrow as June fiddled over the steering and gearshift until she got used to the feeling of driving on stilts and backed out of the parking spot.

"It was a post-coital murderer theory conversation," June admitted. "Do you ever get like...super clearheaded after sex?"

"Bell usually runs me until I pass out, but I've always been more of a post-orgasm napper," Josie said, tapping quickly over her phone. "I told Rosa to be ready."

June opened her mouth to object—Rosa wasn't involved in any of this, and they didn't even know if they'd be needed or if it would be safe—and then shut it again. Rosa was part of her coven, not to mention the woman who had been constantly reaching out to June for almost seven years. If she wanted to help, June could get used to that.

"What if we get there and Bell and Ash already have it wrapped up?" Josie asked.

"I still want to know who attacked me. Who killed Amira," June said. She blinked and glanced at Josie for a moment, turning onto Rosa's street. "Do you think they would...do something drastic to whoever it is before we got there?"

"Bell was ready to kill Merryweather. Is Ash protective?"

June's whole body warmed, even as she pressed a little harder on the gas pedal. "Okay, so we're going to speed."

Rosa was waiting by the curb, bundled up head to toe, and she only paused at the sight of the truck before opening the door to the backseat and climbing into the cab with a grunt. "Hey guys, what's the plan?"

"Oh, we definitely don't have one," Josie said, reaching up to grab the handlebar above the window as June squealed over pavement in a U-turn, the right front tire bumping briefly over a snowy curb.

"Fun, improv, I love it," Rosa said, peeling her layers off in the backseat. "Just so you know, Pie Daddy Demon was watching from their window so..."

"Fuck," June breathed out.

"Worry about the drive first," Josie said, patting June's shoulder. "I'll catch Rosa up."

"YOU LIVED IN A *SCHOOL*?" Rosa asked, squinting up at the old brick.

"I lived in a building that used to be a school," June corrected. They had parked farther down the street this time. The coven house was dark, only a few lights sprinkled in windows from the night owl witches of the coven, but Ash's ride was fairly distinctive and she didn't want to be spotted too soon.

"Don't get me wrong, it just seems very...bohemian of you," Rosa said slowly.

Josie disguised a snort as a sniffle and kept her head down.

"It was the closest thing to family I'd really experienced at that point," June said, and both of her friends sobered. In truth, the coven was still the closest, a very low bar, but the one she was planning on raising soon if she could. "Come on."

"So you just left here, right? I mean earlier tonight? And now we're going to bust in again?" Rosa asked.

"We're not going in there," June whispered, pointing to the main building. "I never got any clear taste of what it would've taken to strike Amira in there." They turned left before reaching the school steps, walking quietly up the broken pavement of the old drive toward the back of the building.

"Oh...okay, now I'm feeling the spooky," Rosa hissed.

The old utility building—once saved for maintenance and gym materials—butted out the back of the school, dark and slightly tilted with weary age. Most coven magic was worked together in the converted gymnasium, harmless energy exercises that June now assumed had fed into Brett's overall hold on the group. She'd avoided the outbuilding in her years with the coven. It had reminded her too much of the pulse of power her parents carried, and at the time, she'd believed that was the nature of magic. Brett offered her safety and simplicity to magic, but that didn't mean it wasn't his nature to work with the darker headier ends of the scale. It was fine, as long as she didn't have to.

Now the old structure looked like a massive warning sign, the rust running over the steel thick with the corrosion of the magic worked inside, as if it were rotting away at the building.

"It's quiet," Josie whispered, brow furrowed. "Do you think they're still inside?"

"It's warded for privacy. They're in there. I can... It's like a pounding at the back of my skull."

"Bell's either trapped or ignoring me," Josie said with a hand over her stomach, eyes growing wide. "I tried to pull on him, and he won't budge."

"I can break through the wards, but—"

Rosa set her hand on June's shoulder, brilliant red lips curving. "You break through the wards, I'll punch a witch, Josie breaks the circle. Easy peasy."

"Punch?" June repeated.

Rosa glanced between the two, eyebrows raising. "What?

You thought we had to go in, wands raised like it's Harry Potter? Honey, not everything takes magic. We just need to break the witch's concentration and the circle holding in your demons. I've got a right hook from self-defense classes, and you guys have the woo-woo skills, we got this."

June's nose wrinkled at her magic being referred to as woo-woo, but Rosa was right—a punch would do the trick faster than anything else she could pull out of her sleeve at the last minute.

She hadn't made the wards on the utility building, but they were solid, which meant Brett had always known what was worth hiding in his coven, and it took place behind those rusted set of doors.

"Bell knows we're here," Josie whispered, lips ticking up as June examined the locking structure of magic blocking them. "He went from pissed to excited."

"How can you tell?" Rosa asked.

Josie rested a hand over her stomach. "He never finished healing the hack job of his sigil Merryweather cut on me... I didn't really want him to."

June's eyebrows rose at that news. Josie had a demonic sigil on her *body*. But it was coming in handy, at least. She shook herself and turned back to the building.

This work reminded June of Ella. Simple, elegant, *strong*. Ella's best magic was deceptive in nature. June remembered an illusion the older woman had presented June with as a test, a forking path in the woods that led to the same dead end no matter what direction you chose. Ella had made her try to walk home from that test for an entire day, without food, and June had never solved the puzzle. Later, she'd overheard Ella's explanation to her mother. There was no right answer. It was a trap in both directions.

"Can you break it?" Rosa asked June.

"No, but that's not the point of it," June muttered. Ella's wards locked the door. No one but Ella could break them, which simply meant...

June paced around the building. No windows. No other door. She'd never seen anyone coming in and out of here, had avoided it during her time with the coven.

"June," Josie said, her and Rosa shivering in the midnight cold, watching her circle the building like a lunatic.

"The wards are misdirection," June explained. "Maybe we do have to go into the school, or—"

June stopped abruptly on the far side of the building, staring at the rust patterns carving through the steel, at the way the building leaned a little toward her. Illusions were Ella's specialty. She reached out and ran her hand over the ragged edge of one rusted hole, giddy pride bubbling up in her as it was smooth to the touch, wide and rubbery and easy to hold.

"Found it," June whispered, reaching for another hole farther up the wall.

Josie grimaced and then tilted her head, eyes widening. "Oh, it's like a climbing wall. It doesn't look safe."

"It's safe enough," June said, although it did wobble as she lifted herself up, stepping one foot into another hold. At least it wasn't a very tall building.

Josie and Rosa watched her climb up to the roof, and June had to swallow her laugh. A hatch was open, a ladder leading down into darkness. The bloody flavor of corruptive and manipulative magic was clearer up here, and June held her breath, nodding to her covenmates on the ground before sliding over the smooth roof to the hatch. The summoner would be behind another door inside, based on the quiet, but at least this time she'd discovered Ella's trick.

"All right, we're doing this," Rosa breathed and started to

climb. June waited for her to reach the top before descending the ladder, eyes adjusting quickly to the deeper dark inside.

Now there was a murmur of voices, one thin and feminine, obviously stressed, and then the bite of lower male tones.

"Wait for Josie," Rosa whispered, tiptoeing down the ladder. "We'll have to be fast. This is so Nancy Drew, I can't believe it."

"Rescuing demons and stopping witches is Nancy Drew?" June asked.

"I hate ladders," Josie muttered from above.

"No, but sneaking into old buildings to catch murderers is," Rosa answered. "Also, I would tease you for sassing me, but I like it on you."

It was a shame it was too dark for Rosa to see June's smile.

"All right, let's do this, my man is waiting on me," Josie said, bouncing on her toes, a little moonlight from the sky shining down onto the top of her head.

June was a little jealous not to have that same sense of Ash, but she could guess how he would feel when they burst in together and that was enough. The door to the next room was warded, but this one was more than a trap and not nearly as secure as Ella's. June rested her palm above the knob, picturing her magic as a smooth pool of power in her belly and then pushing it out, sliding it under the spiderweb ward on the door and then soaking in the other witch's magic.

"Ready," June whispered as the woman's voice inside grew frantic. Not Ella, not with that panic. But then who?

"Ready," Rosa echoed with a nod, reaching around June to grab the handle.

The door pulled out, and June stepped back, candlelight inside wavering with the sudden gust of air. A tall figure shrouded in black gasped, spinning around to face them, and Rosa jumped forward, one fist ready and swinging, missing in the tangle of dark fabric, the two figures stumbling back into a wall.

June was too preoccupied about the crowd within the circle. Beleth was vast and shadowy, glowing with power, terrifyingly tall and gruesomely handsome and animal. He had the partially demonic form of Vinny—all red and steaming and twisted—in something tighter than a headlock, the red demon obviously gasping for air.

And there, kneeling on the floor, was her beast. He still had his horns, and he was golden and massive, and every bit the bear Josie had joked he was, smile too wide, eyes too big. Behind him, collapsed on the floor, was the young redhead Jess.

Rosa yelped, and June shook herself, diving forward, grabbing up a handful of black fabric and ripping it away as Rosa wrestled the woman to the ground, one hand fisted around—

A long brown braid.

Christine appeared, red faced and panting, Rosa's knee pinning her to the floor, June gaping at her with her hand uselessly clasped around the shroud.

"You?"

"Took you long enough, Cupcake. I said the cavalry had arrived ten minutes ago," Beleth growled.

Josie huffed and knelt, scrubbing at the white circle that bound the demons. "That's what you get for trying to use snappy one-liners."

"Starling, you all right?" the big golden beastly demon

asked her in a slightly rougher and even more growling version of Ash's voice.

"Fine. Jess?"

"I think she's spelled. There was a lot of screaming and she never woke up," Ash said with a grimace.

June nodded at that. She probably would've screamed too if she'd been summoning one demon and instead, three had shown up.

Speaking of, she whipped around to where Rosa held a struggling Christine to the floor. June reached a hand into her pocket, pulling out a length of string, creating a series of loops into a chain knot, and then knelt, grabbing Christine's kicking legs and trapping them in the noose, the woman's whole body going limp.

"Why did you come back here?" Christine choked out, her chest panting for air.

Behind June, Josie had broken the circle and stepped quickly away as Beleth wrestled Vinny to the ground. Their forms were human again, and Ash joined Bell in subduing the large redheaded demon.

"I told you to stay away. I told you from the beginning like I tell all of the girls, and not one of you ever *listens*!" Christine cried, thrashing briefly before June pulled tighter around the noose.

"If you were trying to protect us, why *kill* Amira? Why attack me? You could've helped her leave. Could've given her more information to take to the authorities."

Christine moaned and shook her head. "This is my home. This is my family. I made the choice to stay."

"With Brett."

"With the *coven*. We didn't need him."

"Then why not help her put him in jail?!" June shouted. "Why kill a woman?"

Christine scowled. "Jail? For what? This is Virginia, June. It wasn't even statutory rape here. All the girls were over fifteen. He knew what he was doing. And how would it look in court, the ex-girlfriend accusing him years after the fact? He'd get a slap on the wrist."

June's head shook, stomach turning. "No. There were so many of us. It was a pattern."

"Oh yeah. Were *you* going forward with Amira? Were you going to help her? Was Imogen? Because no one in this coven offered to join her. Ella gave her your name, thought maybe you would—But no. You refused too. Amira wanted him in jail so badly, she could help me make it happen. And she did. Murder is a *real* charge."

"Except you failed to account for his alibi," June murmured, staring at the older woman, the horror spreading cold and numb in her veins.

"He told me he was going to be working in here alone," Christine whimpered. "Jess wasn't supposed to be caught so early. He'd only just started his routine with her."

Bile rose up, and June swallowed the gag. All these people watching Brett seduce one girl after another, knowing it was a matter of when not if.

"I thought I could make another pattern for him. Angry ex-girlfriends dying," Christine said, glaring out of red-rimmed eyes up at June. "He'd be the prime suspect no matter the alibi, not when it was just from a young girl."

Except that Jess had announced in front of them all that she had undeniable proof. Proof that would've landed some kind of sentence on Brett, if not the murder charge. But Christine was right—maybe it would've only been a year in jail, at most.

"A short sentence might've given the coven its freedom," June said, lifting her chin. "It would've put him on the sexual offenders registry. Not to mention giving him a reputation that would've helped protect other young women!"

Christine screamed, bucking on the floor. "It wasn't enough!"

"That wasn't for you to decide!" June yanked the noose around the woman's ankles, and Christine groaned and fell still again.

"Ladies, I hate to break up story time, but we are about to be interrupted with visitors," Beleth said quietly. "The rest of Hell's Bells appears to have followed us."

"This room can't fit anymore people," Josie said.

June caught her breath and stepped back, a slow sigh slipping out of her as her back met a warm, solid, and familiar figure. Ash.

"Ash, take the witches back, I'll deal with Vinny and Pie—"

"No," June said, turning her stare to Beleth. "What happens to these two if we leave them with you?"

Bell's lips pursed, eyes narrowing, and he grunted as Josie elbowed him in the stomach. "I'm not sure," he admitted.

"We need to get Jess inside to the coven," June said. "And Christine..." She hesitated then. Christine was responsible for Amira's murder, in a manner so calculated and so intricate, she wasn't sure the police would even believe it if Christine confessed. She had betrayed vulnerable women in a convoluted attempt at revenge. And if Bell and Ash hadn't come with Vinny, what would've happened to Jess?

"Christine I will leave up to you," June said softly.

"I didn't realize we were taking unbound orders from our enemies, Beleth."

June shivered, and Ash's arm slid heavily over her chest, drawing her further into his broad frame as a tall, pale figure stepped out of the shadows and into the doorway, candlelight reflecting eerily off of Paimon's round glasses.

A warm, tingling protective layer of power draped over her head, soaking into her with the same ease as Ash's declaration.

"June isn't my enemy."

19

MIDDLE MANAGEMENT

Enough was enough, Paimon decided, as Vinny vanished from Grimsby House at a witch's call for the third time in the span of a month. Bell's interest in the kitchen witch was becoming an impediment to their work. Ash had made no apparent progress, in spite of June Byrne's binding being now removed.

"Where is Ash?" Pie asked Dante, the handsome demon sprawled out on a chaise, watching a game show on the small and static ridden television set.

"Huh? Oh, I dunno. Think he's after that witch. It's Zeboim, you asshat!" Dante barked at the contestant on the screen.

We're becoming domesticated, Pie thought with a frown.

"And where is Bell?" Pie asked.

Dante rolled his eyes and turned his head. "Look, not to be a dick... Actually, yeah, why not. It's not *my* job to keep track of everyone. Aren't you, kinda, middle management in this situation?" A quiet moment later, after the walls of Grimsby House closed in and the shadows grew tall and the pressure lay thick in the air, Dante sat up straight on the chaise, head bowed. "Right. Sorry. If I'm honest, I've been getting some vibes from our leader. I assume he's following his stomach or his dick, but either way, they're headed in the same direction."

Pie nodded. He'd guessed as much. Bell had warned him when it started that his connection to the baker was uncomfortably potent. At least Dante had the sense to notice too.

Bell had promised to keep Pie apprised of any developments, but demons weren't loyal to promises exchanged between them. That was fine. Pie would act with or without Bell's leadership. He stood, preparing to head for the basement where he might follow the thread of Vinny's travel, when movement out of the living room window caught his eye.

Rosa Velasco was out, bundled into a soft cocoon, marching for the street. Pie moved to the window, peering through horrible lace curtains as Rosa bounced on her toes at the edge of the sidewalk, leaning out to watch the road. She was a dark little blob on the curb, and his mind itched to pull away the colorless filter he kept on the world, but he resisted.

It was the dead of night. It was freezing cold.

Who was the green witch waiting for?

The answer came with the roar of an engine a minute later, headlights high and tires kicking up a splash of slush and ice that Rosa backed away from.

"That's ours, isn't it?" Dante asked, appearing at Pie's side, snooping on the witch with simple curiosity.

"It is," Pie said, studying the massive vehicle that had been more or less adopted by Ash like a loyal dog.

"And that's not us driving," Dante continued.

"It's not." It was the stitch witch and the kitchen witch.

And now Rosa, climbing up into the backseat, a screech of rubber on the road as the truck made a sudden U-turn.

"Um. Should we be concerned?"

Pie stepped away from the window, heading for the basement. "Find Aim and Barbie. Meet me downstairs."

There were too many variables, but Pie knew one thing.

It didn't pay to underestimate a witch. Bell and Ash had landed themselves into some kind of trap, if the witches were running around in their vehicle. Perhaps, at last, this war had found a battle worth fighting in.

IT WAS NOT the scene he'd expected to discover, and Pie could admit he was a little disappointed. And confused.

He'd caught enough information in the rush of conversation as he watched with the others behind a wall of shadow.

The witches were here to rescue demons. The demons—Bell and Ash—had also apparently arrived to rescue the witches, or at the very least, perform them a service. Vinny was, difficult as it was to believe, innocent in the situation, merely victim to the laws that ruled their kind.

"I didn't realize we were taking unbound orders from our enemies, Beleth."

Bell shifted a fraction, but it placed his shoulder in front of the diminutive kitchen witch. Rosa was in the corner, booted foot resting on top of a stranger, a bound witch and apparently the one so partial to summoning Vinny.

And Ashtaroth, the reliable, loyal, clever demon who'd never sought power or challenge outside of work he seemed to genuinely *enjoy*, draped a possessive arm over the blonde, June.

"June isn't my enemy."

Even Bell looked surprised by that one. Paimon stepped into the cramped room, revealing the three other demons behind him, who shifted at Ash's declaration.

"You're defecting?" Dante asked, squeezing forward as much as he was able into the tiny closet and frowning at Ash.

Ash shrugged. "I'm with the witch."

"I'm with the other witches," June said and then glanced at the bound one. "Not her."

"I was aware of your loyalty, yes," Pie bit out, and Ash grew larger, moving to June's side, prepared to defend her.

Curious. Such a strong response for one of their kind.

Bell straightened, his hand on the cuff of a silenced, irate Vinny's neck, pushing them into Paimon's face, blocking the view of the witches and Ashtaroth the defector behind him.

"We have the witch who's been summoning Vinny. The Sweet Pea coven witches are leaving."

"Just like that?" Paimon asked, arching an eyebrow. *Say it,* he thought. *Declare yourself like Ash did.*

"Just like that," Bell said, low and quiet, pretending he was still in charge of the mission. Bell turned his head to the side, but remained locked with Paimon's gaze. "Ash. Go on."

Paimon's stare flicked to Rosa in the corner, her wide eyes and ruffled curls, the slight swollen side of her cheek. And for a moment, just to see if that really was a *bruise* marking her, he let go of the control on his vision and allowed color to seep in, one brief glimpse of red on her mouth shining first. But it was too late, Ash caught the three Sweet Pea witches and the young collapsed girl in a grip and tore them out of the room, a little whiff of sugar and ice and roses hovering in the air before it too vanished.

"All right, Vinny," Bell said, twisting roughly and

throwing Vinny away from him, letting the rabid demon loose after days of holding control. "Have at her."

Vinny's teeth were bared, eyes wild, and Paimon thought Vinny might dive for Bell rather than the trembling woman bound on the floor.

"Please," she whimpered.

That was all it took, Vinny growled and spun, and the woman shrieked as he dove for her, a sudden crackle of lightning and wavering heat building around them, turning the sight of Vinny's limbs claiming and tearing into her hazy, and then they were gone, sulfur and brimstone eating away the last of the sweetness left on the air.

"Why did you follow?" Bell asked, expression flat and hard.

"Because, Beleth, I am not an idiot," Paimon answered, peeking at his supposed superior over the rim of his glasses. "It's time for you to make a decision."

Bell scowled at him, jaw grinding as he glanced at Dante and the others. "Yeah. Well...yeah. I guess it is."

"I'll give you this much. At least tonight has been interesting," Aim said.

If Bell acted as Paimon expected him to, it might make the future even more interesting. This was not the kind of trap he was expecting to find his fellow demons in. It was time for Pie to make decisions too.

He really hated middle management.

20 RISK AND REWARD

"Will she be all right?" Rosa whispered at June.

Ella looked up from where she sat at a sleeping Jess' side, a handful of other women moving in and out of the room, bringing herbal teas and candles and hand quilted blankets.

"She'll be fine. The coven will be here for her if she wants it," Ella said. "I know her family, and I'll make sure they are aware that she may require extra support too."

June crossed her arms over her chest, and Ash's hand squeezed tenderly on her shoulder, checking in with her. "I'm going to come back. I'd like to speak with her," June said

Ella's eyes narrowed, a hard smile on her face, but she nodded. "I understand. I know you don't like me, June."

"I don't trust you."

"But I was only trying to teach you to survive," Ella finished. "That's why I'm still here."

June pursed her lips and breathed out her nose. That may have been true, but it wasn't the whole reason. Ella's interests wouldn't leave her welcome with most covens. She carved herself a place with the ones who would welcome her, no matter how she justified it.

"And Christine?" Ella asked.

June shrugged and found that the lie came to her tongue easily. "Christine ran. I don't know what happened to her."

"She'll show back up, and then we'll have to decide what to do with her," one of the other women muttered.

Ella only stared back at June, unconvinced but apparently willing to go along with the story. "That's all then. Brett left not long after you did."

"What happens to the school?" June asked.

Ella scoffed. "He was twenty-four years old. *I* bought the school. The coven will be fine. We will all be fine. Go home, June."

June took another longer look at Jess—she was turned to the wall, and June suspected Jess wasn't really sleeping. There was no getting around the trauma now. June had arrived and torn part of this girl's world open, led to her being attacked by Christine. Ella might make Jess let June come to talk to her, but she probably wouldn't be able to make the girl listen.

That was okay, that would be June's burden, not hers. She would still come, try and make sure the girl was safe with the rest of this coven.

She nodded and turned away. "Okay. Okay, home."

"Come on, witches. I'll give you a ride," Ash said, forcing a smile as he tucked June into his side and ushered the group of them out the door and down to the school entrance.

"What *did* happen to Christine?" Rosa asked.

Josie's gaze was distant, and June ducked her head, determined not to wonder, leaving Ash to answer.

"Whatever she deserved."

Rosa paled, and then hissed as they stepped outside, huddling into her coat and hurrying to stand behind Ash and his windshield body.

JUNE WAS EXHAUSTED. It was closer to dawn than it was midnight, her whole body was sore between the use of magic and the admittedly awesome sex, and...

And emotions were *tiresome*.

"I'll check on you tomorrow," Josie offered as they paused outside her door.

June nodded, tongue a little numb, and then stopped Josie with a hand on her wrist. She stepped forward, and Josie met her in the middle, arms swinging around one another.

"It's not easy," Josie whispered in her ear. "It's not easy to do, but it's not wrong, either."

At that hour, after that week, June could've applied the statement to any number of problems in her life.

"I'll text you tomorrow," Josie said. "See if you're up for company."

"I can't remember what day tomorrow is, but sure," June said, nodding.

Ash was waiting for her a few feet away, hands in his pockets, looking so...impossibly human. Too big, too handsome, too good to be true.

He arched an eyebrow. "You need me to carry you back to bed?"

June sighed. God, that sounded wonderful, but she still had a thread of dignity and she used it to pick her feet up and propel her forward to her own door. Her wards were loose.

"Starling—"

"I know," June answered, heart hammering in her chest for a moment before immediately slowing, hiccuping as she recognized the work. "Fuck. I don't need this tonight."

"Let me go—"

"No! No," June said, an arm held out in front of Ash.

She pushed open the door and found Imogen curled up on the steps inside, leaning against the wall with a book on her lap. Now it was June's turn to step in front of her demon as Imogen rose from her seat.

"What the fuck is he—"

"Imogen, go home," June said, too tired to be gentle or kind or reasonable, or to even talk it out.

"What?" Imogen gasped, eyes wide and clear.

"I said go home."

"June, if you think I'm going to let that—"

"Imogen, if you think, after everything we've been through, after you *bound* me, that you get any kind of say in my life, you are wrong. And if you think you can use magic to manipulate this, you are wrong," June rushed out, moving up the steps to face her sister, nose to nose.

"Junie, he's a demon, what is he doing here?"

"Whatever he and I want him to," June said, shrugging, trying to spread herself a little further out on the steps as she heard Ash's footsteps thunk up the stairs closer to her.

Imogen's brow furrowed and then softened, eyes going wide again, feigning innocent. "Junie, *we* protect each other. Us. Just you and me."

Ash held back, which June appreciated in the moment. He was there if she needed him, but he wasn't going to get between her and her sister.

"We tried," June said, reaching out and taking Imogen's hands. "We *tried* to protect each other, and...we failed. We couldn't protect each other from our parents. We couldn't protect each other from Brett. We can't protect each other from moving on. I don't want to, Gin. I'm sick of living in that glass bubble you made for me. And you've been sick of me trying to control you for a long time too." June shrugged and swallowed hard.

Imogen's expression was blank, eyes flicking between Ash and June, narrowing. It wasn't enough. Imogen would never trust Ash. She probably wouldn't ever trust June to make her own choices, just as much as June wouldn't trust her. They weren't good for one another, even as sisters, even as hard as they tried to be. They had to learn how to have real relationships before they could form one together.

"Imogen, if you intervene in my life again, I will—"

Ash stepped up, not blocking June but reaching out to Imogen. "I vow to do no harm to your sister, nor to let any harm come to her. On my seal and body as a demon."

June shot Ash a glare. He thought he was clever, putting the vow into Imogen's hands rather than hers. Maybe he was clever. Maybe she was a little grateful too.

"Imogen, go home," June repeated. "I want us to be sisters, not keepers. But...but I'm not ready to forgive you for what you did. And I don't care how talented you are, I am not letting your power touch me again."

Imogen flinched at that, eyes dropping to Ash's offered hand. "Just because you're declawed doesn't mean you won't bring harm to her," Imogen whispered. "June, I—"

June blinked and held her breath as Imogen looked up again, gaze scanning over June's features, brow furrowing in a way that made June want to reach out and smooth the trouble away.

"I only wanted to keep you from doing something you'd

regret," Imogen said softly. "I will always carry the consequences so you don't have to."

"Gin," June snapped, but Imogen twisted and pushed past Ash's broad shoulders, retreating back down the stairs. "Gin!"

Ash waited with June on the stairs as Imogen let herself out.

"She made that ominous so I would go chasing after her," June muttered, frowning, staring at the closed door.

"Are you going to?" Ash asked without judgement, just a simple question.

June blinked, and Ash remained quiet as she let the storm pass through—anger, shame, sorrow, worry, love—and then she caught her breath and shook her head. "Not tonight."

His arms wrapped around her then, lifting her off her toes and carrying her up the stairs.

"Don't think I didn't notice you try to slip that vow in," June mumbled, resting her head on his shoulder.

"She should've taken it," Ash said, the door to the apartment popping open as he approached. All the lights were still on, and a moment later they were off again.

"You told the others you were *with* me," June said, smiling. "I like that version better."

"I am with you, starling."

June hummed as he headed for the bedroom, pausing at the bathroom door and then stepping inside. The tiny room was far too small for both her and Ash together, never mind the actual tub, but then the walls did something funny, and suddenly there was plenty of space.

"You're going to make me lose my deposit," June said, eyes growing wide as Ash rested her on her toes and began to undress her.

"I am increasing the property value," Ash answered.

"*Why* are you with me?" June asked, briefly brave as her face was hidden inside of her own shirt as he pulled it over her head. "And don't say I make things interesting because I'm not a big fan of all the excitement."

Ash reappeared, grinning, and June batted his hands away to finish undressing herself, preferring the show of watching him do the same.

"I like you," Ash said. "You're grumpy, critical, a perfectionist. You have poor social skills, you're secretive—"

"Wow, thanks," June growled out, hands on her hips.

Ash stepped out of his jeans, still beaming like the asshole he was, and then yanked down her pants and underwear, bending forward and scooping her over his shoulder as she yelped. He pulled the rest of her clothes off and then reached up, patting her ass with one hand and stepping into a mysteriously full and steaming tub. Sneaky bastard demon.

He shifted her down again, her chest against his, his arm banded around her hips, her toes brushing the hot water. His nose nudged at hers, eyes crinkled with laughter as she tried to hold onto her glare.

"I admire the survivor, your fight and strength," Ash said, voice heavy and solemn in comparison to his usual grin. "But I think you've had enough battles and it's time for you to rest."

It was absurd for this damned soul, who had only come to Sweet Pea to curse it, to make June feel safe. Safe, and steady, and sometimes like she was about to combust too.

Ash performed the physical feat of settling into the bath, June in his arms and the water inexplicably up to their shoulders.

"Did you carve space out of my shop for this tub?" she asked.

"I did not. Is that all I get for my very charming declaration?" Ash countered.

"Hmmm." June shifted, climbing over Ash's bent legs, combing wet fingers into his dense beard and smiling when his gaze flicked down to her breasts as they rose up near his mouth. "You get *me*, beast. Thank you," she said, bending and kissing the center of his brow, sighing into his skin as his hands rubbed at her lower back.

"Your sister might be right—Hell may have something to say about my defection," Ash said lowly, his grip tensing, pulling her closer.

June's hands slid down to his neck, around to cup the back of his head, tangling into his hair and tugging so his face lifted to hers. She recalled the somewhat terrifying version of him in the summoning circle, golden and animal, grinning and feral. She felt a kind of kinship to that beast, her beast, and she dipped her head to nuzzle against his bristly cheek.

"Then we will answer them. I like having you on my side, but that doesn't mean I won't keep fighting. For Sweet Pea, for myself, and now for you too."

Ash's chest rumbled with a soft growl, almost a purr, and his arms twined around her, sinking into the steaming water. His mouth reached for hers, tongue stroking in and lips claiming, and June let herself drown in the kiss, overwhelmed by one perfect, complicated, dangerous union.

21

RECKONING

Hesitation was a rare concept for Beleth the Warlord King. Patience was irksome but acceptable, waiting for the right moment to strike. But *hesitance*?

He scowled at the alley door.

He was a demon. He was millenia old—not that he chose to feel it. He was a king.

He had been stalling for months and was now wondering if the decision he'd been avoiding was still on the table.

I'm with the witch.

Fucking Ash made it sound so simple. Just a few days of whatever that power was that the witches struck them with and *ta da!* Ash was sold. Converted. Betraying his service to the Bowels in exchange for...a human woman.

Bell's temples were starting to hurt from frowning. His stomach was growling as it always did when he stepped too close to Josephine's Bakery. Even at three in the morning, the alley teased him with whiffs of butter and pastry and chocolate. Josie would be sleeping, it could wait...

No. It had waited and waited and waited and—

Bell would deny later that he jumped at the sudden throwing open of the alley door.

"Josie."

"Bell?"

"You should be in bed," he bit out. What was she doing out? She'd barely gotten any rest tonight.

Josie's eyes were wide with dark shadows below, and she stood with her arms crossed over her chest, one hip cocked in that 'don't give me any bullshit' stance he found so frustratingly appealing. He wanted to tackle her to the stairs until those tight and guarded limbs were wrapped around him, begging him closer.

"I couldn't sleep, and I've gotta be working soon enough," Josie said, sighing and softening as she raised a hand over her eyes.

"Why can't you sleep?"

"What are you doing out here?"

Bell stepped in close, forcing Josie to lean against the door jamb, her face tipped up to his, eyes narrowed in suspicion. "Why weren't you sleeping, Cupcake?"

Her expression twisted, pained one moment and then hard and impassive the next. "How bad is it going to be for June and Ash?"

"June and *Ash*?" Bell growled out.

Her shoulders straightened, and Josie's chin butted out in defiance. "He stuck up for her. What are you going to have to do to him?"

The question struck Bell hard in the gut. Ash had stuck up for June. Ash had, and Bell...hadn't. Not outright.

Not yet, he thought, taking in a deep breath. He didn't have to make a decision, it was made. Ash was right about that—he'd only been delaying the announcement. Possibly *too* long, if Josie's prickly gaze was anything to judge by. That was fine. He liked when she was pissed with him, liked the way he could melt her like she melted butter.

"I don't know how bad it will be. It won't be up to me," Bell said, shrugging.

"What? Why the hell not? Can't you—" Josie huffed and shook her head, trying to turn away from him, growling as he braced his arms around her waist to hold her in place.

"Cupcake, what am I supposed to do? I'm in the same shit they are," Bell said, ducking to catch her eye.

Josie had a hand on his chest to push him away when she stiffened. Bell fought his own grin as her eyes went wide and her fingers dug into his collar.

"What?" she breathed out, face still turned away.

"I'm on your side," he said. He'd expected to grind the words out reluctantly, but no, it was a relief, like taking off an uncomfortable disguise.

"Secretly," Josie said, glancing at him out of the corner of her eyes.

That was fair, but a bit galling. "It's not a secret anymore, Josie."

"You didn't say—"

"I *will*, next possible opportunity. But I wanted to make sure you and your friends got out first," Bell said. Josie was still glaring at him, but her fingers had hooked into his collar possessively now and he was taking it as a win.

"If you're on my side, you're on Sweet Pea's side," Josie said.

He wanted to tease her, say something like 'don't remind me,' but for once, he thought it through. He needed to be... sincere. Just for the moment. Just so she would know he wasn't fucking around and she was safe with him.

"I know." He bent and pressed a kiss to that pursed and irritated pout of hers and then straightened again.

Josie's expression opened, eyes wide and lips slightly parted, cheeks flushing. "And it's not a secret?" she repeated.

"Fuck secrets," Bell said, shrugging.

Josie's eyes narrowed, cheeks swelling with a smile. "You're mad Ash did it first, aren't you?"

Who gave this little witch the power to see right through Bell's bullshit? It was...fucking delightful.

"I maintain that he was following in my footsteps by Ian—" Josie's hand clapped over his mouth.

"Mr. Bad News, if you want to come upstairs, you better stop right there."

He grinned behind her fingers. She hadn't called him that in weeks. He'd fucked up not doing this sooner—yes, he was a little annoyed Ashtaroth made the leap first—but at least Josie wasn't one hundred percent fed up with him. He preferred when she was at a solid twenty-three percent.

Josie sighed and pulled her hand away, arching an eyebrow. "You're sure?"

Maybe at some point, he would admit that it was long since too late for him to *deny* that he was too close to Josie to do his work here properly. But he didn't want her to think he was forced to her side. He'd picked it the night Merryweather attacked her, the night he'd kissed her for the first time and vowed to keep her safe. He just hadn't recognized the decision for what it was then. Somewhat embarrassingly, he had needed Ash as an example of how easy it would be to step over the line. He'd make that up to her, provided Paimon or Curson didn't drag him back to the Bowels.

I'd come back, he realized, stunned and calm. *I'd come back for her.*

Now *that* was shocking.

"I'm sure."

He didn't wait for her smile, not after his revelation. Bell dove down, hauling Josie off her toes and ducking inside, her squeak muffled against his lips, the door banging shut behind them.

"I should let you sleep," he rasped, with absolutely no intention of following through.

"Just jazz me up before you go," she gasped out, arching and offering him her neck.

His arms tightened around her waist and he turned, sitting halfway up the stairs with her on his lap. "I'm not *going*, Josie."

"Ohh," Josie sighed out, a little giggle in the sound as he found his favorite spot at that blade sharp corner of her jaw. She squirmed and pushed Bell back till his shoulders hit the edge of a stair. "Wait, so what are you going to do all day?"

And because it would stir her up, he answered, "Hang out in the bakery. I can sample."

"What?! No way, buddy," Josie barked as her hands slipped under the hem of his T-shirt to stroke up his chest.

"I could even help you bake," Bell added, grinning.

"Ughhh."

"Give you back rubs."

"You are turning me off, Mr. Bad News."

Considering she was playing with his nipples and rocking over his hips, he didn't take that so seriously.

"Or I lie around in your bed, naked, waiting for you to come back and serv—Yow!"

"Shut up," Josie gritted out, his now abused nipples pinched and twisted in her delicate fingers. "Before I send you back where you came from."

I never stood a chance against her, Bell thought, sighing as she loosened her twist and moved one hand down to his belt.

"Conquered by a five foot nothing baker with pink throw pillows," Bell mused, brow furrowing.

Josie beamed at him, yanking open his pants a little *too* enthusiastically, and then stripped her coat off followed quickly by her shirt with his help.

"Yeah you are," she said gleefully as he tried to drag her up to his mouth.

They'd never fucked on the stairs before, but Bell figured they should try it out. Twice, from both angles. Maybe a third too.

"You should leave the shop closed."

Josie's fingers slid into his hair, short nails scratching over his scalp and making him growl as he licked and bit at her collarbone and down to her breast through her bra.

"That's not how running a business works, baby."

Then he would have to make a very compelling argu-ment for the plan. A long and thorough argument. There was no rush now. He wasn't going anywhere.

22

DEFECTORS

"Now who's the beast?" Ash asked, watching June lift another enormous bite of food to her mouth. Her elbow jerked into his chest, and Ash grunted and nipped her shoulder, getting a mouthful of wool for his effort.

"Youm'ever said you cood cook," she mumbled out.

"I never said I made a good chair, either, but here we are," Ash said, and he squeezed his arms around her waist in case she tried to get up.

She did not, just shot him a flash of a glare over her shoulder and then went back to eating the breakfast he'd scrounged up from her thinly stocked kitchen. Fried eggs, drop biscuits, tater tots, leftover fried chicken, and white gravy. He'd been cooking for *his* stomach, not hers, but June matched him bite for bite. And then stole some of his.

"Don't get yolk on my sweater."

"My sweater," June mumbled.

He couldn't deny it. He'd started it for himself, but somewhere along the line, infused with protective knots and cables, decked with delicate baubles...

Well, it looked better on her, even with the sleeves rolled up to find her fingertips.

"You're going to have to make me one in return," he said.

June snorted and twisted in her seat, widening her eyes and exaggerating her shrug. "I can't because of the curse."

"The curse?"

"The sweater curse."

He squinted at her, his own lips threatening to break as hers twitched with laughter.

"If you knit your significant other a sweater, you'll split up before it's finished," she explained, shrugging again and going back to her plate, frowning when she realized he'd somehow snuck away a few tater tots. He stuffed them into his mouth before she could steal them back.

"Thassnot a thing."

"It is. Just ask Diane."

Diane was one of the knit night crew with good taste and a healthy yarn hoard.

"I'll knit myself a giant comfy sweater and you can borrow it," June offered.

"That's the same thing."

"It's not."

Ash growled, and June ducked her head to hide her grin. She was chipper, in spite of the short sleep they'd actually shared. She'd clung to him through nightmares and then wrestled him away in her restful moments, spreading out over the expanded mattress like she'd always had so much room. He was going to have to build them a very big bed.

"Do you...work now? Or... I mean, can you go back to the others after last night?" June asked, sobering and pushing away her now empty plate.

"I'm honestly not sure. They're not banging the door down. I'll have to find out," Ash said.

She swallowed and let him turn her to face him, wrestling her around on the stool, her bare legs hanging on either side of his. "But you'll come back...to me?"

Ash nodded, holding that bright new gaze he was already so familiar with. June mimicked the nod, but there was a line of worry between her brows. Ash considered pushing the vow again, but June would take it when she was ready.

"I'll come pick out the yarn for my sweater when I'm done," he said, triumphant as she huffed out a laugh.

"Maybe I should let you wear this one today," June said, glancing down and digging possessive fingers into the cables.

Ash kissed her forehead. "Nope. It's yours now. Curse and all."

"That's not how that works!" June laughed as he lifted her off his lap.

"Go on, get dressed. I'll clean up."

"You're going to use magic aren't you?"

"I'm going to use my demonic talents," Ash corrected.

June glanced at the mess of pans and trays and plates he'd created. "For dishwashing?"

He raised his hands in front of him. "Do these look like the kind of hands that wash dishes?"

Her eyes narrowed. "No, you're right—they're too big and clumsy."

Ash grinned. "Big I'll take, starling, but *clumsy*? Need I remind you what these can do?"

June glanced at the clock on the microwave and sighed. "You'd better not, I don't have time. Later?"

There was that note of worry again, less than before. "Later," he promised.

BELL WAS WAITING for him in the alley as Ash followed June out. She paused in place, glancing between the two, and Ash stiffened for a moment as Bell pulled a box out from behind his back.

"From Josie," Bell said.

It was a white pastry box, and June made an intriguing moaning sound at the back of her throat, leaping forward and snatching it out of Bell's hand.

"Thank you," she said, staring with open suspicion at the demon king. "And for covering for us last night."

Bell nodded and then turned to Ash. "We're going to the Inferno."

June tried to step between the two of them, and Ash drew her back by her shoulders, guiding her to the shop door. "I'll see you later," he reminded her.

"But—"

He ducked, pressing his lips to hers, trying not to laugh at the way she scowled against his kiss. "I prefer blues and grays," he said.

June rolled her eyes, tugging once on the collar of his jacket for another kiss and then turning away.

Ash headed for the end of the alley without checking to see if Bell was following. When the door of the knit shop clicked shut, he spoke. "What's going to happen?"

"I have no idea."

"Should we even turn ourselves in then? What if Pie sent for the cavalry?"

"Think of the paperwork. It would take too long for them to show up," Bell answered, but his shoulders were tight too, boots stomping hard with each step. Ash wasn't the only worried one.

"They'd be smarter to take us out."

"It's what I would do," Bell agreed, and then he let out a huff of breath. "But not necessarily what Paimon will do. He likes to observe. Play cat and mouse."

Ash frowned at that. "He'll try to use us against them?"

"Or them against us," Bell said, frowning as they neared the door.

The bar was quiet, not open yet, but the five remaining demons of the mission were out on the floor, seated around tables pushed together. Ash mulled over Bell's warning as they approached. June had been wearing a target on her back since October, but it didn't feel great to know he might be making it larger.

It would've felt worse to be the man firing at it, Ash decided. At least now he could try and deflect some of the shots.

"I wasn't sure you'd come," Paimon said, watching from the far side of the table, a steaming cup in front of him. Dante was sitting at his right, arms crossed over his chest, still wearing that same confused frustration from the night before. Aim showed a little curiosity, and Barbie absolute boredom, one foot propped on the corner of the table. Meanwhile, Vinny...

Vinny was still leashed, this time by Paimon, face flushed and practically foaming at the mouth, eyes wild. *Like a rabid dog*, Ash thought, and wondered if June could ward her whole side of the block to keep Vinny safely out of reach.

"I don't give my enemy my back," Bell said.

Paimon's eyebrows lifted. "Is that what we are now? Enemies?"

Ash shot Bell a glare, but Bell just stared back at the other king. "I don't think we'll be able to avoid it. Sooner or later, you'll have to make a move."

"And you'll stop us?" Paimon asked, head tipping.

"I'll be standing with the witches who do," Bell said, simply. And then he shrugged out of his leather jacket, the one that labelled him *Prez*, holding it out in front of Paimon. "You'll want this."

"You're deserting the mission. You won't be allowed back into Grimsby House," Paimon said, sitting up straighter and laying his hand flat on top of the table.

"I think I'll live," Bell said lightly.

"Yeah that's not much of a punishment, boss," Aim agreed amiably.

"As for Hell's Bells and the bar," Paimon continued, ignoring them both and slipping his glasses back up his nose, "The business is a necessary evil to disguise our presence. Your name is on the paperwork. And the club has human members. I don't see why it can't have defectors too."

Ash swallowed hard. That was too easy, right? They could just...continue to hang around?

Bell grinned. "Did you report last night?"

"I did," Paimon said, making Bell's smile falter. "I'll wait for the officials to decide anything further."

"Keeping us under your noses," Ash noted.

"Or underfoot perhaps, time will tell," Paimon said with a shrug. Bell withdrew the offered jacket slowly, and Paimon only watched. "You've already made one mess and left me in a position of leadership, Beleth. You'll have to continue your role at the bar. I plan on keeping busy."

Ash's hands fisted at his side, and Dante's eyes landed on them, head shaking in warning. Ash didn't have much of a role at the bar, and at the moment, he was glad of it. He didn't want to stick around for Pie to drop ominous threats as the others all stared at him like he'd grown two heads.

No, that wouldn't have surprised them.

Ash had grown a *heart*, and that was so much stranger for their kind.

"I'm heading out, I'll..." Actually, he wasn't sure he *would* be back later. Ash turned and headed for the door, a last muttered exchange between Pie and Bell before he heard footsteps jogging to keep up with him.

Ash hurried out of the bar, head spinning, and Bell kept pace just behind.

"Why do I feel like that was worse than them sending hellhounds after us?" Ash asked Bell.

"Hellhounds are my business, not Pie's," Bell said simply and then caught Ash's irritated expression. "He's gambling. Arm wrestling. Testing to see which of us can best the other in close quarters. It's fine. We've got time before it gets official. And we outnumber them."

"How do you figure."

"The two of us plus the witches."

Oh. Bell was counting Imogen in that. "Maybe," Ash allowed.

"And we also know something else valuable," Bell said, his steps bouncing a bit as he jogged across the street.

"What's that?" Ash asked, twitching toward June's shop doors. She was inside, facing the cubbies of yarn, and he wanted to duck in and spend the day distracting her.

"Demons are susceptible to witchcraft," Bell said, grinning. "We're proof of it. I think Pie wants to keep an eye on us to know how serious it is. To know the signs in case it catches with any of the others."

Now there was a thought.

Bell was still bouncing on the balls of his feet, and Ash stared at him a moment, realizing that wasn't Bell's predatory battle face but something entirely different.

"What are you so excited about?"

"All the shit Cupcake is gonna give me when she finds out I have nowhere to live," Bell said, grinning.

And with that, Bell spun on his heel and marched for the end of the block. The wind gusted down the road, carrying a not quite natural whistle with it, and Ash rolled his eyes.

The knit shop was quiet, but for the first time, there was music playing in the corner, something old and vaguely familiar. June turned, her arms loaded with a yarn a shocking shade of marigold yellow that had been buried at the back of a cubby.

"No," he said, shaking his head.

"No?"

"No, you're not making my sweater out of that."

"I am not making you a sweater at all," June laughed.

"I'm gonna dye that yarn."

"You're not touching it! It's not for you. And it's *happy*. I like it."

She was still wearing the massive sweater, now paired with black leggings and a simple pair of sneakers. Her hair was pulled up, swinging as she hurried her bundle for the yarn winder, and Ash grinned at the red spot of beard burn where he'd been kissing her this morning while she ate breakfast.

"Are you happy?" he asked.

June glanced at him over her shoulder, eyes growing wide and mouth opening without an answer.

He shrugged out of his leather jacket, draping it over the back of a chair, and went to help her wrestle the swift.

"I am. I'm happy," June said. Then she laughed and shrugged. "For now."

Ash frowned. "For now?"

"No, I don't mean—" June bumped her hip against his.

"I'm not expecting the worst. Or maybe I am. I just mean... being happy right now is enough. It will be enough if I'm happy tomorrow too. Or if I burst into tears in an hour over something meaningless, it was still enough. I'm embracing the spectrum of emotions, that's all."

It was understandable but not quite enough to satisfy Ash. He would work on that until June trusted that the good could outweigh the bad. It would be a challenge.

"You're still here," she said, rising up to her toes, hands reaching for his face to draw him to her.

Ash leaned into the kiss, taking every brush and bite and press she offered, pushing the shocking yellow yarn out of her arms. He would wear it, and he would give her shit for the color and enjoy the victory when it made her laugh.

"You're stuck with me. Speaking of, how do you feel about me working with power tools in your apartment? I need to build a new bed."

"I feel like you're absolutely not going to do that," June said, a little breathless. "Wind that for me?" She had a teasing smile on her kiss swollen lips as she pointed to the yarn on the swift.

"You just want to watch my muscles," Ash said, but he grinned when she didn't deny it. "I'm serious about the bed."

"You're seriously not getting sawdust all over my place," June tossed back. "But while we're on the subject of carpentry...what can you do about that?"

Ash twisted and found June glaring at Mrs. Montgomery's rocking chair. "Wood chipper?" he suggested.

June's eyes lit up, and her head shook. "Tempting, but too extreme. I'd settle for it being silent."

"Done," Ash said with a shrug.

He wondered how long it would take June to notice that Mrs. Montgomery would also remain silent while sitting in the rocking chair. It would be his most devilish feat in Sweet Pea in quite a while, but he knew it would work. He was doing it for June's sake, after all.

"You're going to be very handy to have around, beast," June murmured, leaning up against the yarn shelves and watching him crank the winder.

"I plan on it, starling," Ash vowed.

EPILOGUE

Eucalyptus, heather, pennyroyal, and juniper. Spanish moss around the rim of the vase. A little sprig of winter witch hazel for good measure.

Rosa Velasco missed the heavy lush blooms of summer, but spring might start popping its head out of the sleeping ground in another week or two. At least many of the best protective plants were evergreens.

"You're going to keep my place nice and tidy and safe from our neighbors, aren't you?" Rosa murmured to the arrangement, wiggling the eucalyptus into place.

Flora Fresca was closed now, but she liked to play with the day's scraps. No bloom, branch, fern, or twig would go wasted on her watch. Protective wreaths and bud vases had become a bit of a hobby for her ever since the demons had rolled into Sweet Pea. Hobby or...compulsion was probably the better word for it.

"Abuelita would scoff at you," Rosa said, replacing the witch hazel. "*Yuma* nonsense. But I'll cover my butt as many ways as I can find, thank you very much."

Rosa glanced up from the work, staring out the

windows, across the dark and empty street, to Josie's shop. She was tempted to hurry over and see if Josie wanted help with dinner—or if she had anything she wanted to send home with Rosa—when a shadow appeared from the kitchen of the bakery.

The demon—Bell, Mr. Bad News—hurried over to Josie's glass case, ducking out of the way of her swatting hands, and Rosa watched with a pained curiosity as Josie's head tipped back, what must've been laughter pouring out.

It was wrong to be jealous of a friend's happiness, but Rosa wondered if the whole 'demon' thing provided extenuating circumstances. She wasn't jealous of Josie and Bell exactly. She had concerns—some residual worry left from being raised by devoutly spiritual Catholics and suspicion by being raised by those same women in their role as Orisha priestesses.

That kind of man was bound to bring trouble with him.

Unfortunately, as Rosa was well aware, normal men brought plenty of trouble when they wanted to as well.

Josie could handle a little trouble, and she had the coven. They were doing all right against the demons.

"Two down, five to go," Rosa mused, grinning and turning to head for her coat and purse.

She had her back turned to the door when the breeze entered her shop—too warm for the end of February in the mountains—carrying with it the scent of metal and blood. The back of Rosa's neck prickled with warning, and the display bouquets on shelves rustled.

Rosa caught his reflection in the mirror behind her counter. Almost tall enough for his shining head to brush the exposed beams, deep umber skin gleaming, eyes glinting like polished black pebbles. The heavy chains around his neck and hips sang a deceivingly light introduction as he moved to the heart of the store, examining one of her burst cattails in its tin bucket.

"San Pedro," Rosa murmured, closing her eyes and bowing her head low, turning slowly and tracing the sign of the cross over her chest.

Santiago. Ogun. Saint Peter.

Abuelita's family saint and the God of War.

It should've been honor making her heart hammer, watching the red of his robes trailing on her floor like blood. But an unsolicited visit from the family saint usually wasn't a good sign. Most often, it meant you were fucking up in a big way.

"Hermana," San Pedro greeted, voice heavy and solemn. "When were you going to tell me you had demons at your door?"

Rosa swallowed hard, her brain taking an unpaid vacation as she lifted her gaze to the iron chains around San Pedro's throat and tried to think of an answer that wouldn't turn Sweet Pea into an immediate battleground.

ALSO BY KATHRYN MOON

<u>COMPLETE READS</u>

The Librarian's Coven Series

Written - Book 1

Warriors - Book 2

Scrivens - Book 3

Ancients - Book 4

Summerland Series

Summerland Stories, the complete collection plus bonus content

Standalones

Good Deeds

Command The Moon

Say Your Prayers - co-write with Crystal Ash

The Sweetverse

Baby + the Late Night Howlers

Lola & the Millionaires - Part One

Lola & the Millionaires - Part Two

Bad Alpha

Sol & Lune

Book 1

Book 2

Inheritance of Hunger Trilogy

The Queen's Line

The Princess's Chosen

The Kingdom's Crown

SERIES IN PROGRESS

Sweet Pea Mysteries

The Baker's Guide To Risky Rituals

The Knitter's Guide to Banishing Boyfriends

Tempting Monsters

A Lady of Rooksgrave Manor

The Company of Fiends

ACKNOWLEDGMENTS

Firstly, I want to thank so many of the women who taught me to knit, who encouraged me to fill every corner of my free space with yarn, who fostered my obsession with fiber and hand-dyes. It's a skill and a refuge to be able to create something with my hands. Also, gosh I love the pretty colors.

And for this book, thank you to:

KellieArts, my incredible cover designer.

Meghan Leigh Daigle, my precise proofreader.

The Beta Babes: Desiree, Chloe, Lana , Helen, Jami, Amanda, and Ash.

My amazing Moongazers who cheer me on each and every step!

All my writing babes, near and far, who inspire and motivate me.

My Momma Moon for loving me and my stories, but especially this series, and giving me someone special to write it for.

ABOUT THE AUTHOR

Kathryn Moon is a country mouse who started dictating stories to her mother at an early age. The fascination with building new worlds and discovering the lives of the characters who grew in her head never faltered, and she graduated college with a fiction writing degree. She loves writing women were are strong in their vulnerability, romances that are as affectionate as they are challenging, and worlds that a reader sinks into and never wants to leave. When her hands aren't busy typing they're probably knitting sweaters or crimping pie crust in Ohio. She definitely believes in magic.

You can reach her on Facebook and at ohkathrynmoon@ gmail.com or you can sign up for her newsletter!

www.ingramcontent.com/pod-product-compliance
Lightning Source LLC
Chambersburg PA
CBHW022116310726
48972CB00007B/2059